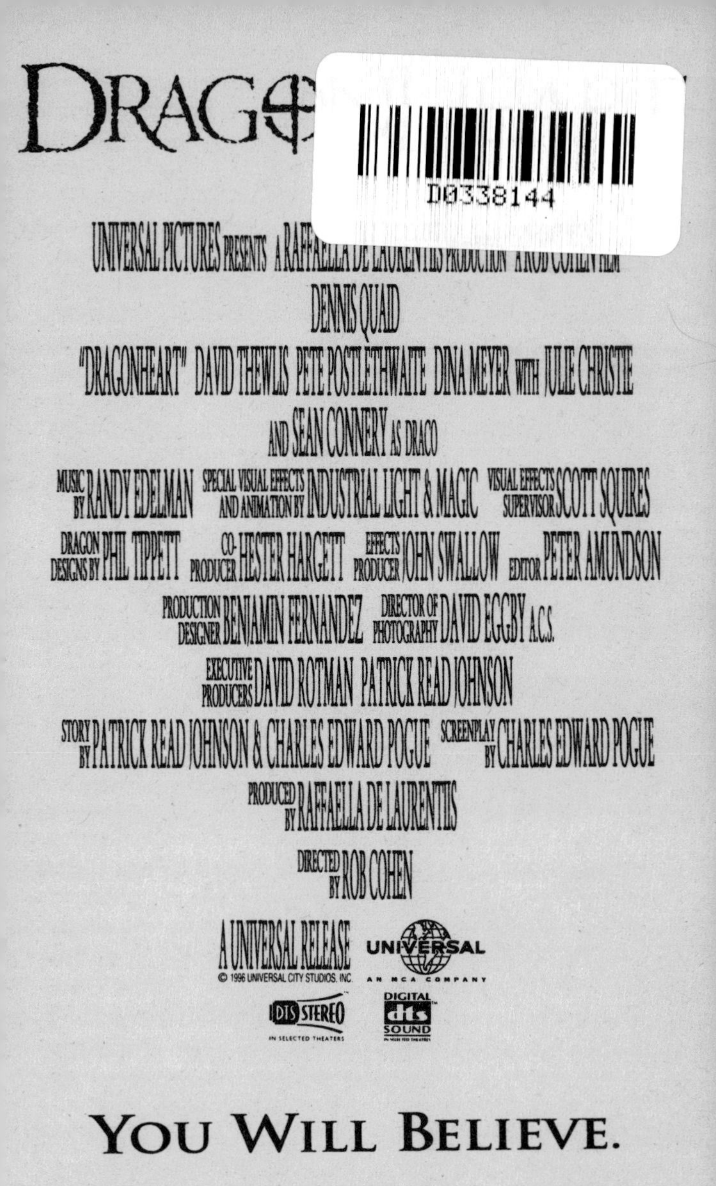
DRAGO
D0338144
UNIVERSAL PICTURES PRESENTS A RAFFAELLA DE LAURENTIIS PRODUCTION A ROB COHEN FILM
DENNIS QUAID
"DRAGONHEART" DAVID THEWLIS PETE POSTLETHWAITE DINA MEYER WITH JULIE CHRISTE
AND SEAN CONNERY AS DRACO
MUSIC BY RANDY EDELMAN SPECIAL VISUAL EFFECTS AND ANIMATION BY INDUSTRIAL LIGHT & MAGIC VISUAL EFFECTS SUPERVISOR SCOTT SQUIRES
DRAGON DESIGNS BY PHIL TIPPETT CO-PRODUCER HESTER HARGETT EFFECTS PRODUCER JOHN SWALLOW EDITOR PETER AMUNDSON
PRODUCTION DESIGNER BENJAMIN FERNANDEZ DIRECTOR OF PHOTOGRAPHY DAVID EGGBY A.C.S.
EXECUTIVE PRODUCERS DAVID ROTMAN PATRICK READ JOHNSON
STORY BY PATRICK READ JOHNSON & CHARLES EDWARD POGUE SCREENPLAY BY CHARLES EDWARD POGUE
PRODUCED BY RAFFAELLA DE LAURENTIIS
DIRECTED BY ROB COHEN
A UNIVERSAL RELEASE
© 1996 UNIVERSAL CITY STUDIOS, INC.
UNIVERSAL
AN MCA COMPANY
DTS STEREO
IN SELECTED THEATERS
DIGITAL dts SOUND
YOU WILL BELIEVE.

DRAGONHEART™

Charles Edward Pogue
BASED ON HIS
SCREENPLAY

BOULEVARD BOOKS, NEW YORK

DRAGONHEART
A novel by Charles Pogue.
Based on a screenplay by Charles Pogue.

A Boulevard Book / published by arrangement with
MCA Publishing Rights, a Division of MCA, Inc.

PRINTING HISTORY
Boulevard edition / June 1996

For information address: The Berkley Publishing Group,
200 Madison Avenue, New York, New York 10016.

The Putnam Berkley World Wide Web site address is
http://www.berkley.com

ISBN: 1-57297-130-4

BOULEVARD
Boulevard Books are published by The Berkley Publishing Group,
200 Madison Avenue, New York, New York 10016.
BOULEVARD and its logo are trademarks
belonging to Berkley Publishing Corporation.

PRINTED IN THE UNITED STATES OF AMERICA

10 9 8 7 6 5 4 3 2 1

For Julieanne,
My Muse, My Champion, and My Lady Fair.

And in memory of Hotspur, who was Draco,
And my father, who taught me the Old Code.

This is the tale of a Knight who slew a Dragon and vanquished evil.

The Chronicles of Glockenspur, Detailing the Historie of King Einon and the Rebellion Under His Reign as Set Down by One Gilbert, a Friar.

Part I

THE KNIGHT

Inside the table's circle,
Under the sacred sword.
A knight must vow to follow
The code that is unending,
Unending as the table—
A ring by honor bound.

—*The Old Code*

Chapter One

THE FALL OF KINGS

". . . No one will take arms against my crown."

Bowen caught the sword against his own, a slice away from his smile. Sunlight and sparks slashed along the blades as they shrieked down each other in a skittering slide, locking at their hilts. From behind their wedged embrace, Bowen's gray eyes gleamed like the sunlit steel.

"Not bad." He grinned, then disengaged with a swift flare and a blurred sally that drove his visored adversary into the dirt.

"But not good enough to live, Prince." Bowen emphasized the taunt by poking his sword tip against the royal coat of arms emblazoned on the downed man's surcoat . . . a dragon's head impaled on a sword.

An oath lurched out of the helmet and the prince's boot lurched against Bowen's thigh, shoving the knight back. The prince spun from under Bowen's jarred blade and sprang to his feet in one swift swirl of motion.

But even as he lunged, Bowen's sword was there to meet his, deflecting it away from his broad, bare chest by inches.

"Better!" Again, Bowen smiled through their crossed blades. Pleased.

So was the prince. More by the compliment, thought Bowen, than by the skill of the maneuver. Bowen could make out the toothy, lopsided grin behind the visor grate. He could also take advantage of it. For basking in the praise, the prince had let down his guard. Just slightly. But enough. Bowen's blade arced down and struck him . . .

. . . with the flat of his sword.

"But you'd still be dead, Einon!"

Prince Einon reeled from the blow. Snarling another oath, he wildly charged Bowen, who, laughing, effortlessly parried the violent but awkward assault.

"Purpose, not passion, princeling! Fight with your head, not your heart!" Bowen mocked the prince, punctuating each maxim with a slap of his sword flat against Einon's body.

Even so, Einon was good. He'd learned the mechanics well. It was only hotheadedness that made him sloppy and predictable. And made Bowen's mastery of him easier than it should have been.

Bowen allowed the prince to drive him back through the ruins of the old Roman castle to a crumbling stone wall. He perched on it, fending off Einon's frenzied blows.

"Mind if I sit? Your exertion exhausts me."

Another indecipherable mutter shot out from behind the helmet. Bowen easily caught the blade that shot out and, with the force of his own blade, sent Einon sprawling through the tall, uncut grass to the ground. The helmet clanked against a stone.

"Nobody ever found victory in the dirt," Bowen barked at him, and bracing his sword against the wall, reached for the waterskin laid there.

He took a healthy swig, the water running down his tanned chest and mingling with the glistening sweat. He stared into the afternoon sun as it started its descent behind the mountains. Its waning rays crept down the rocky bluffs below where King Freyne's wooden stronghold nestled and kidnapped it from the sheltering shadows. But even the sun's shimmering gold could not brighten the grimness of the fortress. It seemed to shun the light, preferring the dark caresses of the cliffs. Crude and primitive, it suited its master well.

Freyne would never be a builder like the mighty legions who had crafted the fine stone upon which Bowen sat. Even in its disrepair, the remnants of the old castle bespoke the glories of the conquerors who raised it. In victory, they left a legacy of their greatness on the land . . . broad roads and mighty walls and proud blood. From this last had come a king whose legacy was even more far-reaching than the empire of his ancestors. A legacy that once bound all Britain by a dream. A dream of the heart and of the spirit.

But that king, those days, were now a faded ruin—like this castle and like Imperial Rome itself. A memory. No more. And in their place had risen overlords like Freyne, whose conquests extended no further than their bloodlust or their greed. No, Freyne was no builder like the Romans. It was meet that his dark fortress—Bowen could not call it a castle—hang among the lurking hills below, like a bird of prey perched and waiting to rake its talons across a shuddering land.

Bowen gulped at the waterskin to wash away the bad taste in his mouth. He heard Einon rise and whirl and charge once more. He didn't even stop drinking; he merely snatched up his sword in his left hand and smote Einon back to his knees. The prince was getting careless; toying with him had ceased to be amusing.

"Kneel in battle and you'll never kneel at your coronation." Bowen slapped his sword rapidly against both sides of the helmet, making it ring. Einon shook his head wildly and roared. From where he knelt, he took a weaving swipe at Bowen's legs. Bowen leapt onto the wall and the blade scraped along the stone. Einon twisted back with a vicious uppercut. Glowering at the prince's pathetic show, Bowen caught the blow on the waterskin. The bag shredded on the blade, spraying its contents into Einon's visor-veiled face. Bowen threw the sopping sack at him too.

"Cool off, princeling. Remember! Nerve cold blue; blade blood red."

But the dousing cooled neither Einon nor his nerve. And

his blade, though deadly, was desperate and clumsy. Bowen sidestepped another lunge with a dismissive laugh.

Then the wall crumbled beneath his boot heel.

The fall was neither far nor hard. The tall grass on the other side of the wall had cushioned his landing, but it scratched against his bare torso. He heard Einon clamber over the stone, then his plaintive, "Sir Bowen?"

And in that cry of anxious curiosity, Bowen knew the advantage was his. He lay utterly still. His eyes closed. Waiting for Einon to come to him.

Einon swallowed the bait. Down off the wall. Through the overgrown grass. Bowen heard it rustle against the prince's body. Closer. Closer. Utterly guileless. Unususpecting. It was almost too easy. Bowen peered through slit lids and the mud-blond mop of hair that had fallen in his face. Einon leaned down over him. The visor was up. The fighting demeanor of his pimpled fifteen-year-old face had surrendered to worried gravity. His fair skin was splotchy red, flushed with exertion and sunlight. The boy had none of his mother's beauty. He was all broad angles and rough curve, with a feral aspect that he shared with his father. Physically, there was no doubting that he was Freyne's son. Bowen was determined that he would not turn out to be Freyne's son in other respects as well.

Again: "Sir Bowen?" Bowen could scarce repress his smile. A moment ago that timid, tentative voice had been snarling curses at him.

Einon knelt to examine the knight. But a noise distracted him. Bowen heard it too. Hoofbeats. Coming from behind. Coming fast.

As the boy whirled to the sound Bowen whirled up behind him, his sword glinting at Einon's throat.

"Dead again, Prince!" Bowen leered over the lad's shoulder. "How many times must I tell you?"

Einon mechanically recited it with him. "Only expose your back to a corpse!"

But the fencing lesson was over. Einon pointed at the

riders as they galloped through a weather-wasted arch into the ruin of what had once been a tiled courtyard. "It's happened."

Einon took off his training helmet and ran his fingers through a thick whitish-yellow shock of hair, damp with sweat. Bowen scowled as three men rode up. Two soldiers led by a massive brute of a knight: Sir Brok. All dressed in battle regalia. Bowen knew why they had come. So did Einon.

"The peasants are revolting."

Brok grinned sourly.

"They've always been *revolting,* Prince. Smell one sometime. But now they're *rebelling*."

Brok's men laughed at the jest. Bowen still scowled. Brok still grinned. At Bowen. It was still a sour grin. He disliked Bowen. Bowen didn't care. He disliked Brok.

"King Freyne would have his son witness his noble victory."

"Noble . . . ?" Bowen's scowl curled into a sneer of contempt. "Crushing desperate, frightened men . . ."

"Traitorous scum!" Brok corrected Bowen. His horse snorted nervously at the sharp snap of his voice. "The king commands! Bring him! . . . You can watch too, nursemaid."

The sour grin was back. Brok whipped his horse and rode off with his men into a splash of setting sun. Bowen turned and walked to where his and Einon's mounts were tethered to a piece of decaying timber. Taking the tunic flung over his saddle, he started to pull it on.

"Why do you let him insult you like that?" Einon's voice tensed in hurt agitation. "You, a knight of the Old Code! You're not afraid of him!"

"Nor of his opinions." Bowen laughed. His head poked through the neck of his jerkin with a shake of his unkempt mane. He'd already proven himself against Brok. They both had vied to be the prince's mentor. Freyne's choice of Brok would have gone unchallenged had it not been for Queen Aislinn. She had wanted Bowen. She had wanted a knight of the Old Code. Freyne had only agreed to a competition because he thought Brok would defeat the young knight who had lately come into his service in the trial by combat. Freyne had been wrong. By rights, Bowen could have killed Brok that day. But he let him live. Brok would never forgive him for it.

Bowen threw on his leather surcoat. As he belted it he caught Einon staring glumly at its emblem—a silver sword, hilt up, within a golden circle. He wanted the boy to respect the symbol, not be disappointed in it. He had taught him the words: "Inside the table's circle, under the sacred sword . . ." But Einon was still a boy, and words were subtle things, and boys didn't appreciate subtleties. Honor is honor. And an insult an insult. And it must not go unanswered. Bowen gave the only answer he could, knowing it would not satisfy.

"I expect no less of Brok. He is the king's man." The distaste in his voice was too obvious, as Bowen well knew. He saw it register in Einon's uneasy frown. Hard to be the son of a barbaric tyrant. Hard to serve one. The boy caught him looking at him and managed a smile.

"When I am king, you will be my man, Bowen."

"I am already your man, my prince." Bowen clapped the lad warmly on the shoulder and helped him into the saddle.

The shriek of battle shattered the night. Clanking steel and shouting men and groaning horses clamored in a cacophony of violence and death.

Gray smoke smudged the black sky. Fire tinged it blood red. Out of the slate-and-crimson haze flared a glint of gold. A crown. Spiraling to the ground. Into the mud and blood.

Feet scrambled past it. Stomping hooves nearly trampled it. A body careened down next to it. An armored knight. Emblazoned on his surcoat was a dragon's head impaled on a sword. As he collapsed, mud splattered across it, mingling with the blood that was already there. Blood also trickled from his mouth, flecking his beard. King Freyne had been struck a mortal blow. He was dying.

But even in his death throes, his glazed eyes spied the crown. His gauntleted fingers clutched for the golden orb, falling limp just short of it. His eyes stared vacantly at the unreached goal. His mouth went slack, a gurgle of blood bubbling on his lips. The king was dead.

"Father!" Einon's wild wail pierced the battle din as he whipped his mount through the carnage of the field. Armored warriors clashed against a motley rabble whose only weapons were crude farm implements. A scythe, wielded by a red-bearded peasant giant, had sliced Einon's father from the saddle. Einon had witnessed it all from the safety of a hillock above the fray. Bowen had insisted they watch from there . . . and watch only, though Einon had longed to be in the thick of things, if for no other reason than to see Bowen in action. He was the best swordsman of all the knights. The best, and the least liked. Einon attributed it to envy, but he also knew they could not stomach Bowen's pristine disdain for their ways. It was the same disdain he felt for this battle. Still, he should have been down there. If Bowen's blade had been at the king's side, the red-bearded dog of a rebel would have never cut him down.

He knew Bowen was somewhere behind him. He had heard the knight shout after him when he spurred his horse down the hill. But Einon had lost his mentor in the confusion. He was glad—Bowen would only steer him to safety again, and he had to get to his father.

Einon galloped through a veil of smoke, surging past blades and bodies to the spot where the fallen king lay. Dismounting, he scrambled to his father, laying a hand to his breast . . . and with a shudder pulling it back, covered in blood. Stunned, Einon stared from his hand to his father and then . . . to the crown.

It lay an arm's length away, catching firelight and

spraying it back. The glinting spokes of light that emanated from it like golden fingers dazzled Einon, seeming to beckon to him. Trembling, he reached over the limp corpse of his father to pluck the golden chaplet from the mud.

It made a sucking slurp as Einon pulled it loose. It felt heavier than he had expected. As he lifted it to him metal-encased fingers suddenly clamped onto the circlet and yanked it . . .

. . . down! Einon went with it and found himself staring through the golden ring of the crown into the fierce eyes of his father! Alive and determined. Startled, Einon instinctively jerked back. The crown came with him. Freyne clutched for it possessively, but Einon swung it from his reach. Freyne's fingers convulsively clawed at the air for a moment, then his outstretched arm fluttered and flopped onto his chest. A hoarse rattle seeped from his bloody lips and his eyes gazed at his heir in deathly astonishment.

Einon pulled back from his dead father. He realized he was still holding the crown aloft. Again, flamelight flickered across it, making it burn brightly in his hand. Then a hulking shadow behind him snuffed out the glow.

"The pig's brat. Come to wallow in the mud with his father."

Einon turned. A lean, sinewy giant hovered over him. The rebel's hair and beard were the color of the blood that dripped from his scythe. He was flanked by a barrel-chested bear of a man who wore a blood-soaked rag tied over his left eye and a gangly youth perhaps a few years older than Einon. The youth wore a bucket on his head with one side cut out as a crude helmet and watched the red beard in nervous uncertainty. Others crowded behind them.

"Thank Riagon, piglet." The one-eyed bear sneered. "His stroke made you king." This elicited laughter from several of the others.

"Hush, Hewe!" Riagon commanded. His eyes were hard and hateful and bore into Einon. "My stroke will unmake you."

Riagon the red beard raised his scythe. Einon cringed. From the corner of his eye, he saw Buckethead squeamishly turn away. Einon wished he could do the same, but his eyes were transfixed by the stained blade above him. Stained with the blood of his father. As Einon watched death arc down at him he suddenly felt himself catapulted backward; the scythe swooped past his head, carving only a jagged slice across his hand. Einon winced at the sting and the crown went flying from his fingers. But miraculously he was alive. Alive and ahorse! Bowen, grim determination distorting his handsome features, hauled the boy into the saddle behind him and whirled to meet the swishing scythe of the red beard.

He nimbly ducked the swirling blade, grabbed the shaft of the scythe, and with a rough jerk, cracked Red Beard under the jaw with the blunt end. The rebel lost his grasp on the scythe and staggered into the arms of Buckethead, driving them both to the ground, dazed.

"Only expose your back to a corpse!" Bowen growled at Einon as Hewe the Bear charged him. "Will you never learn?"

Hewe's barrel chest collided with the heel of Bowen's thrusted boot, which sent the peasant lurching back. Not forgetting his charge, Bowen continued his lecture, even as he clouted another rebel with the dull end of the scythe. "Do you forget everything I teach you?"

"Don't teach! Show! Kill the scum!" Einon screeched, his temper exploding in the aftermath of his grief and fear and the quivering humiliation of his own near death. He snatched the scythe from Bowen and wildly swung at another attacker. Bowen grabbed the weapon back and swatted the peasant with the shaft.

"I don't need to kill them!" Bowen sharply admonished, and flinging the scythe away, spurred his horse out of the melee and across the field.

• • •

Bowen whipped his horse up the hillock under the spectral shadow of a dead tree. Reining the steed, he leapt off and turned to Einon, still ahorse, anxiously examining the boy's cut hand.

"Are you all right? Do I waste my breath on you?" Bowen's angry reproof could not hide the tense concern in his voice. "Use your head—"

"—or lose my head," Einon timidly recited the rule, like a chastened schoolboy. It did not soften Bowen's stern sermon.

"And your first battle will be your last . . . if you call this bloodletting a battle!"

Bowen spat contemptuously, glaring down on the field. The peasants were determined fighters, but woefully outmatched. The king's men were slowly devastating them. He turned away in disgust to find Einon gazing at him in curious confusion. The boy spoke quietly, with both familiarity and deference.

"Is that why you do not fight, Bowen?"

Bowen's glare melted into a smile, then a hearty laugh.

"What did you think that was back there, little warrior?"

"I mean with this!" Einon leaned over in the saddle and, grabbing the hilt of Bowen's sword, yanked it from his belt, holding it aloft in boyish admiration. "Yours is the finest blade on the field!"

"Too fine to foul with the blood of helpless men." Bowen tore off a piece of his tunic sleeve and wiped at the bloody cut on Einon's hand. The boy winced. "My blade serves your safety, Prince, not your father's slaughters."

"He *was* my father, Bowen." Einon faltered, his tone quiet and hurt. "And he was . . . the king."

Bowen accepted the gentle rebuke in silent chagrin. In the chaotic fury of the last moments he had forgotten the boy's grief, and it seemed that Einon had too. But Bowen's thoughtless remark had pierced the wound afresh. Einon's lip trembled as he tried to hold back tears.

"*You* are king now." Bowen spoke comfortingly, gently

wiping away the tears with the bloody rag. "Be brave, Einon. Remember today. Remember the difference between battle and butchery. And remember the Old Code. Restore its forgotten glory so that the crown will shine with honor once more and never again will men have to take up arms against it. Then you will be a greater king than your father."

Bowen turned back to the raging battle with weary eyes. Silhouettes of clashing men flashed out against the dark and smoke, framed in firelight.

"I promise, Bowen, I will be greater. And no one will take arms against *my* crown."

A strange, harsh lilt in the boy's voice made Bowen turn to him. For the briefest instant he imagined a dark glint in Einon's gaze. But it must have been night shadows and fire glare. For Einon's eyes suddenly bulged in startled remembrance.

"The crown!" he gasped, startled as if by sudden remembrance.

"—will do you no good without a head to plop it on!" Bowen grabbed the horse's reins, anticipating Einon's intention before he could act on it. He would not have the boy hurt—or tainted—in the bloody brawl below. "Victory—such as it is—before the spoils, my prince."

"Your king!" Einon coolly corrected his mentor. "I want what is mine!"

Still holding Bowen's sword, he slapped his blade flat against the horse's haunch. The stallion whinnied and reared, tearing the reins from Bowen's hands.

"Einon!" Bowen's shout was smothered under the pounding hooves of the horse as Einon whipped it down the hill to the fray.

Through the smoky haze, Bowen spied Einon riding for the corpse of his father, still sprawled in the mud. He had sped down the hill after him and onto the field. Though weaponless, he had encountered little opposition. The king's men had the rebels in rout and most of the peasants gave an armored knight wide berth. One fool had come at him with a quarterstaff, only to have it wrenched from his hand and to be knocked breathless when it was thrust into his gut. Another had swung at him with a knife. Bowen had easily ducked the blow and run on.

He still ran as he watched Einon ride toward the crown perched on its side in the sloshy earth. Einon leaned low in the saddle, thrusting out Bowen's sword to scoop up the prize. The circlet looped the blade.

"Einon!"

Bowen's cry came too late. A gangly body, helmeted in a bucket, sprang off a small rise above Einon onto the horse. Bowen's sword flew from Einon's grasp and, still ringed by the crown, embedded itself into the ground. The two boys spilled into the mud, a jumble of arms and legs. The bucket helmet clattered off Einon's attacker, who flopped face-down, a cascade of red hair falling to his shoulders. First to his feet, Einon lunged for Bowen's still-vibrating sword, its point fixed in the ground.

Buckethead shook his red locks and whirled toward the blade. The rebel had his back to Bowen as the knight rapidly covered the distance between himself and the youths. From over the boy's shoulder Bowen saw Einon grab the sword hilt, then suddenly hesitate as he turned toward his enemy, jaw dropping in surprise, as . . .

. . . Buckethead's hand tore the hilt from Einon. The young king seemed to come to his senses in that moment and clawed at Buckethead's hand, struggling to tear the sword from it. The blade flipped out in a spray of mud and Buckethead awkwardly thrust it forward, plunging it into Einon's chest. Einon gasped, still staring with startled eyes into the youth's face, and lurching back off the blade, sagged to his knees, then pitched forward.

Bowen's rage and grief were unleashed in an anguished scream as he swooped up behind Buckethead, one hand tangling in the youth's long red hair and the other ripping his sword from his grasp and raising it back to strike in one fluid motion.

But as he jerked the young rebel back by the hair, he suddenly hesitated even as Einon had, now knowing why.

Buckethead was a girl!

A girl . . . only a year or two older than Einon. Even the grime of battle could not hide her beauty, haloed in the splendor of gleaming red hair. Bowen trembled above her in anger and stunned surprise. Her bright eyes were wide with fear, but eerily resigned, asking no mercy and expecting none. Bowen could not stand to look at them.

With a tormented wail, he flung the girl roughly from him, her hair ripping from his clutching fingers. She went spiraling to the ground and lay there, gasping, her bright eyes staring back at the knight in confused amazement. Again Bowen yelled and menaced her with his waving blade. She tore off into the night, no longer questioning her miraculous fortune.

"Bowen . . ." Einon gurgled weakly, his mouth half-full of mud. Bowen knelt beside him and gently turned him over. As he did so, something clanked against the metal studs of his belt. It was the crown. Einon clutched it in his hand. It was sticky with blood—Einon's blood—which oozed from a gash in his chest, seeping a scarlet ribbon across his surcoat, across the severed dragon-head crest of his ancestors.

"Bowen . . . ?" Einon murmured his name again. Bowen braced the limp, half-conscious body against his own, wiping mud from the boy's face.

"I'm here, my prince . . . my king!"

Chapter Two

MOONLIGHT PILGRIMAGE

"It has the stench of dragon!"

"Dead, madam . . ."

Aislinn watched the blood splatter on the floor, pool around the hem of her gown. It dripped from Brok's wounded shoulder as he knelt before her bedchamber altar. It seemed odd to see Brok bowed in such a sacred place. Of course, the brute had not come in reverence for the great silver cross that decorated her candlelit holy table, nor for the wood-carved, gold-trimmed dragon icons that flanked it. Piety compelled him not at all, merely protocol. He knelt there because he had interrupted the queen at her prayers. It was to her he knelt, not God. Still, the sight of Brok on his knees before her altar seemed odd, almost sacrilegious.

"King Freyne, your husband, is slain." Brok's words spilled out in a rough, breathless ramble. The blood from his wound spilled out in a steady *tap, tap, tap* onto the stone floor.

Aislinn gazed at him impassively. He had obviously fought long and ridden hard. He was filth-smudged and weary. His stark gaze searched her face for a reaction to his news, but he was disappointed. She accepted it with stoic resignation and motioned him off his knees, then turned to the altar, crossed herself, and lit the thick candle at the base of the cross. The jeweled eyes of the carved dragons glittered in its yellow light. Their shadows loomed on the curved wall of the small alcove. The shadow of the cross stretched between them, as though they were its guardians.

Aislinn blew out the taper and moved to her open window. She could hear the distant sounds of fighting, still, and could see the battle fires that pocked the dark plain below. Sudden worry trembled on her lip.

"The prince?" she asked of Brok, not turning around.

"With Sir Bowen."

"Safe then."

Her sigh of relief was drowned out by the echoing clank of her chamber door slamming open. At the sound, both she and Brok spun. A slant of light spilled across the floor of the long room—a torch from the hall outside. In the halo of the open door stood a silhouetted knight, a limp form cradled in his arms.

With a gut-sinking premonition, Aislinn stepped from the altar alcove and slowly, then quickly weaved to the door. A single tear trickled muddily down Bowen's battle-grimed face as Aislinn gasped at the sight of her crumpled son in his arms.

"Forgive me, my queen," Bowen whispered huskily.

Aislinn sagged against the door, speaking with quiet, bitter anger. "It's not your fault. The cruel excesses of his father brought him to this end."

She gestured to her bed. Bowen strode across the room, wordlessly shoving past Brok, who had bustled up to help, and gently laid the boy down among the sleeping furs. Aislinn sat on the edge of the bed. She saw the bloodstained crown still clutched in the hand that flopped across his chest. As she tried to lift it back Einon stirred, and a feeble whisper slid from his unmoving lips.

"My crown . . ."

Aislinn whirled to Bowen.

"He lives."

"He dies, madam." Bowen shook his head and knelt beside the bed. "Beyond all help."

Aislinn turned back to her son, probing his wound with

unflinching fingers. Her voice was curiously calm, even hopeful.

"Not all . . ."

A scarlet moon loped along the black path of night like a marauding wolf, hungrily eyeing the snake of flickering light that slithered through the mountains behind the castle.

"Inside the table's circle,
Under the sacred sword.
A knight must vow to follow
The code that is unending,
Unending as the table—
A ring by honor bound."

Bowen's voice was clear and strong against the wind, against the distant echoes of the battle far below. Aislinn looked down on the knight from her horse and smiled. Bowen had dismounted and led his horse so that he could walk beside Einon. The young king lay on a hide pallet borne by four royal guards. Torchbearers led the way up the tortuous mountain trail as Brok guided Aislinn's horse through the ancient Roman ruins.

In the glow of the wavering torches and under the strange crimson moonlight, the crumbling stones loomed out of the night like suspicious red-faced sentinels, as if gravely challenging the procession for trespassing. Bowen preferred them splashed with sunlight—pale and chalky, bleached of all their mystery. Was it only hours ago that Einon had dashed among these stones, lashing out with his blade and his oaths? Bowen longed to hear those murmuring lips curse him once again.

"Speak the words with me, Einon." Bowen plucked the crown from where it bounced on the stretcher and, placing it in Einon's hands, took up his recitation. "A knight is sworn to valor. . . ."

". . . sworn . . . to valor." Einon murmured the litany.

"His heart knows only virtue. . . ."

". . . virtue . . ."

"His blade defends the helpless. His might upholds the weak. . . ."

Einon's mumble slid into a groan. Bowen shook him. "You must stay awake, my lord. You must! Recite the code. . . ."

". . . code . . ." Einon breathed out the word, his fingers flitting absently over the crown.

"Yes!" Bowen continued. "His might upholds the weak. . . ."

"His . . . word speaks only truth. . . ."

"Yes . . . yes . . . His wrath . . . ?" Bowen prompted.

"His wrath undoes the wicked." They recited it together. Then the crown slipped from his fingers once more and Einon slipped into unconsciousness.

"Einon?" Bowen leaned over him. The boy was still breathing, but barely. Aislinn must have been mad to think he could survive all this jostling. He wondered if the ancient arts of her clan could truly save Einon. More, he wondered what those arts were and why they necessitated this nocturnal journey. Where was she taking them?

She sat her horse proudly—head high, eyes straight ahead. The wind caressed her yellow hair, tinged pink under the scarlet moon, blowing it back from her graceful neck and smooth jaw. The night embraced her beauty, which was only enhanced by her quiet, eternal melancholy.

Her people had come from the lands of the North Seas. Old in their ways and old in their knowledge. Some whispered that they were magicians. Aislinn only smiled when she heard such talk, saying one man's witchery was merely another's wisdom.

Bowen was suddenly jarred from his thoughts by an eerie trilling. It seemed to echo from farther up the mountain, its music haunting and mournful. The others heard it too, halting in their tracks.

"Proceed," was all Aislinn said. Her voice was placid, her

face composed. But her blue eyes sparked excitement as she listened to the trill. She turned and caught Bowen watching her.

She stared at him as though she were stealing his thoughts. And her sad smile strangely stole his fears.

"The right can never die. . . ." She spoke softly. "You also proceed, Knight. Teach my son the code. . . ."

Bowen obeyed.

"The right can never die,
If one man still recalls.
The words are not forgot,
If one voice speaks them clear.
The code forever shines,
If one heart holds it bright."

For another hour they climbed up the mountain, Aislinn directing their path. At intervals, the weird trill floated, ghostlike, through the air, bouncing off the hills, sounding as though it came from everywhere. And each time it was closer.

Now it was very close. Aislinn had led them to the dark maw of a cave. From within came that forlorn song. Bowen now knew what was singing it. And he suddenly feared Aislinn's magic.

"I know what place this is." He eyed the queen warily. "It has the stench of dragon."

"Not the dragon's stench," Aislinn calmly remonstrated. "Merely man's pollution of him."

She took a torch from one of her guards and disappeared into the cave. Bowen and Brok exchanged uncertain glances. Aislinn's voice issued out of the blackness beyond. "Come and fear not."

Bowen looked at Einon's limp, still form on the pallet; then he scooped the boy into his arms and followed Aislinn into the dark unknown. With a grunted sigh, Brok reluctantly motioned the others into the cave and brought up the rear.

Chapter Three

THE DRAGON

"Witness the wonders of an even greater glory."

Even the torches could not dispel the gloom. Their flickering blaze illuminated bubbling mud pits and bones. Steam misted off the gurgling muck holes and writhed through the maze of stalactites and rock formations.

Bowen's darting eyes hunted the dismal shadows for a sign of life. He spied it in the cave's farthest recesses—a faint iridescent ripple of movement. And the sighing, lonely trill. Toward this Aislinn discreetly, humbly, approached.

"Lord! Serene One!" Her voice reverberated through the hollow chamber. The trilling stopped. Bowen heard the guards murmur uneasily. His eyes never left the glow at the back of the cave. It seemed brighter, defining some uncertain shape. Aislinn signaled for silence.

"Your song is sad tonight," Aislinn said respectfully.

"No stars in the sky tonight."

The voice came from the large, eerie shape shimmering in the shadows. It too was large and eerie, yet strangely soothing and sad.

"No bright souls glitter on this dark night." Aislinn moved toward the glow. "Only a moon. Blood red."

Bowen had followed cautiously behind the queen. He eased Einon down on a flat stone beneath the ledge where the creature stirred. Placing a hand on his sword hilt, he hovered protectively over the boy, suspiciously listening, his eyes always on the shadowy presence above. He could see now that the peculiar iridescence was the beast's scaly hide. It emitted the wavering glow every time the dragon shifted, as it did now, cocking its head and appraising the woman below him.

"Aislinn. Daughter of Athelstun."

"Yes, Lord," Aislinn answered warmly, pleased that the dragon had recognized her. "Whose people loved you and called you kind friend."

"Once," hissed the dragon. "Long ago. No more. No longer fickle man's friend. Feared. Forgotten."

"I have not forgotten," Aislinn replied. "I do not fear."

"You warm the bed of him whose ancestors first drove us to dank holes and night's shadow."

"Politics, Dragon Lord, not love. A bride of conquest, my betrothal bathed in blood, my people driven out and slaughtered even as yours."

"My crown!" Einon shuddered out in sudden delirium. His cry ringed the cavern walls, as though spoken by a thousand tongues: *Crown, crown, crown* . . . Both Aislinn and Bowen knelt to comfort the boy.

"Peace, Einon," Aislinn murmured sweetly, stroking his brow.

"No peace," Einon muttered, feverishly fondling the crown. "Red hair. Red hair. Like fire. Like blood."

Einon slumped back, semiconscious. Only Bowen knew where the boy's mind wandered. Only he knew of the red-haired assassin. The assassin he had let go. Suddenly sensing motion behind him, he reeled back.

It was the dragon, leaning over the ledge. His half-hooded eye glinted in the darkness, surveying the prince . . . his bloodstained surcoat . . . the severed dragon's head on it.

"Freyne's child," the dragon droned wearily.

Aislinn whirled on the dragon in desperation. "No! Mine!"

"Is this why you come, dragonslayer's wife?"

"Dragonslayer's widow!" returned the queen emphatically, then softened her tone, though it remained husky with emotion. "Please! He's not his father." She pointed to Bowen. "This knight is his mentor. He has taught him the Old Code. And I will teach him *your ways*!"

The dragon turned to Bowen. Entranced by the creature's luminous stare, the knight did not see the taloned claw that loomed out of the darkness until it was almost too late. He went for his blade, but held back as the dragon also went for a sword . . . the sword within the circle on Bowen's surcoat. The talon plucked gingerly at the symbol.

"The Old Code . . ." mused the dragon with a raspy sigh, then withdrew his claw. Bowen noticed the middle talon was half-severed. A whispery hiss escaped the dragon, sounding strangely like laughter, and he held the jagged talon up before his shiny eyes.

"An old wound from the boy's father," the dragon said wryly. At that moment the glow in his eyes seemed to dim and he turned them balefully on the boy's bloody breast . . . on the beheaded dragon emblem.

"The wound is deep. . . ." The dragon turned to Aislinn as he spoke. She nodded and a look of understanding passed between them. A long silence ensued as the dragon considered her plea. "You know what you ask?"

"I know." With this, Aislinn slowly knelt before the dragon as Bowen and her retainers stood by, shocked. "I swear. He will grow in your grace. Grow just and good."

The dragon's shadowy head inclined toward Einon.

"*He* must swear. Your sword, Knight."

Startled and suspicious of the request, Bowen looked to Aislinn for guidance. The queen calmly nodded for him to comply. Still uncertain, he reluctantly unsheathed the sword to hand it to her, but the dragon's scaly claw emerged once more from the darkness and gripped the blade between his talons. Bowen instinctively let go.

The dragon swung the sword over the still form of Einon. The shadow of its hilt and blade framed the boy in a silhouetted cross. Einon stirred and, seeing the shadowy creature above him, gasped. Aislinn moved to his side, with a calming whisper.

"Fear not, child, he will save you."

"But first, boy, by the cross of the sword, you swear." The dragon's breath throbbed through the cave. "Swear your father's bloodlust and tyranny die with him. If you live and rule, live and rule in mercy. Swear this. And that you will come to me and learn. The Once-ways. That my kind may leave the gloomy dark and spread their wings in sunlight once more. That man and dragon may be brethren as of old. Swear!"

Swear, swear, swear . . . The word echoed through the darkness, and the dragon extended the hilt of the sword to Einon, who clutched it.

"I . . . swear. . . ." the young king gasped, and leaned up to kiss the pommel. But before his lips could touch it, his fingers slipped off the hilt and he slumped back. Bowen caught him in his arms.

"Einon?" Bowen shook him. "Einon!"

He laid the limp form of the boy on the stone and staggered back in dazed grief.

"All this jabbering and empty mummery! You are too late! He's dead!" The words jerked out of Bowen in halting gulps, their echoing bounding back on him as if to remind him that Einon was dead. As if he could forget. He glared at the queen in searing rebuke. "Why have you brought us to this devil creature to dabble in his dark witchery?"

"Hush!" Aislinn coolly commanded. "Curse not what you know not!"

"I know evil! I know my charge, your son, is dead!"

Bowen wheeled in wild despair and violently grabbed his sword by the hilt to wrest it from the dragon. But as he yanked, the dragon's talons scraped down the length of the blade with a whining screech, scoring a groove in it from guard to tip.

"Peace!" The dragon's powerful breath held the knight at bay with a shuddering blast that blew the torches out. The cavern was immersed in utter darkness, save for the occasional glint of the dragon's shimmering scales and his glowing eyes. They blazed into Bowen—not in anger, but with a strange, fierce serenity.

"Peace, Knight of the Old Code," the dragon urged quietly, "and witness the wonders of an even more ancient glory."

The dragon released the sword and placed his ragged talon against his breast, impaling it in the scales of his hide. As he sliced down his chest a red glow issued from the wound. Not blood. But light. The dragon reached into the cut. Sighed. Groaned. And captured a pulsating scarlet brilliance in his claw as the wound closed over.

He held the glowing orb over the boy. Einon's eyelids fluttered open. He smiled as the beast gently reached down and the glowing redness seeped into the boy's wound.

"Half my heart to make you whole," the dragon intoned. "Its strength to purify your weakness. Live and remember your oath."

The dragon pulled his claw back and a thin sliver of fire shot from his mouth along Einon's wound. Bowen lunged forward to protect the boy, only to be halted by Einon's calm smile. The young king felt no pain. The flame was cauterizing his wound.

When it ceased, the gash was sealed by a crusty smoke-blackened scab. Aislinn gasped a sob and hugged her resurrected child. Einon struggled to rise, but the dragon gently restrained him.

"Rest. Sleep and renew," the dragon enjoined, and covered the boy's face with his scaly claw. When he withdrew it, Einon's eyes were closed in peaceful slumber. Bowen was startled from his state of dazed disbelief when the dragon shot forth another burst of flame.

It relit the torches in the startled attendants' hands. The queen motioned Brok to bring forth the stretcher. The bearers came forward and lifted the sleeping king onto the pallet. Aislinn turned and, in deep reverence, bowed once more to the dragon. The dragon's shimmering head nodded in acknowledgement, then Aislinn rose, leading her entourage toward the entrance of the cave. Bowen hesitated, glancing at the deep groove the dragon's talon had scratched in his blade. Turning, he followed Aislinn's example and knelt before the mysterious creature on the ledge.

"I've served the father only for the sake of the son," Bowen said, surprised by the sudden rush of emotion in his throat. "In him go all the hopes of my heart. Forgive a doubting fool. Call when you've need of me, ask what you will of me. My sword and service are yours."

The dragon had already faded back into the darkness. Only an occasional shiny scale flickered from the gloom. But the dragon still had one message to deliver. "Only remind him always of his vow, Knight of the Old Code," he said.

Brok scratched his thick beard as he watched Bowen and the queen riding ahead of him, the torchbearers lighting their way. Bowen leaned over in his saddle and pointed out a crumbling arch that stood amidst the ruins of the old Roman castle. Aislinn nodded as she listened, smiled appreciatively, and spoke animatedly with the knight. Brok frowned as he brought up the rear with the stretcher bearers and the sleeping king.

To his untrained mind, Aislinn seemed a disturbingly learned woman. She knew all about architecture and art and letters. Not at all like the women Brok was used to. Good healthy bawds who liked a joke and a romp and a raucous feast. He could never understand why Freyne had made this white dainty his queen. Oh, her beauty would inflame any man; but toss her in your bed, not on your throne.

Brok snorted and spat. He didn't like thinking like this. He wasn't an introspective man. And certainly not a scholarly one. He knew nothing of architecture and art and letters, knew nothing and cared less. So as he sourly watched the swishing tails of the horses, he neither knew nor cared that he had been inspired to fashion a figure of speech: My sudden shift at court, he thought, is like the back ends of those horses ahead—full of dung.

Bowen was the king's mentor and had the queen's ear. To Brok, this meant that things were soon going to be dull around the court. No more bawds and brawling banquets. Now would come the interminable invocation of codes and courtly niceties . . . and, perhaps even more strange, dark rituals with dragons. Freyne would moan in hell if he knew the blood of his ancestors' ancient enemies now flowed in his son and heir. Of course, it hadn't looked like blood. Just a dazzling glow of light; and back in the cave, Brok had been dazzled like the rest. But now, out in the good night air and among familiar things, he shivered with distaste and distrust. He now knew why Freyne had annihilated Aislinn's witch clan.

Brok remembered this dragon. Indeed he had been a member of the hunting party several years ago when Freyne had wounded it. The king had been furious at its escape. He had wanted that trophy . . . to be a recognized dragon-slayer like the rest of his blood. Brok mused how he might gather some of the others and go a-dragoning soon. They would get Freyne his trophy. What a funeral gift that would make! What a monument on his grave!

Of course, such behavior might not sit well with the new monarch and his mother. Or with their right hand—Bowen. And Brok had felt Bowen's right hand himself. He spat again. It had been a long night. He was worn to the bone. He didn't like thinking on all this. It made his head hurt.

Fate kindly relieved him of his weighty ruminations by providing a distracting clank. Brok turned around. The crown had slipped from Einon's hand and fallen against a rock. It caused Einon to jerk awake, sitting bolt upright. There was a strange, fierce light in the boy's eyes. He was tense with coiled energy. Brok signaled the bearers to halt and knelt beside the pallet.

"Your Majesty?" he asked. "Is all well?"

Einon unconsciously slipped a hand through the tear in his clothing, feeling the scar on his chest. He gazed at it and remembered . . . and smiled at the memory. "All is very well. The crown."

He gestured for the fallen chaplet. Brok picked it up and offered it to him. Eyes afire, the boy snatched it and plopped it on his head. It was too big, but Einon seemed to like the fit nonetheless. Or perhaps, thought Brok, he just liked possessing the crown, period. "Anything more, Your Majesty?"

"Much more." Einon turned from his regal regard to smile grimly at Brok. It warmed the cockles of Brok's heart. It was Freyne's smile.

Brok looked down the trail. Bowen and Aislinn were some distance ahead, unaware that the others had stopped. He turned back to the king to find him hesitantly rising off the stretcher. Brok leaned in to support him, but Einon pushed him away. The boy was shaky on his feet, but he stood.

"The Romans built a great castle here," Einon said, looking out on the moon-clad ruins. "Mine will be greater."

Brok heard the conviction in the boy's voice and found it intriguing, even encouraging. "It will take many men, milord, to rebuild this ruin."

"Yes . . ." Einon smiled his father's smile again. Brok smiled back. Perhaps his new place in the court wasn't the horse's rump after all.

Chapter Four

THE KING RESURRECTED

"Burn the insolence out of his eyes!"

Firelight licked the gray edges of dawn. Brushing aside a lock of her red hair, Kara shifted in the branches of the tree and peeked through its concealing leaves to watch her village burn. Women wailed and children shivered in the cold morning, staring fearfully at the corpses littering the muddy paths between the huts. Kara stared at them too—friends, neighbors, people she had known all her life. So far Riagon, her father, was not among them. Nor was he among the menfolk being rounded up and shackled in wooden neck stocks.

But she wondered how long he would be safe. He had been the first to see the riders coming and, against her protests, had insisted she run. She had obeyed, as she always obeyed him, but had run only as far as the giant oak, hiding in its heavy green boughs. She had lost sight of her father when the king's men swarmed in, putting everything to the torch. Resistance had been brief, futile, and quickly disintegrated into panicked chaos. Riagon had disappeared into the smoke and flame and crush of fleeing bodies.

A towering brute, who seemed to command the foray, steered his horse through the trampled shambles of a hut and scraped away debris with his sword, ferreting out a trapdoor beneath the charred clutter. He motioned to a pair of soldiers, who jerked the door open, exposing a disheveled-looking red-bearded giant, huddled in a root cellar full of cheese.

Kara gasped as the brute jabbed his sword downward. But he was aiming for the cheese, not Riagon. Impaling a round, he brought it to his mouth and took a hearty bite right off his sword as the two minions herded the redbeard out of the hole.

Kara wanted to run to him. But as they shackled him in a neck stock with two other captives, he raised his head and looked directly up at the tree. She saw the almost imperceptible shake of his head from side to side. To any observer, it would merely have seemed a look of dazed disbelief at his fate, or maybe trembling fear. But Kara knew it for what it was. A signal to stay put.

Her fingers flicked nervously through her thick red locks. As she debated defying Riagon just this once someone rode out of the smoky haze and approached the brute and his new prisoner. Kara recognized him.

It was the prince—the one her father had called piglet—the one she had stabbed. How had he survived? How could he sit a horse? She would never forget that startled thrust of hers. The slithering, liquid squish it made as it sank deep into his chest. Yet here the piglet was, the crown of Freyne perched awkwardly on his head, glaring at her father in malevolent satisfaction. But the young king could not match the cold contempt of her father's gaze. Piglet rubbed the cut on his hand. Riagon the Red saw the movement and smiled. "You remember me, boy? Pity I didn't make a deeper impression."

The brute yanked Redbeard's head back by the leather band that bound his wild mane, exposing the rebel's neck to his blade. "Your grave will make a very deep impression."

"No!" the piglet ordered the brute, then asked: "The girl?"

"Must have run off with the rest." The brute scowled.

"Or was slain in the battle by your butchers," Riagon suggested with a snarl. Kara knew he wanted them to accept this suggestion as the truth. Better that they should think she was dead. "Search the slaughter field, Piglet."

Again, the brute's sword was at Riagon's throat.

"We'll send you there to search."

Again, the young king called off his dog.

"Enough, Brok!"

Brok the Brute withdrew his blade reluctantly. The king glared at the redbeard. "I want no martyrs. And death is a release, not punishment."

The boy smiled evilly at Riagon. But the rebel's steady gaze did not waver as Piglet wheeled his horse to snatch a torch from one of his men. The blaze of the torch washed Einon's pale skin even whiter. In its harsh light, he looked like a dead soul come from hell as he sneered down at Kara's father.

"It's an insolent gaze. Look good, dog. And remember. I am your king. The man who crushed you. And the last thing you will ever see."

"Pity," spat Riagon the Red, defiant to the last. "Your crown is cockeyed, Piglet!"

The boy flung the torch down to the brute, shouting, "Burn that insolence out of his eyes!"

Grinning, Brok picked up the torch. And as the flame came near his eyes Riagon, pale but proud, looked to the trees . . . to the giant oak that towered on the village outskirts . . . to Kara . . . and his eyes ordered her to stay.

Kara disobeyed.

"No!" came her sobbed scream, and she leapt down from the oak. But Kara's scream was not heard. Another cry fractured the gray morning and drowned it out.

Bowen rode in like a whirlwind, shouting wildly. Brok barely saw the sword blade sweep past his face before it had struck the torch from his hand and came shattering down on the neck stock of the three prisoners, splintering it.

"Run," Bowen yelled as the redbeard and the others

broke free. But they needed no encouragement and were already scattering for the woods. Bowen's daring had confounded and momentarily paralyzed Einon's men. Finally one snapped from his stupor and spurred his horse toward the redbeard, who had suddenly stopped in his flight, stunned by the sight of a young girl with hair as red as his own rushing out of the foliage toward him.

"Kara! Quickly!" the rebel shouted, and wheeled to confront the man charging at him. But Bowen sped between them and cut the man out of the saddle, grabbing the reins of the downed man's steed.

"Take the horse!" he snapped at the giant . . . and then recognized the flame-haired girl at his side. He was not the only one to do so.

"I want those red devils, Bowen!" Einon galloped toward them, his sword slithering from his scabbard. "Stop them or I'll have your head!"

Bowen flung the reins of the horse at the peasant. "Get gone!"

Redbeard mounted and pulled his daughter up behind him, whipping the horse toward the forest as Bowen stood his ground, waiting for Einon and for what he dreaded and did not want to believe.

He had awoken early this morning and had gone to the royal chambers to check on Einon's condition. Einon was gone. Bowen's search for the boy had led him to the stables, and there he had learned of this expedition from a groom who had overheard Brok and others talking. It had been the groom's understanding that the new king would lead the raid, but Bowen figured the churl had gotten it wrong. He had come to stop Brok, not to seek Einon. He knew his charge would not be here, would not be party to this. Even now, as Einon bore down on him, the knight knew it wasn't, couldn't be, true. It was a mad dream and he would wake from it as soon as the swords clashed.

But they clashed and Bowen found himself already

awake and the nightmare real and the only escape from it was to defend himself.

"How dare you defy me!" the enraged boy screeched, and rained down a mad sally of blows.

"Einon! You're unwell!" Bowen reluctantly but skillfully defended himself, pleading, "You've been bewitched! Don't do this! Remember the code!"

"The king is above the code!" Einon growled.

Dismayed by the declaration, Bowen dropped his guard for an instant and Einon unseated him with a stab in the shoulder. The knight toppled between the skittish horses. Einon rode over him, whirling triumphantly to acknowledge the cheers of his men. A mistake . . . for a muddy hand reached up and yanked Einon's leg from the stirrup, shoving it out and up, heaving the boy off his horse. Einon reeled over the right flank of his horse, flopping to the ground. He pushed his oversized crown back from his eyes to find Bowen grimly grinning at him through the legs of the horse.

"Dullard! Only expose your back to a corpse!" Bowen, bleeding from his shoulder and his head, braced himself on his blade and tried to stagger up. Einon angrily leapt to his feet and, whipping his horse away, struck at the still-kneeling Bowen. But even kneeling, Bowen deflected Einon's wild charge.

"Control, little warrior!" Bowen countered Einon's undisciplined sallies, critiquing the boy's technique as he did so. "Purpose, not passion!"

He slashed Einon's scabbard. It slid down his legs, tripping him up. Bowen savagely lunged atop the tottering king, forcing him down, poising his blade against the boy's chest. He glared Brok and the others back, sword arm tensing.

"Should have been a better fight. I was a better teacher! But I thought you were a better student," Bowen barked in bitter disappointment. His eyes smoldered with pained hurt. His blade pressed into Einon's chest, which heaved with panic.

"How many times?" Bowen harshly queried. "Fight with your head, not your heart!"

The heart. Bowen watched Einon's dragon crest rise and fall along with his blade in chaotic rhythm with the boy's racing heart. The dragon's heart. The dragon. It was almost as though he could hear the cursed thing beating. *Thump. Thump. Thump.* Pulsing with treacherous life.

"No one is above the code," Bowen rasped in choked emotion, staring at the petrified youth with sorrow-filled eyes. "Least of all the king!"

He leaned down and kissed the stunned boy.

Tears welled in the knight's eyes as he whirled and sharply whistled. As Bowen's steed galloped up, Einon scrambled away, grasping his cheek where the knight had kissed him. His confused fear quickly turned to anger once more as Bowen mounted and spurred off into the forest.

"Seize him! Bring him down!" Einon shrilly bellowed the command and straightened the cockeyed crown upon his head.

Aislinn had been alone all day, with only the rumors of her servants to keep her company. Uncertain, confused whispers about reprisals for Freyne's death. And certain, clear lies that Einon had been at the head of his father's knights when they rode out before sunup. It was true that the knights and Einon were gone. But not for bloodletting. Not after the miracle of last night. Not with Bowen gone too. She would talk with Bowen. The king should still be resting from his ordeal. It was unconscionable of the knight to allow him up and out. It was irresponsible of him not to keep her informed. Where had he taken the king? Why hadn't he told her? Where were Brok and the others? What were they doing that had taken the full measure of the day? Where was Bowen?

A clatter of hoofbeats and rough laughter sent her rushing to her chamber window. Freyne's knights galloped into the courtyard below her window. Einon was in the lead. He leapt from the saddle, scowling, and slapped the reins of his horse into the hands of a groom.

"Not a bad day, milord," Brok said, trying to cheer the king. "Sixty men for the quarry. And the redbeard and the wench can't escape us for long."

Aislinn saw Einon wither Brok with his stare. "And what about our friend Sir Bowen?"

But Aislinn could detect no friendship in Einon's voice, and again she wondered where Bowen was. She could not know that at that very moment he was close. Nor could she know that she would never see him again.

"We'll find Bowen too, Your Majesty," assured Brok, dismounting.

Einon snorted a sharp laugh. "In a pig's eye, you will. . . . Ah, let him go. He's served his turn. I don't need him anymore."

Aislinn's son caught sight of her in the window. She did not like the truculent way he shoved the heavy crown back off his forehead. Suddenly he winced and pulled his right hand off the chaplet, clenching it in his left. Brok hurried to his side.

"Something wrong, milord?"

"A cramp in my hand, that's all." Einon flexed his fingers and looked at the scab on the back of his hand where Redbeard's scythe had bitten it. "Probably where the rebel dog sliced it." As he shook the pain out a tortured trilling came tumbling down the hills into the courtyard.

Einon and his minions listened to the low, ominous keening, glancing curiously about them, as it bounced from crag to crag, obscuring its origin. But Brok knew where it came from and he shivered at the sound.

Aislinn also knew and her sad eyes scanned the towering mountain beyond the ancient ruins. The sinking sun impaled itself on the high peaks and its purple-red blood oozed out across the horizon as the strange, wailing dragon cry echoed across the darkening sky.

• • •

The dragon clutched his claw to his scaly breast. His shimmering color dimmed as his shadowy form sagged against the rock wall. He slid his talons underneath the plates and felt his chest, felt the fresh sore scar . . . felt the emptiness inside. Moaning, he tore the claw back from his chest, glaring at the maimed middle talon and, with a shuddering trill, resumed banging it against the jagged cavern stones . . . relentlessly pounding in agonized fury until it was shredded and swollen. Crimson light seeped from tattered flesh and his half-severed talon cracked and broke off, clattering down the rocky ledge to the cave floor.

But the dragon was suddenly aware of something more than the echoing bounce of the talon. He ceased his groaning lament, and even as he sensed the intruder's approach, his skin shed its natural color and blended into the multishaded rock, becoming one with the cave. His inner eyelids shuttered down, their gauzy membranes masking his eyes, yet still allowing him to observe the uninvited visitor undetected.

Waning rays of daylight drifted in from the open mouth of the cave and captured the interloper's long shadow as he cautiously entered, his unsheathed sword gripped in readiness. He edged past the burbling mud pits, twisted around a stalagmite. His eyes focused on the ledge where the dragon lurked and watched, quiet and invisible.

It was the knight of the Old Code. . . .

Chapter Five

A DREAM AND DESTINY

"Not my betrayal."

Bowen crept toward the cave ledge, ever on guard. His eyes furtively searched the shadow-darkened recesses for some hint of movement. There was none, but he knew the dragon was here. His boot struck something then and a faint flash of red rolled across the ground. Bowen jumped back into a crouch, his blade flickering up like a snake's tongue.

But nothing came at him and the red glow stopped, growing dimmer. Bowen inched toward the iridescence and, reaching down, snared it in his free hand. It was the dragon's broken talon. The red glint emanated from its ripped base. But even as Bowen turned it curiously in his hand, the glimmering light dulled and seemed to fade into the viscous bloodlike liquid that dripped from the torn talon. Closing his fist around it, the knight rose.

"I know you're here, dragon!" Bowen called out. "I heard your dark song. It was still echoing off the walls as I entered. Come forth!" Bowen's own shout rang throughout the cave. "My oath will not save you! All bonds are broke with your betrayal!"

"Not my betrayal," the dragon droned bitterly. Bowen swerved to the sound of the voice, glaring up at the ledge.

"Lying hellspawn!" Bowen peered into the shadows above. For a moment it seemed as if the rocks rippled vaguely—a trick of the fading sunlight, no doubt. There was nothing there, but the voice had sounded as though it came from that direction. Bowen clenched his sword and wished he had not come here at day's end. He had ridden all day, eluding Einon's men, and his shoulder still stung where the boy had pricked him.

"Show yourself!" he demanded tensely.

And the dragon complied . . . in a swooshing glittering flash, the color flowing back into his scales as he swooped off the ledge, over the startled knight, and out of the cave.

Bowen tore from the cave to see the dragon lunge past his rearing horse and out into the twilight clouds. The frightened horse whinnied as Bowen frustratedly clanged his sword against a rock, shouting after the sun-speckled shape, "No matter where you fly, dragon, no matter where you hide, I will find you! I make a new vow! I will undo your treachery! . . . Even if I must spend the rest of my life hunting you down!"

The echoing oath was answered by a mournful trill. Every mountain seemed to reverberate with the haunting song as Bowen watched the dragon drown into the fiery flood of the sinking sun.

He felt the heat of its light upon his face, was deafened by the intense crackle of its blaze and . . .

. . . woke up!

He had dozed off. Well, it had been a long day. But a profitable one. He looked out across the lagoon by which he camped. The water shimmered in the firelight. The flame's gleam sparkled hotly over the thick scarlet liquid that dripped from the gashes of the burning dragon carcass and pooled into the green water like crimson lily pads.

The blaze burned furiously over the huge mountain of flesh, half-submerged under the placid pond. Bowen had used a fire arrow to cremate the kill, piercing one of the flopped wings. The fire had devoured the thin membrane rapidly and soon the entire carcass was engulfed in flame. Dragons always burned swiftly . . . and brightly, shooting off strange, almost supernatural sparks of light. Perhaps their foul blood caused the phenomenon; whenever a wound was inflicted, it flowed out as glowing light before liquefying into a dull, oozing gore. Whatever the cause, it made a glorious pyre. It meant one less dragon.

Bowen picked up the talon he had severed from this kill—the middle right talon—and affixed it to the shield in his lap; the task he had been about before he dozed off. This would make eleven. He didn't need to count the other talons already mounted on the shield. He knew how many there were. Eleven. Knew where he had killed them. When. How. Eleven. Eleven in three years. Einon would be eighteen now. A man. His reputation as king was already made. He had built a magnificent castle upon the Roman ruins of the mountain, it was said. And the borders of his realm stretched far beyond those of his father's domain. He was a great and powerful king. And a hated and feared one. Yes, his reputation was made. Carved in blood and brutality.

But someday Bowen would put an end to it, put an end to this curse. He looked at the dragon talons mounted on his shield. Eleven. This was the first in a long time; dragons were harder to come by of late. But he would go on searching, no matter how hard it became. He would search until he was finished. Eleven wasn't enough. There were more out there. There was *one* out there. With each kill he had checked the breast for the telltale scar. He had checked the right claw . . . and the middle talon. No, it wasn't enough.

Only eleven . . . no . . . *ten.*

Only ten. Bowen studied the centerpiece of his trophy shield, ran his finger gingerly down the jagged edge of the broken talon. The one lie among his victories. Merely a promise of victory. An unrealized dream that beckoned him . . . or taunted him. Mocked him and haunted him. Like the dream that had come to him tonight as he had dozed, as it had come so often in the last three years. Not a dream at all, actually. A memory. For it had happened. He had stood upon that mountaintop and watched the dragon wing its way into the setting sun and disappear with it into the darkness beyond his reach. And he had shouted those words after the fleeing figure. "I will undo your treachery." Made his vow. A memory. A dream. A nightmare. A destiny.

Bowen flung the shield aside and, kneeling by the pond, dipped his hands into it, splashing his face with water. It was warm. Probably the heat of the fire. As the ripples he made settled he stared at the face frowning back at him from the pool. He barely recognized it anymore. The laughter in the eyes had dimmed; the gaze was cold and cynical. The frowning mouth tight and hard set. The face was still chiseled, but freshness had fled the sun-leathered flesh and the smoothness of the still-firm jaw was marred by a unkempt beard. Gray tinged the brownish-blond hair that tangled down his neck.

Bowen puddled the water with his hand and drowned the frowning face. He gazed across the flame-flicked pond to the burning dragon. A fiery lump of flesh slid off the exposed rib cage, hissing into the water. The carcass flared with unsettling incandescence. It was almost too pretty. Magical. Melancholy swept over Bowen like the fire swept over the dragon. How bright the blaze!

Part II

THE QUESTS

Oh, Avalon! Bright Avalon! End my soul's dismay.
Return forgotten glories that once held noble sway.

—Gilbert of Glockenspur, "Lost Avalon"

Chapter Six

ONE LESS DRAGON

"Never have I seen such skill!"

The wheat waved gently in the morning breeze. Or perhaps it merely bowed to the bombast of the recitation that disrupted the serenity of the day.

> "So lost the world when lost its code,
> So lost in evil cruel!
> But one back dared to bear the load
> And seek the golden rule."

The poet was a priest, Brother Gilbert of Glockenspur. He rode his mule down the brown path between two fields of wheat, composing as he recited, scratching with a quill across a vellum scroll unrolled on a writing tablet braced against the mule's neck.

> "A solitary pilgrim rode
> Upon his lowly mule . . ."

Both the mule and monk were laden with scrolls and manuscripts. Bundles of parchment protruded from four saddlebags flapping against the mule's flanks. Slung about the priest's middle was a cloth sack filled with scrolls. As the mule plodded down the path Gilbert pondered his next line, tapping the quill against his pursed lips. Inspiration struck; he dipped his quill in the inkwell on the tablet, and scribbled across the scroll, speaking aloud the words as he wrote them.

> "Content with this, his humble mode,
> His quest was spiritual . . ."

It came out "spirichool," a tortured attempt at a rhyme with "mule." The mule itself shook its head with a short snort, as though in derision. Gilbert frowned at the animal.

"Everyone's a critic." Gilbert scratched out the line. But his editing didn't seem to satisfy the mule, who whinnied nervously and stamped his feet. Gilbert's writing tablet and its contents clattered to the ground, ink spilling over his composition as it went. Gilbert yanked the reins, trying to control the beast.

"Whoa, Merlin! It wasn't that objectionable. Whoa!"

But Merlin responded with a rambunctious buck. Braying, he sent the priest flying after his writing tablet. Gilbert tumbled cassock over crucifix, the manuscripts spilling from his pouch into the wheat with him.

The priest sat up with as much dignity as he could muster and, thrusting aside a clump of wheat from his face, glared at his disturbed mount, quivering and stomping the ground.

"I'm not in the mood for any of your tantrums, Merlin," Gilbert chastised as he crawled about gathering up his scrolls, quite oblivious to the animal's blatant distress. Or its cause.

He did not hear the creeping rustle in the field behind him. He did not see the curling smoke that weaved through the tendrils of wheat and, like a snake, slithered toward him.

Totally unsuspecting, Gilbert wagged an admonishing scroll at the shivering mule. "I realize that, thus far, this has been a rather uneventful, if not altogether fruitless and boring, quest. But remember its goals, its glory! Soon something's bound to happen!"

Something did.

Gesturing grandly with his manuscript, Gilbert caught it

on something behind him. As he turned to inspect the obstacle he was engulfed in a puff of smoke. Coughing, the priest fanned the smoke away with his hand . . . and struck something. A shiny tooth. His manuscript was snagged on it.

Actually, it was a fang. A very sharp and very long fang, as Gilbert discovered, sliding the rolled parchment off of it. The fang jutted out of the grain stalks just below a scaly snout and a smoke-spouting nostril. Down the snout, peeping out from the crisscross web of wheat and smoke, glared a gimlet reptilian eye!

Saliva slid down the tooth onto Gilbert's shaking fingers. In slack-jawed fright, he jerked them back from the fang as a sudden roar rumbled up from behind the tooth. The wheat trembled in the growling blast.

So did Gilbert, collapsing to the ground with a whimper. Just in time too. For the roar was followed by a jolt of flame that just missed the buckling Gilbert's skullcap and hit right in front of Merlin's forehooves.

With a panicked hee-haw, Merlin turned tail and bolted into the wheat. With a yelp, Gilbert followed the mule's example, scrambling for the dubious haven of the field, now ablaze.

One backward look gave him the only glimpse of his pursuer he wanted. The dragon raised himself up above the wheat. And up. And up. Head cocked, he glared at his fleeing prey with one good eye. The other was covered with milky film. Ribs protruded beneath his mottled, scarred hide. His wings flapped in reflex only. Their membranes were shredded and pocked with holes, their flying days long over. His tongue flicked across his lips. Crammed between his teeth or in spaces where his teeth once were were half-chewed stalks of wheat. No wonder the old boy's ribs were showing. Another drop of spittle slithered over his open jaws as, on gimpy legs, he hobbled after his prey.

Arms laden with his precious scrolls, Gilbert crashed through the stalks. The fire was rapidly spreading and the smoke confused his direction. He heard the rustling of pursuit. Caught sight of hide in one spot, then a glimpse of thrashing wing in another. A flickering tail. That glaring eye.

The smoke was like a fog. And the rustling seemed to come from everywhere. All around him. Then right in front of him. Charging down on him. The wheat quivered as swift clomping pummeled the soil.

Gilbert's sandals slapped to a sliding halt as something long, slender, and sharp speared out of the stalks at him. But it was not a fang or talon. It was a lance! Wailing, the frenzied friar flung himself to the ground in a welter of flying manuscripts and fevered prayer.

"Jesu!" Gilbert crossed himself and flopped his face in his hands, awaiting the inevitable. But when impalement eluded him, he peeked through his fingers to find the lance had skimmed over his shoulder, its point still burrowing in the soft soil behind him. On the other end of it was a knight charging through the wall of wheat on horseback. Gilbert blanched. At least impaling would have been a tidier death than trampling. But the knight reined his horse just short of the priest and yanked back his lance, shooting the priest a surly scowl.

Gilbert's already-pounding heart nearly thumped out of his chest when he spied the faded emblem of the sword within the circle on the knight's tattered surcoat. He had never thought to see that glorious symbol adorn a living man's breast. He had only seen it depicted in drawings or on ancient tapestries, read about it in his books and scrolls . . . a dream of dead ages to be wondered on and mourned by historians and poets like himself.

Of course, Gilbert would have expected—and, if truth be told, wished for—a more worthy representative of the Old Code. His poet's fancy had always held an idealized version and this tousled-maned, unshaven wreck of a knight did not come close. Oh, he was a decent-enough-looking fellow. Run a comb through his bedraggled hair, clean him up, put some new clothes on him. Besides the torn surcoat, the fellow wore a dull coat of mail, dirty patched breeches, and scuffed boots.

Both he and his steed were laden with assorted weaponry. Broadsword, lance, bow and arrows, mace, battle-ax, and buckler. The shield gave grim evidence of his trade . . . on its face was mounted an awesome assortment of dragon talons.

Of course, Gilbert's appraisal had been instantaneous and instinctive. Other thoughts dominated his mind, so when the knight snapped at him in curt irritation, "Fool! What are you doing here?" Gilbert stammered out an answer.

"Dra . . . dra . . . drag . . ."

"Yes! Where?" the knight barked impatiently.

Gilbert gestured wildly with a bent scroll clutched in his shaking hand. But before he could pinpoint the direction, a shaft of flame belched out of the wheat, flashing between the knight and the priest, setting the crop behind them ablaze.

Gilbert screeched and the knight whirled his mount through the smoky haze, seeing the dragon's plated spine dip down behind a ridge in the field. Raising his lance, he gave chase.

A dazed Gilbert realized the dragon's fire burp had set the scroll in his hand ablaze. He blew on it frantically, then stuck it in the dirt to extinguish the fire.

A painful yowl jerked the priest up, shivering. The wheat rustled in manic agitation. Smoke from the burning field wafted by. A flash of dragon tail whipped in the air, then snaked out of sight. Then the stalks began to quiver in front of Gilbert. Something was coming toward him!

It was the knight's riderless horse. Gilbert knelt in prayer.

His prayer was answered. The knight was alive . . . for the moment. He rose on the end of his lance, which stopped perpendicular to the ground.

It was an easy guess where the other end was embedded, for there was a terrible growling and thrashing. The lance shaft trembled so violently that the dragonslayer lost his grip and was thrown down out of sight.

Gilbert followed the waving, snapping stalks that marked the tussle. A sword flashed up. Down. There was a hoarse gasp. Then no more waving. No more snapping. No more tussling.

The priest stopped. Listened. Not a sound. Absolute quiet. He took a chance and peeked through the stalks . . .

And a dragon claw loomed up!

Gilbert leapt away. Fell. Somersaulted backward. His head bobbed up in time to see the taloned claw clutch convulsively, waver in midair, spasm again, then come careening limply down toward him. A talon slid past Gilbert's frightened face, just missing his belly, slicing the rope belt of his cassock, then flopping between his splayed-out legs, just below the point where they joined, just missing what Gilbert had euphemistically dubbed his "staff of life." Of course, as a priest, he had no real occasion to use it for that purpose, and thus, since it had never achieved its full propagating potential, it was hardly the most crucial part of his anatomy. Still, it had certain practical functions that might have been inconvenienced by its destruction, so he rejoiced that the claw had missed it.

He stared at the limp limb, finally summoning a modicum of courage to poke it with a tentative finger. It did not respond to his touch.

"It's dead, monk." The knight emerged through a haze of smoke, clamoring over the back of the dragon, which curved above the wheat.

Wreathed in smoke, he stood atop the dead beast, his chest heaving from his exertions. Firelight and sunlight splashed across his face, making the sweat and blood on his cheeks and brow glisten. He hadn't made much of a first impression, thought Gilbert, but now he looked every inch a knight of the Old Code. The monk scrambled to his feet as the knight descended from his kill.

"Magnificent! Marvelous!" Gilbert's enthusiasm ran ahead of him as he struggled to knot up his severed belt and retrieve his scattered scrolls along the way. "Heroics befitting the days of Arthur and the Round Table. Never have I seen such skill!"

"Then you've led the sheltered life that becomes a monk." The trace of a tolerant smile broke the knight's stern mask. With his sword he prodded at the dragon's exposed chest.

"Also scholar, scribe, historian, and poet," Gilbert bowed, dropping several scrolls while his knotted belt came undone again. "Brother Gilbert of Glockenspur, your servant, Sir . . . ?"

"Bowen . . ." The knight brushed back the scales over the dragon's heart.

"My humble life, Sir Bowen, is in the debt of your exalted prowess, daunting courage, and superb, swift sword."

"You have a poet's gift for exaggeration."

"Oh, sir, you should read my histories!" What a complimentary fellow, thought Gilbert. "But you belittle your own talent. A great victory for you and the Lord!"

"Then let the Lord savor it." Bowen frowned as he ran his hand along the smooth pale breast exposed under the scales. It was the only part of the dragon that wasn't scarred or discolored. Bowen examined the pocked, shredded wing in weary disgust. "There's too little glory to be shared in this kill."

"Modesty as well as valor," Gilbert was impressed. "The code of ancient Camelot still lives."

At this, the knight jerked his head up with a hostile glare. Then the glare was suddenly tinged with wistful sadness. He seemed to shake the melancholy from him with a sardonic grin and chopped the middle talon off the dragon's claw with his sword.

"No modesty in it, priest," Bowen said flatly, retrieving his severed trophy. The talon and wound seeped a ruddy viscid ooze. "I merely hurried this relic of the devil down the path he traveled. Sick and starving . . . Still it's one less dragon—"

"And meat for a month!"

Both the priest and knight turned at the sound of the intruding voice. A ragged peasant quickly ran past them and leapt onto the dead dragon. Several more, all armed with knives, followed him. Swarming over the dragon carcass like vultures, they quickly whittled away scales and hide and stripped off morsels of flesh. Gilbert found the desperation of the ritual repugnant. But he noticed Sir Bowen was actually aghast and ran to stop them.

"No! Are you mad? You mustn't! It's vile!" Bowen warned.

"You're wrong, Knight." An elderly man took a bite out of a severed slice of raw meat. The thick dragon blood dribbled down his chin. "It's good."

Bowen shook his head in disgust. "Nothing good comes from a dragon."

Clattering hooves interrupted Bowen's admonishments. An effete lord in a ridiculous feathered hat rode up on a gaily bedecked horse, flanked by three burly men-at-arms. He shouted at the peasants in shrill contempt, "No gorging until those fires are out, you laggards!" He turned to the brutish minions beside him. "Beat them back to the fields!"

"Yes, Lord Felton." The man grinned and he and his fellow ruffians descended on the hungry peasants, chasing them off the carcass with whips and sword flats. Other peasants had already rushed down from the village on the hill to fight the fire.

Felton jabbed an imperious, bejeweled finger toward the smoky field. "If King Einon's wheat burns, you will too."

The three bullyboys beat the peasants off toward the fire. Bowen approached the haughty lord.

"Don't let them eat that meat," he insisted tensely. "It's foul."

"Appropriate for their prosaic palates." Felton smirked at the knight's concern. "They're peasants, knight, not gourmets."

"They can ill afford to be, lord," Gilbert offered humbly, idly picking up his scrolls. "These are hard times."

"For some." Felton yawned. He turned his horse to go.
"For me." Bowen caught the reins.
"Oh, not for you, Knight." Felton smiled. "Not with your skill!"
"Indeed, milord, Sir Bowen's skill is passing rare!" Gilbert exuberantly agreed. Bowen glared at the priest, seemingly unpleased with this trumpeting of his talent. Felton still smiled.
"Sir Bowen, eh? Thank you, priest. I'll put in a good word for you with the king, Sir Bowen. You've done well. Our gratitude. Mine and King Einon's."
Again, Felton turned his horse to leave. Again, Bowen restrained him.
"Keep the good words and the gratitude," said Bowen. "I'll take gold. Yours or the king's."
Felton looked at Bowen's hand on the reins and cocked an eyebrow. He was still smiling. Unpleasantly.
"Gold, Knight?"
"We struck a bargain. One dragon put down, one pouch of gold."
It suddenly seemed to Gilbert that the sword within the circle on the knight's surcoat was more faded than he had first noticed. The mention of this mercenary motive dismayed him. Chivalry was gilded with glories; not gold. Unable to restrain his shocked disappointment, he blurted out, "Your honor has a price, Knight?"
"It has expenses!" Bowen snapped hotly at the pouting priest. "Honor cannot fill my belly. Or shoe my horse. Or keep my sword edge sharp or my armor shiny." He wheeled back to Felton. "I ask no more than any man. A fair price for a fair skill."
"The priest is right." Felton's thin lips curled from a sneering smile to a smiling sneer. He jerked the reins from Bowen's grasp. "It is your duty to protect Einon's vassals as a knight of this realm!"
"Not of this realm! I bend no knee to Einon."
"Ah! Merely another landless vagabond cluttering up the

countryside." Felton sniffed disdainfully. The smile was gone. Only the sneer was left. "Then be gone before I arrest you for . . . for . . ."

For what? Gilbert waited impatiently, curious. Bowen had done nothing. Felton's rings sparkled in the sunlight as he jabbed a finger at the dead dragon.

". . . For poaching the king's wildlife!" Felton's smile returned. He was pleased with his inspiration. Gilbert was outraged. He stepped forward to protest, but Bowen's firm hand smacked his chest, slamming him back. The priest watched the knight watch the lord. A tight smile played on Bowen's lips, as though he were biting his lip to keep from laughing at the ludicrousness of Felton's trumped-up charge. He fingered the hilt of his sword and Gilbert knew the knight was debating whether to cut this popinjay down to size. But Felton's thugs-at-arms, through with pummeling peasants, rode up to give their master's threats weight. Bowen did laugh then and, bowing to Felton, turned and strode to his horse, which was grazing nearby.

"I may yet have a word about you with the king, Sir Bowen," Felton called after the knight; his tone conveyed the fact that it would no longer be a good word. "You see, I've not forgotten your name."

"I commend your excellent memory, Lord Felton." Bowen grinned, adding cryptically, "I wonder if Einon's is as good as yours."

Gilbert was suddenly startled from the drama unfolding before his eyes by a rustling jolt in the wheat behind him. It was the wayward Merlin, nuzzling the back of his neck. He gathered the mule's reins and approached Bowen, who was mounting up.

"Forgive me, Sir Knight, for questioning your motives," he apologized. "Times are topsy-turvy and the world is not as it once was."

"You noticed?" Bowen's wry grin seemed to offer pardon for any affront.

"You saved my life," Gilbert replied sincerely, and dug

into one of his saddlebags. "If I could share some of the charity others have shared with me . . ."

He pulled two coins out from between a sheaf of manuscripts and held them out in his open palm. Gratitude in his eyes, Bowen looked at the proffered coins, then at the priest. He leaned over in the saddle, but did not take the coins. Instead, he folded Gilbert's fingers around them and gently pushed the monk's hand away.

"I've not sunk so low, friar, as to take money from the church."

Gilbert found himself staring again at the emblem of the sword within the circle. It was not quite as faded as he had thought a few moments earlier. He knew he could not let the knight go. He must talk with him more. There were few enough dreamers like himself. How did such a young man come to embrace such an old ideal?

"No dishonor meant, sir. I've some meal and mutton and a fair culinary flair. Please join me in my evening repast."

"Come evening, I shall be far from here, priest."

"So shall I. For I am on a pilgrimage!" Gilbert, leading Merlin, trotted alongside Bowen, who spurred his horse and headed up the ridge toward the main road. Gilbert's belt was coming undone again and it was all he could do not to trip on the dragging hem of his cassock. "Might we travel together?"

"Unless Einon's taxed it, the road's still free"—Bowen addressed this last to Felton as he passed by the lord—"and a man may travel which way he chooses."

His horse broke into a canter and topped the ridge crest. Clambering onto Merlin's back, Gilbert urged him forward with a kick in the haunches. Passing Felton, he nodded with cool deference. His brows arched in bemused pensiveness, the lord bestowed upon him an indifferent flick of his glittery fingers while he watched Bowen disappear over the hill.

Chapter Seven

REDBEARD'S RELEASE

"I am a disobedient child."

"A road tax, Your Majesty!"

Felton had forgotten the knight's name after all. But he had remembered something much more important. Encumbered by his hunting gear and the jostling of Brok and his fellow ruffians, Felton struggled to keep pace with the king's long strides as Einon led the hunting party from the shadows of the portico into the courtyard. It buzzed with workmen and servants. Masons and carpenters crawled about the warren of scaffolding erected against the buildings and walls, hauling beams, angling braces, fitting stones. Einon's prediction had been right. His castle was greater than the Roman one. And it was not even completed yet.

The coterie of knights followed the king through the hubbub and debris to where the grooms awaited with the horses and the falconry masters attended to hooded birds of prey on perching racks.

Felton hated these bloodletting frolics of the king. A lot of sweaty stalking, squatting on an uncomfortable saddle all day under a broiling sun, reeling from the stench of horse piss, dead animals, and unwashed knights. It all seemed so senseless and silly. After all, what were servants for, if not to go out and provide game for their masters' tables? Felton bemoaned the rigid customs and politics that necessitated his indulging in activities that were beneath him. He also bemoaned the fact that he wasn't any good at them. He rarely, if ever, came back with any kill across his horse's flanks.

Once he and a servant thumped an arrow into a deer corpse and hid the thing in the woods the night before the hunt. The next day, Felton made a big show of spying a deer concealed in the brush and shooting it. Unfortunately, his masquerade was exposed when he dragged several of his fellows over to the bushes to envy his kill. There they discovered only half a carcass—some scavenger had eaten the other half sometime during the night—and the arrow he had actually shot was still prominently vibrating in the nearby tree it had struck. At the feast that night much was made of "Felton's magic arrow" that could not only turn itself into two arrows but a cleaver as well and tear half a carcass away.

"Keep that fancy feather out of my face, fop." Brok swiped at the feather in Felton's hat and tried to muscle past him to usurp his place at the king's ear. Felton muscled back as best he could and promptly tripped over his bow. Brok smirked as he slipped by him. Felton cocked an imperious eyebrow at the clod and turned to the king, who had mounted his horse.

Einon had finally grown into his crown, which tightly ringed his ashen-yellow hair. His wispy beard was of the same pale shade, almost transparent against his womanish-white skin. He had cultivated the beard in an attempt to look older than his nineteen years, but it only made him look more boyish. But a very big boy nonetheless. He had grown tall and tough. Eyes sharp. Mouth cruel. He was armed with sword, dagger, bow, and quiver.

Apparently oblivious to his knights' petty jostlings for position, Einon chewed the insides of his cheeks as he scanned the ongoing construction of his castle. The fingers of his right hand idly stroked up and down his chest, as was his habit in moments of distraction. There was a jagged scar on the back of the hand, an unflattering memento of his youthful victory over the rebels.

Felton watched the royal hand slide back and forth over the royal coat of arms and wondered if the king had even heard his suggestion.

The king had.

"A road tax?" Einon weighed the proposal as he pulled on his hunting gloves. Slipping under Brok's arm, Felton squeezed forward to fan the flames of his idea.

"They use it. Let them pay for the privilege." Felton gestured expansively and, once more, got caught up in his bow. Untangling himself, he indignantly flung it to a nearby servant and finished his thought. "And those that can't, can work it off!"

All waited for Einon's response. It came in a sly smile. He leaned over and, removing Felton's hat, playfully thumped a finger on Felton's skull.

"Ingenious, Lord Felton!"

Felton was pleased that the king seemed to like his idea, and his new hat as well. Einon admired the feather, stroking it between the tips of his fingers. Felton was particularly proud of the feather—it was peacock—his own suggestion. The king smiled and plopped the hat back on Felton's head, arranging it at a careful angle. "You shouldn't hide such a good brain under such a bad hat."

Brok and the others chortled. Felton made a gracious bow and a mental note to get a new milliner. As he struggled out of the bow Brok leaned in front of him and took a falcon from the rack, sweeping it in front of the noble's face. The bird screeched and flapped its wings. Felton cringed.

"He likes to bring down peacocks." Brok smirked again. Felton huffed and haughtily clambered into his saddle—or rather tried to. The weight of his equipment hampered his swing in the stirrup.

"Fly, peacock, fly!" Brok grabbed him by the seat of his pants and roughly shoved him astride. The others laughed as Felton clumsily clutched his horse's neck to keep his balance and, once more, lurched into Brok's falcon. The bird screeched again and snipped at the feather in Felton's hat. Felton recoiled with a screech of his own, eliciting more laughter from Brok and the others. Only Einon did not laugh.

"Lord Brok." The king silenced the revelry with calm command. "Some are good at hunting men. Some are good at hunting *money*. Both have value to me."

Felton straightened his hat and himself in the saddle, savoring a smirk of his own at Brok. It was, however, a short-lived triumph. Einon snatched Felton's bow from the servant and tossed it to the startled lord.

"So don't forget your bow, Felton. You might cross paths with a ferocious coinpurse." Einon joined the others' laughter this time. Even Felton forced a giddy giggle out of himself to prove he could take a jest.

"To the hunt!" Einon spurred his horse out the gate. His minions echoed the shout and followed him down the road. Felton juggled his bow and his reins and reluctantly whirled his horse after them. God, how he hated this sport.

Kara adjusted the hood of her tattered cape and, picking up her water bucket once more, made her way through the quarry. In four brief years Einon had carved an enormous cavity into the earth. His castle had required much stone and had left the place an overworked, withered skeleton. Not unlike the half-starved, ragged peasants who toiled in the sun under the bored gaze of their guards.

She came to visit her imprisoned father one afternoon a week, as permitted by the edict of the king. Not that Einon had issued it out of any magnanimity or pity. But rather because the sight of shackled loved ones put to slave labor proved an effective deterrent to any burgeoning treasonous impulses. The guards tolerated her with the same indifference they showed their charges. Nor did she invite notice . . . she merely shambled among the prisoners, head down in stooped subservience, her strong, lean figure shrouded in a formless frock. Both her beauty and her wild, red mane she buried within the shadows of her hood.

She doled out drinks to the thirsty quarry slaves as she made her way to an emaciated giant chipping at stone with a chisel and hammer. An unruly shock of white hair streaked with stray strands of red hung in matted clumps to his shoulders and was bound by a leather headband. He stopped work as he heard Kara behind him scoop a ladleful of water.

"Drink, Father," she said, proffering him the water. Riagon turned to his daughter. As Kara looked at his scarred, sightless eyes she thought of the knight . . . the knight who had defied his king to save them. All for naught.

It had not taken Einon long to recapture Riagon and carry out his threat. Riagon had known that it was inevitable. So he had deserted his daughter one night and used himself as decoy to save her. Condemned himself to this dark purgatory. Four years had wasted his once-virile body, had choked his proud voice with dust, had buried his haughty defiance under a ton of rock. Kara was grateful he could not see her tears.

"I told you not to come here anymore, Kara," Riagon the Redbeard rasped.

"I am a disobedient child, Father. Drink."

"No longer a child. A woman. And even a blind man can tell a beautiful one."

Riagon's gnarled hand groped for his daughter's face. She gently took it and led it to her cheek. His callused, dusty fingers caressed it.

"One day one of these dogs will notice too. Go home, Kara!" he sternly pleaded.

"You are my home, Father." Kara kissed his blistered palm, then taking some meat from the folds of her frock, stuffed it inside his shirt. "Here, for later. Now quickly, drink. The guard is watching."

She placed the ladle in his hand. As he lifted it to his lips, an arrow suddenly tore it from his grasp. The water splashed upon him and Riagon jumped back in startled confusion. Kara spun to the raucous laughter behind them.

"I don't believe—I mean, magnificent shot, Your Highness!"

A fatuous-looking nobleman in a hideous-looking hat was floundering his way through some flattering remarks. The object of his praise lowered his bow. Though it had been four years, Kara recognized the piglet instantly. His white, sallow features stood out clear across the quarry. Apparently, he and his men had been out hunting. They were laden with game. Pheasants, boars, even a stag.

"Magnificent! Truly . . . uh . . . magnificent!" The fop was still flattering.

"And profitable," Einon cut him off. "Unless you care to double the wager, Felton."

Felton took the bet. "Through his legs!"

Einon took the dare, notching another arrow and letting fly. Kara had no time to warn Riagon before the shaft whizzed through his legs and clinked on the rock behind him.

"Kara!" The redbeard whirled frantically.

"Stand still, Father!" she ordered him.

"The bucket!" Felton shouted out another target, hoping to recoup his losses. Kara saw the arrow slice the air and strike the bucket next to Riagon, sending it clattering off the stone, its contents splashing at his feet.

"Kara!" Riagon jumped back.

"Don't move!" Kara stepped in front of him and . . .

. . . headed for the piglet.

She saw him scowl, surprised and indignant that someone should interfere with his sport. He notched another arrow and loosed it. It struck before she had time to react—or even think—in the dirt before her feet. She hoped her shuddering sigh of relief had not shown and kept moving forward. Einon fired another arrow. Only inches from her left big toe. She kept moving forward. Another arrow. This time aimed at her. She still moved forward. Not a flinch. After all, the die was cast. He either was or wasn't going to kill her. And if he was, better this way, neat and quick, than some other. But he didn't kill her. He lowered his bow. His chalky brows knitted in intrigued confusion.

"You've got nerve for a spoilsport," Einon muttered with grudging admiration.

"There's no sport in tormenting a blind man," Kara admonished him, amazed at her own fearlessness. "I beg Your Majesty. Let him go. He can do you no harm. Nor will he raise your castle any faster. He is sick and tired and his hands suffer from the crippling disease. Let him go."

Einon's eyes intently penetrated the shadows of her cloak as he listened to her plea with curious attention. He absently stroked the fingers of his right hand along his chest . . . where she had stabbed him four years ago. She worried that he was thinking of that wound . . . and that he knew who she was.

True, she was not the child he remembered. Time had transformed her more than it had transformed him. The ensuing years had merely molded Piglet into a bigger version of himself. But out of her gangly awkwardness they had fashioned a lush supple femininity and sculpted the childish curves of her face into the graceful angles of youthful maidenhood.

And in that blossoming maturity, her fierce boyish habits and rough-and-tumble manner had slowly yielded to the force of beauty. At first she saw it mirrored only in the glances of others—admiring glances, jealous glances, awed glances. But then she began to notice it herself. The fullness of her lips, the fullness of her breasts, the sweep of her brow, and the thick lashes of her eyes. It was never anything she consciously aspired to, or thought about, or even made an effort to enhance. It was just indelibly there one day. She found it frightening and strangely wonderful, but she was still uncomfortable and did not know what to do with it. No, she was not the child the piglet remembered. She had greatly changed. In many ways. And not all were physical.

Searching the pale intensity of Einon's gaze, she wondered if he could strip away the altering years and unmask the truth. And if not, would he connect her to Riagon and, in so doing, prompt his memory of that day on the battlefield?

"Who is that dog, Brok?" Einon shifted his gaze from Kara to Riagon, poised in blind uncertainty, confused by what was happening around him.

Brok shrugged, "One of those rebels you crushed, isn't he?"

Kara smiled. No, there would be no connection made between her and Riagon the Red. Nor even a connection between the white-haired, sightless skeleton and the red-maned giant who had slain Freyne. Piglet didn't remember him at all. His vendetta had been merely a moment of mindless violence, forgotten once the toll had been exacted. Now Riagon was just another rebel he had blinded, another peasant he had maimed, or whipped, or slain. Just another faceless body among a heap of faceless bodies in his charnel house of tyranny. They meant nothing to him; she meant nothing. There was no savoring of Riagon's fate, only indifference to it. And in that indifference, Kara saw hope.

"He is of no further use to you, milord." Kara pleaded her suit carefully. "And he will remember your punishment always as he gropes through your kingdom in darkness."

"True," Einon mused amiably, staring at her.

Put a crown on a pig, he's still a pig, thought Kara. "For pity's sake, Your Highness, release him."

"Release him?" Those pale eyes stared at her curiously, then sparkled. "Granted, wench!"

In one flashy blur of motion, Einon notched another arrow and sent it flying . . . straight into Riagon's heart, pitching him back over the very stone he was shaping. Kara stood dumbstuck.

"I always said death was a release, not a punishment," the king philosophized.

The laughter of his sycophants could not shut out Kara's scream.

"Father!" She ran toward the fallen man, her hood flying back, unleashing her wild red tumble of hair.

"Father . . ." Kara knelt beside Riagon, cradling him to her.

"K-K-Kara . . ." The redbeard's gnarled hand clutched for his daughter, then flopped back, unrewarded. His head sagged against her breast. Kara rocked his lifeless body, weeping. His headband fell off and his hair spilled down over his blind eyes.

Hoofbeats intruded upon her grief. She looked up to see the piglet and his flunkies riding out of the quarry. Einon spurred his horse around for one last look, then sped off to overtake the others. Leaving her to her mourning. The crackling of the smithy's fire sounded the dirge. Kara picked her father's headband out of the dust. Pressing it to her face, she washed it with her tears.

Chapter Eight

AVALON

"Avalon is a fable, priest."

"In Avalon, lost Avalon, so the legends say
In mystery and mist, there valiant Arthur lay.
And resting with him, the vanquished heroes of his day."

The grease on Gilbert's pink, plump cheeks glistened in the firelight as he stuffed more meat into them. Without swallowing, he swung back into his florid recitation of the scribbled parchment in his hand, spraying bits of half-chewed food along with his poetry as he waved his mutton joint in time to his suspect meter.

"Oh, Avalon, fair Avalon, this poor world's astray.
So in honor of your dead, I bend my knees to pray
To seek your shining wisdom, to find your secret way!"

Gilbert rose and paced, still flailing out the dubious rhythm with his wagging mutton bone. He began his third stanza with a piercing, declamatory wail that caused Bowen, eating Roman style, to jolt up from his reclining position.

"Ohhhh, Avalon! Bright Avalon! End my soul's dismay.
Return forgotten glories that once held noble sway.
And sweep the world's dank darkness away, away, away!"

Gilbert looked at his audience expectantly. Bowen settled back on his elbow and gnawed at his meat joint. Gilbert gobbled greedily on his own, squatting by the fire and still waiting for a reaction. Only the crackling of the flame and the stream rushing over the pebbled shore where they camped held back the silence of the night . . . the fire, the stream, and the smacking of their lips as they chewed their mutton. Finally, Gilbert could stand it no longer.

"Well, what do you think?"

"Your mutton is very good. . . ." Bowen threw his bone in the fire and picked up his shield. Laying it in his lap, he resumed sewing on his latest dragon talon with a piece of thick leather cord. "Avalon is a fable, priest."

This ruffled Gilbert's ego. One could dispute the merits of his poetry, but not of his research.

"A fable? That's uneducated piffle, Bowen," Gilbert snorted haughtily, and went to his saddle packs, scrounging through a plethora of parchment. "I can prove it. I have it right here . . . somewhere here. . . . Never mind, I quote from memory: 'Arthur unto the vale of Avalon was swept, to lie among his brother knights in a grove of stone upon a tor.' From the venerable history of Gildas the Scribe. Facts, my friend, facts! Avalon is a holy place. And my pilgrimage a sacred duty. I will find it."

"And when you do?" Bowen cocked an eyebrow, intrigued. It was the first time in two days' travel together that the knight had actually shown more than polite interest in anything. Gilbert realized that his plans to draw the fellow out had somehow gone awry. It wasn't that Bowen was an unpleasant or even a reticent companion. It was just that he had a disarming knack for deflecting the conversation away from himself and inquiring about Gilbert's opinions. And the problem with that was that Gilbert had opinions. And he was never reluctant to express them. After all, he was a man of letters and learning. It's what he did. And while it was flattering to be listened to—and Bowen was a very good listener, which made expounding on things all the easier—he had learned nothing of the knight's history.

But now they were getting to it. He'd finally hit upon a

subject the lad seemed inclined to open up on, providing Gilbert led him into it properly.

"What will I do?" The answer struck Gilbert as obvious. "I will pray to the souls of all the sainted men buried there—Arthur and all the knights of the Round Table!"

"It is said not only Arthur lies at Avalon, but also Anwnn—Gateway to the Underworld." Bowen tossed his shield aside and stretched out on the ground, pillowing his head on his saddle. "So be careful, priest. The spirits you call may come."

"Would they might and with them bring back the days of chivalry and the Old Code."

"No prayers can resurrect that pale ghost." Bowen's voice was laced with wistful melancholy. He pulled a blanket over him and stared into the fire. "Good night, priest."

Gilbert sighed. He had lost him. "Good night, priest" definitely signaled the end of the conversation. But Gilbert had caught the regret in Bowen's tone. The reflected flame had exposed the desolation in the knight's eyes.

"Ride with me, my son," Gilbert gently implored, scooting closer. "All knights need a quest. I think ours is the same."

"Men of faith may follow a fable, priest," came the hollow reply. "But my only faith is my sword arm. . . . And besides, I already have a quest."

"What quest?"

"To slay all dragons . . . And one, in particular . . ."

The soft sorrow in Bowen's face had fled. Firelight flickered across his hardened visage.

Einon gulped his wine and glowered into the fire. The flashing daggers of flame brought to mind the smithy's fire at the quarry and the red-haired girl framed in its blaze, cradling a dead man. Red hair melting into red fire. So striking. So familiar . . .

. . . As familiar as the savory smells and rowdy sounds that drifted up from the banquet hall. He had left his knights there, gorging on the table-bending bounty of their hunt. He heard their belching laughter. He heard the screeching titters of their bawds. He heard the lutes of the minstrels. He heard the wail of the red-haired girl as he slew her father. . . .

Einon took another deep swallow of wine and idly rubbed his chest. He noticed the old scar on the back of his hand. The girl had said the blind man suffered from the crippling sickness. He often wondered if his hand was afflicted with it too. He remembered the first day he felt the pain in it. The day Bowen left him. His first day as king.

Then, just over a year ago, the great pain came. Terrible shooting pain that had sent him into screaming collapse. Three days he spent writhing in bed, recovering from it. The doctors had been hopeless dolts. Even the mysterious ointments and salves of his mother could not ease the pain. But she had known it would stop. "Give it time, my son, the wound must heal," had been her strange advice. Strange, because it wasn't a wound at all. Just vicious pain. He had not cut it, or bruised it, been bitten or stung. Just a phantom pain coming from nowhere and leaving no mark.

But Aislinn had been right. The pain subsided after a week, leaving only a numbness in his fingers that lingered for months. It affected his sword grip for a long time, and fearing the injury permanent, he painstakingly taught himself how to wield a blade in his left hand. He was not as proficient as with his right, but a "sinister" assault was so alien to his opponents, it proved unusually effective.

Eventually he regained the power and flexibility of his right hand. Every now and then there was a twitch, a twinge, a little stiffness. But when it grasped a blade hilt now, it was as formidable as ever. Perhaps his mother was right. Perhaps it was a wound and not the crippling disease. He ran the bottom of his goblet across the white scar on his hand back, even paler than his white skin.

Perhaps his hand had never healed properly after that rebel chieftain sliced it. That dog who killed his father. He had blinded that peasant too, Einon recalled. He wondered what happened to him. Probably died in the quarry long ago. Most did. Prey to rock slides or the elements or just the brutal grind of the work. Odd. Einon was unable to remember the man's face. Only his towering height and the color of his hair. It was red. Red like the hair of the girl today.

She had nerve, that girl. Facing his arrows like that. Nerve and pride. He had seen it in her eyes. It was her eyes that had held back his bow hand. Eyes that were older than her youthful face. Grim and weary of life, yet alluringly defiant. He didn't even know if she had been pretty or not. All he saw were her eyes. And they were beautiful . . . and bitter . . . and knowing . . . fringed with thick lashes and arched by fine brows. Deep brown moist pools that threatened to drown him in their flooding contempt. That was why he had shot the old man; so he wouldn't succumb to those eyes. To reassert his mastery over this brazen, peasant wench who dared to shame him with her haunting gaze.

But, in truth, it was her hair. Even more than her eyes. Her hair flowing out from her hood as she ran to her father. Her hair, falling in a tousled riot about her face as she knelt by the old man. Her hair. It fascinated him, seeming to entwine its red locks about his brain until he could not untangle his thoughts from them.

Her red, red hair. A scarlet starburst captured in the burning shimmer of the smithy's fire. A halo of flame within a halo of flame. The image had evoked a memory in Einon. It had stopped him, made him rein his horse to stare at the girl and the fire and grope for the memory. But the girl's defiant eyes had chased the memory from him. Across the quarry she had looked very beautiful. Einon had almost ridden back to her. But he had feared her beauty was only an illusion cast by the fire in her hair. And he had feared her eyes. Even as they had chased his faint memories away, they had chased him from the quarry. He had whipped his horse and ridden off like a frightened child.

Einon cursed and tossed the dregs of his wine into the fire. The blaze lapped it up with a flaring red thirst.

Bowen and Gilbert traveled down a sun-dappled forest path. The priest ambled alongside Merlin, reading from another of his inexhaustible supply of scrolls. All morning he had been trying to reintroduce the topic of last night's conversation. And while Bowen had had no objections to Gilbert's chattering—and, indeed, seemed to tolerate it amiably—it had been another one-sided discourse, with the knight interjecting only to agree or disagree or make a minor comment of no real consequence or self-revelation. But, truth be told, the subject matter was more Gilbert's passion than Bowen's. Avalon was his quest and so, since daylight, he had been unearthing one manuscript after another to prove his quest was not in vain.

"'. . . and dying Arthur was laid in a land cloaked in water and mist . . .' Cenwalh writing in the time of Melwas!" Gilbert punctuated the point with a flourish of his scroll . . . and an unintentional tumble. His manuscript flipped from his hand and he flopped to his knees into a large depression in the middle of the path.

"Kneeling in prayer already, priest?" Bowen laughed and dismounted to help him up. "Is this your holy place?"

"Just a hole, hardly holy." Gilbert took Bowen's hand and struggled to his feet. Bowen brushed the dust from the priest's shoulders and eyed him with serious curiosity. Gilbert self-consciously arranged his skullcap and wiped at his face, worried that something was awry. But Bowen's solemn look was merely the preface to his solemn question.

"If you do find it, friar," Bowen asked earnestly, "what will you pray for?"

Ah, he'd piqued the knight's interest after all. "I'll pray for a savior the likes of those fallen heroes to rid us of Einon's evil."

"Is it Einon's evil?" Bowen frowned cryptically and stooped to retrieve Gilbert's scroll.

"Has the darkness of these times blinded you, Knight?" Gilbert sputtered in disbelief. "It's Einon's rump in the royal seat. Who else's evil?"

"Perhaps he was . . . bewitched."

"You cannot bewitch the devil. Trust a clergyman on that."

Gilbert leaned over Bowen's shoulder to find out what the knight had thought so intriguing. He was clearing some underbrush from the hole. But before Gilbert could get a good look, Bowen thrust the scroll in his face and rose.

"Indeed, good friar." Bowen handed the scroll back and hurried to his steed. "I leave all things ecclesiastical in your capable hands. Farewell."

"Farewell!" Gilbert waved cheerily as the knight mounted up, then realized what he was saying. *"Farewell?"*

"Farewell!" Bowen repeated, as if Gilbert still wasn't clear with the concept. "You've been a pleasing companion, but now our quests take separate paths. I wish you luck with yours."

"Wait! Quests? . . . But . . ."

But Bowen had turned from the trail and was disappearing down a ravine, his eyes keenly scouring the ground. Gilbert grabbed Merlin's reins and started after the knight . . . only to fall into the same hole once more. He shook himself with a frustrated sigh, shedding the mossy debris clinging to his cassock. His eyes went wide as he suddenly saw what Bowen had seen and realized the hole he was in wasn't a hole at all . . . *but a huge dragon track*!

Chapter Nine

A DUEL

"No profit this time, purely pleasure."

The horse slowly sloshed through the stream. Bowen leaned forward in the saddle, staring down into the clear, rippling water. The dragon track was plainly visible, impressed in the mud of the shallow creekbed.

Bowen glanced up and smiled as he listened to the soothing hum of the gentle waterfall that spilled over an overhang of rock downstream. His dragon would be there.

Things were picking up. He had not seen a dragon for over six months. Now two within the week. Maybe the long drought was over at last. He jerked up his lance and reined his steed toward the falls. He regretted his abrupt departure from Gilbert, but the poor fellow had already had one near-fatal encounter with a dragon and Bowen didn't want to expose him to another. He also didn't need the responsibility of another person's safety. The old wreck of a dragon in the wheatfield had been a fairly simple opponent to defeat. But who knew what lay in wait for him behind the falls? The friar had been a pleasant diversion from his solitary purpose. Oh, he was a bit too chatty and a positively wretched poet. But he was an earnest and well-meaning fellow with a good heart. Bowen had forgotten how much he missed affable companionship.

"Yoo-hoo . . ." The voice came from the creekbank, from behind a pile of gray boulders, several of which glistened almost silvery in the sun. Gilbert appeared, huffing and puffing up the ridge of the rocks. He carried his literary sack, stuffed with manuscripts, enthusiastically waving his quill, hallooing for attention. "Bowen! Bowen!"

Bowen muttered an oath and, wheeling in the saddle, rode toward the bank. The monk trod onto a sun-dazzled boulder that seemed to totter slightly as he plopped his bag down and started to rummage through it.

"I'm not too late, am I?" Gilbert asked excitedly as Bowen rode up.

"What are you doing here, Gilbert?" the knight demanded in a snarled whisper.

"Where else should I be when history's in the making?" The scribe smiled, oblivious to Bowen's pique, and flourished his quill. "I've come to immortalize you!"

"Shhh!" Bowen admonished him with a nervous glance back at the cave.

The priest produced a bottle of ink from his pack. "How do you prefer I write this?"

"*Far* away."

The sarcasm went right over Gilbert's head. The priest chuckled good-naturedly and fumbled some more in his bag.

"Oh, please, don't concern yourself with *my* safety," Gilbert's voice boomed out above even the rushing falls, much to Bowen's consternation. "No, I meant style. Verse. Meter. Shall I spice it up with a poetical flourish or just the cold hard facts?"

He unrolled some blank manuscript. Seething, Bowen poked his lance through it and jerked it away. "Why don't you go ask the dragon? Get out of here!"

Bowen realized his curt exasperation had wounded Gilbert's feelings. The friar's face fell in dejection as he stepped out to the edge of the shiny rock to confront Bowen.

"That's a fine attitude!" He pouted as he peevishly snatched his scroll off the lance. The rock seemed to teeter under him slightly. It teetered more as Gilbert stomped his foot to emphasize his indignation. "I come to record your exploits for posterity and you try to muzzle the mouth of chronicle, lop off the tongue of truth. It's all very well to go about hacking and whacking dragons, but if a dragon falls in the forest and no one hears about it, does it make a thud?"

The unstable rock shook under Gilbert's pounding sandal and the priest lost his balance, his rump plopping back onto the boulder. Gilbert recovered with a haughty harrumph, and discreetly pulling the hem of his cassock back around his ankles, he flattened his scroll against the rock, dipped his quill liberally in the ink vial, and began to scribble defiantly across it, as though he had intended sitting down to write all the time. Before Bowen could stop him, he took up his admonishing sermon once more, his disgruntlement droning out across the creek. "You're nothing without the likes of me. Heroics don't make heroes, ballad makers do. The quill is mightier than the sword!"

"Shhh!"

"You can't shush history, lad! Its voice lives forever!"

"Which is longer than either you or I will, if you don't shut up!"

Bowen's frantic whisper, along with his exaggerated rolling of eyes and a jabbed gesture of his lance toward the waterfall, finally penetrated Gilbert's perception.

"Good Lord!" The priest promptly clamped a hand over his mouth in a vain attempt to recapture the escaped exclamation. "So sorry!" he whispered to Bowen with a sheepish grin. "The element of surprise!"

"It *was* the idea!" Bowen sighed indulgently. "Now get you gone, friar."

"I stay, sir!"

"Are you mad?"

"You'll find the courage of I, who witness, no less than that of you, who do."

Gilbert had risen to his feet and gotten into his pulpit again, wildly and insistently waving his quill. Ink splattered from its freshly dipped point across the rock, which suddenly shuddered, and Bowen saw its hard surface crinkle—

crinkle and open up, exposing a giant ink-stained eye glaring up at the priest. Gilbert was still vociferously avowing his courage . . . unaware of the fact that it was about to be tested.

"You will see that I . . . I . . . I—yi . . . yi!"

"Gilbert!" Bowen's warning shout was already too late. The rocks shook with a violent rumble and collapsed into the lake with a giant splash. Trying to steady his frightened horse, Bowen saw Gilbert come careening through the spray of water at him in midair. Bowen ducked as the priest, wailing, pitched over the horse's back into the creek. Bowen whirled his horse to the bank. Most of the rocky mass upon which Gilbert was perched had disappeared, leaving only a sandy beach. He steered his mount back to the sound of more splashing, just in time to see . . .

. . . a dragon tail, slithering along the creek, its dull gray hue transforming to a glittery warm brown. Bowen pursued, poking his lance into the water after the splashing tail. But it disappeared through the waterfall.

His horse shied at the falls and Bowen saw the huge, dark silhouette loom up behind the cascade.

"Come out of there, you skulking brute," Bowen demanded.

"Go away!" came the weary reply.

"Come out or I'll come in. . . ."

"Suit yourself."

A battered breastplate came flying out of the waterfall, splashing in front of Bowen, who steadied his nervous steed.

"That's what's left of the last fellow who entered uninvited." The sonorous hiss snaked through the spray of water.

"That doesn't frighten me."

"No? How about this? Or this? *Or this?*"

A barrage of crumpled armor and bones clattered through the veil of water, half of it crashing into Gilbert, who was trying to rise out of the stream. He scampered out of the debris, floundering to his feet, when suddenly the complete skeleton of a horse and rider jangled out of the falls, splashing in a heap and washing a wave of water over the startled priest that sent him flopping back into the creek. The helmeted head landed in his lap. Gilbert shrieked as he juggled the skull in his hands, then gasped in amazement on closer inspection. It wore the plume-crested helmet of a centurion. He held it up to Bowen with a scholar's delight.

"Look, Bowen, late Roman! I don't believe it!"

Bowen couldn't believe it either. "I'm a little preoccupied, Gilbert, for one of your history lessons."

"It's *my* history lesson, Knight," growled the voice behind the falls. "And you'd best learn from it. Or history will repeat itself. I've quite a collection in here."

"I won't be added to it!" Bowen eyed the shadow, then suddenly cast his lance with a mighty heave. It shot halfway through the falls before jarring to a stop with a loud thunk! The shaft vibrated in midair.

"A hit, Sir Knight, a hit!"

Bowen grinned in cocky victory as the priest waded toward him, jubilantly waving the plumed helmet. The withered skull plopped out of it and disappeared into the water . . . just like Bowen's brief triumph. There was a loud crunch of wood. Bowen and Gilbert turned to see Bowen's lance shaft slowly being sucked behind the falls. There was more crunching and, with each crunch, the lance got shorter until it had vanished completely behind the shield of water. Then no more crunching. Only the rush of the falls, which suddenly spewed out a jumble of broken, splintered pieces of lance. Bowen's horse whinnied and reared. Gilbert flopped back into the creek. With a snarl, Bowen raised his shield and spurred his horse through the falls.

He should have known better. Never go out in the day. But the water had been so cool and the sky so bright. A little swim and some warm sun. So rare these days. He had thought it worth the risk. He had been wrong.

He should have known better. Especially since the Old One's slaying just the other day. The knowledge of the killing had come rippling along the channels of his mystic senses that linked all the ancient brethren to one another. And with that somber sensation came the terrifying prospect of aloneness. Alone. The last.

He should have known better. Should have been cautious. Taken the warning. Instead, it had made him yearn for the so-long-unseen sun. He should have stayed with the night. Clung to the blackness. Sought the shelter of the stars. But the stars were out of reach for him. There would be none to sense his fate when it came. None to mourn his death . . . his dreaded, dreadful death.

Yes, he should have known better. About so many things. But death would not come today. He spewed a bolt of flame as the knight rode through the falls into the cave. But the fellow was quick and deflected it against his shield; sparks hissed and smoked against the moist cavern floor.

"Little damp for fire." The knight grinned up at the shelf of rock where the dragon perched.

"Leave me in peace!" the dragon snapped. "Go rescue a damsel or win a joust! Why must you knight-errants out to make a reputation for yourself always pick on us dragons?"

"I don't need a reputation," the knight retorted. "And I have a collection of my own."

The warrior held his shield into a rainbow of sunlight that prismed through the waterfall. The talons mounted on it glinted in the light.

"Ah!" the dragon breathed a disdainful sigh. "One who kills for *money,* are you?"

The dragonslayer flinched at the assessment and shot back testily, "It's honest enough work! Ridding the country of you lot. One must earn a living."

Strange, how begrudging the fellow sounded. Almost apologetic. As though he were trying to convince himself. Unusual sensitivity for a slaughterer. Still he was right about one thing.

"Yes . . . one must live," the dragon agreed solemnly, almost regretfully. "No way 'round then but to have at it, since you seek profit in this."

"Don't flatter yourself." The knight drew his sword. "No profit this time, purely pleasure."

"Perhaps less pleasurable and more costly than you think."

"It will cost you your middle right talon."

The dragon cackled hoarsely, "I think not, Knight." He extended his right front limb out of the shadows, exposing it to the stunned gaze of the dragonslayer. His hand was a maimed stump, with only the clawlike thumb and fore talon. The other two digits had been sheared off, the little one completely, and the middle one had lost its tip, including its talon.

"Afraid someone beat you to it," the dragon mocked him, and scooped up a skeleton in his wounded claw from the litter of armor and bones heaped upon his perch. "Him here. Much good it did him." The dragon flung the skeleton from the ledge. It clattered down the rocks into the water in front of the knight with a splash. The horse wheeled, and as the knight reined him under control his sword flashed in the refracted sunlight.

The dragon blinked at the sun-sprayed blade and a startled hiss rattled out of his throat when he saw it—*the talon-scraped groove in the blade*! Oh, gleaming stars of heaven, he thought, how our mistakes come back to haunt us! And he lunged off the ledge!

Gilbert came up out of the creek, spritzing water, sitting up in time to see Bowen gallop into the waterfall. His sack went floating by just then, and snatching it up, he began to compose aloud as he rummaged for another quill and parchment.

> "Into the mouth of death he strode,
> Into the gringy gloom,

Into the pit of fear unknown,
To bring the beast to doom."

There was a roaring whoosh, a nervous whinny, and a flash of flame that lit the water screen a shuddering red. A blast of steam rolled out from the falls, slamming Gilbert back into the creekbed. The priest shook the water off him once more and, with ominous speculation, reconsidered his opening.

"Into the pit of fear unknown,
Perhaps to court his doom!"

Gilbert stood up and slung his sopping sack over his shoulder. He managed to find a dry piece of vellum and, juggling his inkwell and quill, scrolled it down his arm and began to scribble furiously.

In this encumbered position, he waddled toward the rushing falls, mystified—and not a little worried—by the sudden quiet beyond it.

Gilbert called out softly, "Sir Bowen?" But he was answered only by the swirling swish of water. He returned to his epic.

"In darkness stygian befell,
The fate of warrior bold."

Again, he called out, "Sir Knight?" Again, only the cataract called back. He fretted to his muse.

"Had dragon flame engulfed his flesh
And left it lifeless cold— *Bowen!*"

Gilbert shouted for his hero once more. This time the answer came in a gush of wind and water that knocked Gilbert back into the creek. The dragon swooped from the falls, water spraying off his magnificent wings as he spread them to their full extension. Patches of his hide glistened. As Gilbert struggled to rise he craned his neck back, watching the glorious awesome creature in slack-jawed amazement.

"Look out!"

Gilbert wheeled to find himself directly in Bowen's path as the knight galloped through the stream after the dragon, twirling a chain-mesh net above his head. The priest plummeted into the drink once more, narrowly avoiding the horse and rider as they sprayed past him in a wing of water and charged down the creek in pursuit of the dragon overhead.

Gilbert bobbed back up to see Bowen cast his net skyward and ensnare one of the dragon's hind feet. Though not impeding the dragon's ascent, the net was attached to a fine chain that uncoiled from a side pouch on Bowen's saddle. The knight quickly wrapped it around the saddle pommel and reined his horse to a skidding halt. The dragon jerked to a halt also . . . in midair.

"Hallelujah! Saints be praised!" Gilbert whooped his elation and inspiration struck, in spite of his waterlogged parchment and his quill floating downstream.

> "Oh, gallant knight! Oh, valor true!
> A hero's end you'll know."

Then the saddle cinches snapped. Horse and rider parted company as Bowen, still mounted in the saddle and still grasping the chain, slid off the horse. The dragon shot through the sky with a spurting lunge and Bowen shot out of the creek, plowed through the muddy bank, and was dragged into the woods, where he disappeared. Gilbert gasped in dismay.

> "Oh, dreaded dragon, dark and foul,
> Is yours the victor's blow?"

Chapter Ten

IN THE DRAGON'S MOUTH

"If your teeth come down, my sword goes up."

Feet in the stirrups, rump in the saddle, Bowen hung on to the chain for dear life, careening through the forest underbrush, bouncing off tree trunks, clobbered by uprooted stones, spitting out leaves and dirt. Once he was flipped upside down with the saddle riding him and the talons of the shield strapped on his back plowing furrows in the dark forest loam. Birds frantically fluttered skyward, small forest animals scurried from thickets out of the path of the human juggernaut.

He came to a sudden groin-bruising halt as the saddle snagged a tree trunk and the chain went taut. Above, the dragon also lurched to a jarring midair stop. He whirled and snorted a blast of flame on the chain, but to no avail. Recovering his wind, Bowen watched the beast hover over him, angrily thrashing and tugging to free himself. The knight quickly wrapped the excess chain around the stump to secure his prey. He heard hoofbeats and turned to see Gilbert galloping up on Merlin.

"Are you all right?" Gilbert asked, fresh quill and parchment at the ready.

Before Bowen could answer, the stump was suddenly uprooted and all three—stump, saddle, and Bowen—were off again. Bowen rolled out of the saddle and found himself dangling from the chain by his hands only, dodging both the stump and the saddle as they collided along with him. They twirled and whirled and sometimes one or all of them left the ground entirely, spiraling in the air as the dragon zigzagged above them, trying to shake loose his restraints.

A blur of ground, forest, sky, stump, saddle, dragon spun past Bowen's dazed and dizzy gaze. Then a swirl of bark loomed into view. A tree. Two trees. A dead one nestled at an angle in the fork branches of the other. The positions were interesting only in that they made a much larger target for Bowen to hit. And hit it he was going to do.

But as the dragon swerved toward the obstacles, Bowen gained his feet and scampered broad-legged up the dead tree, which was positioned like a ramp against the other, the saddle and the stump thumping up behind him. He swung out on the chain as it threaded through the fork of branches and dangled in the air as the saddle and the stump crunched together in the pronged boughs behind him.

Bowen was jostled from the chain as the dragon's momentum partially uprooted the forked tree and freed the dead limb against it. Bowen hit the ground a moment before the huge timber came careening down behind him. A tumble and roll spared him a flattening by inches. He peeked over the trunk to see a flash of dragon, at the end of its chain, plummet down behind a clump of trees.

There was a rapid cracking of tree limbs. A crash shuddered the earth, which belched a brown cloud of dirt into the air.

Staggering, Bowen braced himself against the log as he found his feet. He wiped what seemed like half the forest off him, drew his sword, unstrapped his shield off his back, and still wobbling, followed the trail of the chain.

It led to a small clearing where the dragon, none too steady himself, reeled amid the debris of his inelegant landing and clawed at the netting entangling his foot.

"Fleeing an honorable challenge?" Bowen charged into the glade. "What manner of dragon are you?"

"You won't live long enough to find out, dear boy!" The dragon caught Bowen's sword blow on his maimed right claw and swiped at him with his good left one. "You want my talon. Here it is!"

Bowen caught the upward slash on his shield. The dragon linked his claw with the center talon—the broken one—and yanked the shield and Bowen, still holding on, off the ground. But as he pulled the shield closer to him, his eyes suddenly went wide, and with a hissed gasp, he let his talon slip off the buckler. Both it and Bowen plopped to the ground. Bowen rolled and regained his feet, sword poised. But the dragon had made no move. He eyed the knight in wary shock.

"Recognize an old friend?" Bowen smiled and tapped his sword against his newest trophy. "This one perhaps. He was my last!"

The dragon's eyes glinted with bitter recognition. "So you killed the Old One."

Bowen lunged. The dragon dodged and parried the thrust with a fireball shot from his nostril. Bowen ducked and it struck the ground behind him.

"If you mean that hobbled, gamy-winged, grain-sucking excuse for a dragon, yes, I put him out of his misery." Bowen feinted and dodged another fireball. "He made an even dozen," he lied. It was twelve talons, but only eleven kills. "You'll be thirteen."

"Unlucky."

"For you!"

Bowen's taunt was answered by the dragon's uplifted tail. The scales at the tip folded back and it flanged out, producing sharp curved edges. Bowen caught the first slash on his blade and nearly lost his balance. The next one came low and he leapt over it.

"You're good!" Bowen laughed, hoping the dragon couldn't detect the nervousness in his voice. "Haven't had this sort of challenge in some time."

"Nor likely to again."

Again the tail flailed out. A little too fast. And a little too close. Bowen just barely ducked under it. It sliced a tree behind him in half. It came crashing down with a roaring crack and Bowen dived behind it to evade another blow.

It came in a splintering spray, the tail chopping chunks out of the felled tree as though it were slicing vegetables. Bowen rolled down the length of the log, just inches ahead of the carving tail, until it bit a little too deep and wedged itself in the trunk. The dragon shook his tail, trying to get it loose, bouncing the log up and down.

"Little overconfident, aren't we?" Bowen sprang up, grinning, realizing the brute's tail had been, in effect, "disarmed."

"Hardly, but if you win, you'll be out of work." The dragon maneuvered to confront his enemy as Bowen approached cautiously.

"Ha! I'll keep on till I've exterminated every last one of you."

"I *am* the last one!"

Bowen stopped dead in his tracks . . . and was almost blown dead out of them by the fireball that whooshed from the dragon's nostril. The knight leapt for cover behind the tree and the fire exploded against it.

"You're just trying to save your scaly hide with tricks!" Bowen angrily popped his head over the trunk, then popped it back down as another fireball skimmed overhead and exploded behind him.

"Haven't you noticed the pickings are rather slim these days?"

Bowen had noticed. But it couldn't be true. If this dragon was the last, then that meant "his" dragon was already dead. It couldn't be true. Not yet. Bowen edged toward the dragon and brazenly tapped the latest addition on his shield.

"What about your recently departed friend?"

"And before him? How long has it been?"

Bowen braced himself for a fireball or a talon slice. But there was none. The dragon let him come forward, eyeing him warily.

"The Old One and I were the last. He lived a long time.

It must have been a proud kill, warrior." The dragon's words dripped with disdain. "How much gold did his toothless, tattered carcass put in your purse?"

"What business is it of yours!" Bowen growled peevishly. This was a sore point. The thought of that smirking Lord Felton in his silly hat. He should have cut the fop down when he didn't pay up.

"Couldn't have been much," jeered the dragon. "And you'll kill me for sport. Dragonslaying seems a precarious profession at best."

Keep jabbering, you giant lizard, thought Bowen. You're allowing me to come far too close. A few more steps and you can mock me out of the new mouth I'll slice in your throat. You can't be the last. Just keep talking.

The dragon, unknowingly, obliged. "And when there are no more dragons to slay, how will you make your way, Knight?"

"Shut up, you!" Bowen lunged. He was in perfect position—right where the dragon wanted him. For Bowen had straddled the chain still attached to the dragon. As he lashed out with his blade the dragon yanked his foot. The chain snapped up taut and caught Bowen in the groin. With a yelp, the knight tumbled to the ground, losing his shield as he fell.

The dragon reared up, opening his jaws. And opening. They distended like a snake's, stretching inordinately wide as the sharp eyeteeth fangs sprang out. Helpless, Bowen watched the black maw of the dragon descend on him.

Gilbert coaxed Merlin with a kick in the haunch, riding toward the cloud of dust where the dragon had plummeted. It never occurred to him that the mule might be reluctant to move in the general direction of a dragon, given that it did not share the suicidal whimsy of its master. After all, a mule's instinct for self-preservation could not get swept up in the passion of poetry.

"The sword against the fang and claw.
The flame against the shield.

The man the beast, which one would win? . . .
Uh . . . uh . . ."

Both inspiration and a sense of direction were momentarily lost until Gilbert spied the swath of broken twigs and mashed bushes and churned ground. Bowen, the saddle, and the stump had blazed a trail. The friar kicked the mule down it, searching for a rhyme.

". . . shield, field, wield, peeled . . . Aha! Whose bones would flesh be peeled? . . . Ew!" Gilbert shuddered at his literary desperation. "No, no, no . . . Ah!"

A flash of genius seemed to ignite his imagination. He rolled the words on his tongue, savoring them as he would a tasty joint of meat.

"The sword against the fang and claw.
The flame against the shield.
The man, the beast, which one would win? . . .
Whose fate would soon be sealed?"

Gilbert shrugged; not a lyric feast, perhaps, but a pleasant palate cleanser for the next stanza.

At that moment fire flashed behind a stand of trees and Merlin bucked to a stop. Gilbert saw the stump, the saddle, and the dangling chain point the way from the forked tree. He dismounted. Again, the fire spat behind the trees. Quill and parchment in hand, the priest scrambled toward the fray, hoping to be in time for the kill.

He was.

The dragon was scooping Bowen into his gaping jaws as Gilbert broke into the glade. His own jaw dropped with a screech and he threw up his hands to cover his eyes.

"If your teeth come down, my sword goes up. Right into your brain!" It was Bowen's voice. Gilbert peeked through his fingers and screeched again. This time with relief. Bowen still lay in the dragon's mouth, but his sword tip was tickling the dragon's palate. And neither one was moving.

Chapter Eleven

THE POET GETS A HAND

"Oh, who'd the fatal falter make . . . ?"

Night fell.

They still were not moving.

Gilbert looked up from his parchment. Still in the same positions. The dragon's unhinged jaws remained as before, stretched to their aching maximum, as did Bowen's sword arm, which was propped up by his other arm. It had seemed like hours. Gilbert yawned and continued writing.

"Till moonlight night, the titans dueled.
In deadly combat bound. . . .
Oh, who'd the fatal falter make,
Whose blood . . . would . . . stain . . . the ground?"

Gilbert's quill slid off the parchment even as his head flopped down on it and he fell asleep, his mouth agape in midyawn.

Crouching uncomfortably inside the mouth, Bowen stared at the fangs and tried to sneak his blade up with the utmost discretion.

"If your sworb cums upf, ma teef come down," the tongued-tied dragon garbled. But Bowen understood the message. Sighing, he relaxed his arm, and studied the fangs once more—from a vantage point that he had just as lief not have had. He noticed a piece of cloth stuck between the back teeth. Curious, Bowen gave it a tug. It was a sleeve . . . with a skeletal hand still in it. He recognized the ring on the bony finger.

"Good Lord, Sir Eglamore!" Bowen flung the hand from the mouth in astonished disgust. After all, holding the decomposed hand of a stranger was one thing, but holding the hand of someone he once knew . . . even if he hadn't liked the clod.

"Thanffs!" mumbled the dragon. Bowen felt the tongue tingle beneath him. "Been stug upf dere fa monffs! Cuud you ged you elba aff ma tongue."

"Why should you be comfortable? My mail is rusting in your drool. And your breath is absolutely fetid."

"Wad da you expekd wiff Sir Eglamaa rotting batwan ma molars? . . . Oh? My mouf ith dry . . ."

Hacking grumbles rolled up the dragon's throat as he started to cough. Bowen tried to steady himself on the rocking tongue as noxious waves of breath set him to coughing himself.

"You belch up any flames and the last thing you'll see is my blade coming out between your eyes."

But it wasn't flame that rolled up the dragon's throat. It was a huge ball of yellowish-green saliva. It splashed over him, warm and vile. Bowen shuddered a growl, flinging gobs of the goo from his face and clothes.

"Watch it!"

"Den ged aff ma tongue an' led's tag about id!"

Not moving his blade, Bowen cautiously shifted so that the dragon's tongue was free.

"Ahh," sighed the dragon. "Much better." The tongue flapped up in Bowen's face. He shoved it away.

"Do you mind?"

"Sorry! Seems we're in a bit of a stalemate, wouldn't you say?"

Bowen didn't give an inch. "But I can go three days without sleep!"

"I can go three weeks."

"I'll stab you before I nod off," Bowen, his confidence shaken by the dragon's reply, attempted to recuperate.

"And I'll chomp you!" the dragon snapped peevishly and his tongue slapped Bowen in the face again. "Marvelous. We kill each other, doing neither of us any good."

"What do you suggest?"

"A truce. Climb out of there and let's discuss this face-to-face."

More than happy to leave, Bowen slung a leg over the dragon's jaw, but before he pulled his sword away he had second thoughts. He swung his leg back in.

"How do I know I can trust you?"

"I give you my word."

"A dragon's word is worthless!"

"Stubborn lout!"

The dragon's tongue flapped up in an exasperated snarl and flicked Bowen across the chest so suddenly that his own reaction was the unavoidable one—he tumbled backward out of the dragon's mouth.

As he fell to the ground his sword clattered from his hand. But before he could run for it, a scaly paw clamped down on him, pinning him in place. The dragon craned his neck down, his eyes searing into Bowen as he shook his overextended jaws back into place.

"A dragon's word," spat Bowen. "I should have known. Go on! Kill me!"

"I don't want to kill you! I never did!" the dragon thundered at him. Then his voice got quiet, almost solemn, as his gaze turned wistfully to the star-pocked sky. "And I don't want you to kill me. . . ." The eyes came glaring back at Bowen, the voice taking on a savage exasperation. "How do we gain? If you win, you lose a trade. If I win, I wait around for the next sword slinger thirsting to carve a reputation out of my hide . . . an unenviable inevitability, I assure you." Again, he swung his gaze heavenward, desperately focusing on something in the black night. His words spilled out in a tortured, lisping lament. "I am tired of lurking in holes and skulking in darkness! My life may be miserable, but I must not . . ."

He shook the unfinished thought away with a mysterious shiver and, turning from the sky once more, began to clench and unclench his teeth. Bowen had seen quite enough of those teeth for one night, thank you, and despite the dragon's protestations of peacemaking and his wish for Bowen's continued existence, the knight did not think this ritualistic display of pearly whites boded particularly well.

"Oh, my aching jaws," heaved the dragon, flexing the stiffness from them. Bowen heaved too, relieved that all the teeth gnashing now had a less sinister purpose. The beast leaned down into Bowen once more.

"Now I will let you up and you can retrieve your sword, and if you insist, we can pursue this fracas to its final stupidity. Or you can listen to my alternative."

The dragon released Bowen. Perplexed but still suspicious, the knight staggered to his feet, his legs tingling as the blood flowed painfully back into them. He reeled more than walked to his sword and tried to pick it up. But he was exhausted. And the sword suddenly seemed so heavy. He could hardly lift it. He could barely swivel about to see if the dragon was sliding in for a sneak attack.

But there was no attack; the dragon hadn't moved. He too was spent, and sagged to the ground with another deep sigh, gazing at Bowen with disappointed eyes.

Bowen looked at the sword he leaned on. He'd never be able to get it off the ground in time, much less swing it. He let it fall. Then he plopped down on the soft sward beside it. But he was more than tired. He was curious.

"What alternative?"

The dragon smiled.

The rosy rays of dawn filtered through the forest foliage. Birds twittered. Crickets chirped. Someone snored—Gilbert, lying facedown on his epic ballad.

A pine cone fell from a tree, thudding on his rump.

Gilbert snorted, stirred, and jerked awake. His face was smeared with ink where he had dozed upon his parchment. The parchment was equally blotched. He picked it up and tried to decipher it. "Oh, who'd the fatal . . . *farfromuke*?"

It didn't make sense, but it jogged his memory nonetheless, and he staggered to his feet in panic.

"Bowen!" he called.

But only Merlin answered, contentedly braying from the nearby patch of grass where he grazed. Gilbert scanned the glade. "No bodies, no blood, no sign of battle anywhere!" His words were not quite true. There were the dragon-scorched patches of earth and the whittled tree. But they gave no details about any specific outcome. "What happened to them, Merlin? Worse, who won?" And as he looked at the smeared manuscript in his hand, he realized something even worse. "How am I to finish this?"

Merlin offered no suggestions. But Gilbert noticed something golden glinting in the bush upon which the mule was now munching. He went over and inspected it. It was a ring, encircling a bony finger of a bony hand, encased in a ragged sleeve. Gilbert gingerly plucked it out of the bush. The hand slipped from the tattered garment to the ground. Not acquainted with the late Sir Eglamore or his taste in jewelry, he immediately jumped to the wrong conclusion.

"Oh dear. Poor chap. Picked clean." Gilbert crossed himself in memory of Sir Bowen and sadly crumpled his inkstained manuscript into a ball.

Part III

THE NAMING

A knight is sworn to valor.
His heart knows only virtue.

—***The Old Code***

Chapter Twelve

FELTON'S MISFORTUNE

"Pesky critters, dragons . . ."

Felton lolled on his bed and listened to the growl of the millstone and the crack of his foreman's whip on the hill above his manor, and smiled lazily. The harvest was going well. Einon would be pleased. And pleasing Einon made things pleasant for him.

And things were already quite pleasant. This afternoon had been particularly so. He hungrily glanced over at the pretty little minx who was languorously leaning in the open doorway, lacing up her tunic. The sunlight from outside sprayed her tousled hair an even more dazzling yellow and glowed golden across the tanned globes that no amount of tunic cinching could hide. She hadn't been able to hide them the night she leaned over to pour Felton's wine; the first night he noticed them . . . and her.

And the nice thing was, she had been so compliant. Most of these peasant pretties were reluctant playmates, and Felton found such resistance unflattering, to say the least. After all, he was a rather good-looking fellow, even handsome, if he allowed himself a moment's immodesty. One would think these wretched wenches would gladly prefer the refined attentions of an elegant chap like himself to the fumbling seductions of those brawny dolts in the field. A respite from their drab little lives; a moment spent in a fine house, in a soft bed, eating good food and drinking good wine in the good company of someone who could do them some good and deigned to favor them with the finer things for a few hours.

But Rowena understood the nature of advancement and appreciated it. Or was it Rosamund? Or Ronalda? Ro-something. He could never remember her name. But then he didn't really have to. And that was another nice thing about her. They rarely spoke, and when they did, she was always satisfied with "my pet" or "my lovely." Yes, not only pretty, but clever as well. Clever enough to be in here during the heat of the afternoon instead of outside threshing wheat. Or bundling it. Or milling it. Or whatever her tedious little task was. He could tell she was reluctant to return to it as she dawdled over the drawstrings of her garment, staring wistfully at the wheatfields below. Her golden half-moons arched to a forlorn fullness as her plump little lips pouted a sensuous sigh.

It would be a pity to have that lush skin freckle in that scathing sunlight, to spoil the feathery softness of her playful fingers with blistering labor. Felton grabbed a small pouch of money from his bedside table and rose, holding his pants up; no point in tying them only to drop them again.

He loped up behind his melancholy minx and, reaching over her shoulder, slid the pouch down into the treasury of her ample cleavage. He wondered if it was the feel of his hand or the clunky crush of the coins that made her moan so contentedly. But when she turned and smiled, he forgot the question. A lovely smile for a peasant. She still had all her teeth. Yes, best to get this flower back in the shade before it wilted. Just standing in the door, he could feel the pounding heat of the sun. Or perhaps it was merely his swelling desire.

Or perhaps it was the fiery explosion that suddenly blasted both his pleasant afternoon and a section of his wheatfield.

"Dragon! Dragon!" The cry was taken up across the fields as the workers scattered. None had been in the field that was now ablaze, not that this appeased Felton, who

watched it burn with a dismal frown. Given a choice, he'd much prefer to fry a few churls than lose a grain of his precious crop!

The dragon swept out of the cloud of smoke, a black vortex spiraling in his wake as he winged toward the mill. His pants in one hand, his disheveled minx in the other, Felton exited the house and was just rounding one side of it when he was nearly trampled by the onslaught of peasants pouring down from the mill. His bullyboy foreman stood at the crest of the hill, screaming for the retreating workers to return and save the sacks of milled flour. Felton pitied the minion's dim-witted loyalty, pathetically cracking his whip, hollering, while the wind of the dragon's wings blew a hurricane of chaff in the idiot's face.

Suddenly two fireballs cannoned from the dragon's nostrils. The first blew the roof off the storehouse and sent the bullyboy sprawling down the hill. The other blasted a blizzard of flour into the air, drenching everything in a white downpour.

The fields were in flames, the mill was in flames, the giant mill wheel teetered unsteadily on its stone. Frightened, flour-dusted people dashed about wildly like pale specters.

"Pesky critters, dragons . . ."

Felton spit flour from his mouth, wiped it from his eyes, and saw . . .

. . . the dragonslaying knight, the one he'd cheated not a week before. He was seated on his horse, casually watching the dragon swoop through the wreckage of the mill and alight on the swaying grist wheel.

". . . like big rodents." The knight turned and smiled at Felton. "You never seem to get rid of them."

Felton lost a grip on his pants. They fell to his ankles.

Holding his pants, white powder puffing off his body, Felton stormed through a drifted bank of flour, sidestepping white-daubed peasants who shoveled the stuff back up into sacks.

"Thievery . . . gouging!" Felton dickered hotly with the knight, who sat in his saddle far too casually and seemed far too unconcerned. "You blackmailing blackguard! You'd bleed an honorable man dry?" The smug knight cocked a skeptical eyebrow at him. Felton shoved a peasant out of his way and into the mountain of flour, making his way to the dragonslayer. "You'd take the food out of the mouths of my poor, hungry people?"

The shovelers stopped shoveling and stared incredulously at Felton. The lout he had just shoved spit out a mouthful of flour and stared too. Felton stared back, wild eyes peeking out of the ashen mask of his face, making him look like a corpse risen from the tomb. "What are looking at, you laggards? Scoop it up, scoop it up!" He flung a handful of flour at them for emphasis and wheeled back to Bowen. "In the name of humanity, have pity on these needy souls."

Felton tried to work up a throb in his voice, but it stuck in his throat. He could see that the knight was unmoved by his theatrics.

"You still owe me from the last time and I want *that* in advance too."

Felton's minx was stroking the knight's horse; she now smiled coyly at Bowen. The knight smiled back and winked. Felton yanked her away. Very well. He'd tried to appeal to this knave's better nature; now it was time to threaten. If only he could remember the rogue's name. Bourne. Or Boyce. Bo-something. Never mind. He'd put the fear of the crown in him. "You scoundrel, do you know who you're dealing with? I am Lord Felton, well beloved of King Einon."

"In that case, double the fee."

"I'll have you whipped! Thrown in chains! I won't pay it!"

Felton gestured emphatically with his arms. And again his pants fell down. He leaned over to pick them up, glaring the titters back into the throats of the peasants. A loud rumbling made him jerk up. Peasants were running past him. The dragon had flown off the giant mill wheel, which was rolling down the hill, gathering momentum. Felton jumped aside. His pants went down again as he, the knight, the minx, and the horse all turned and watched the twirling juggernaut crash into the side wall of Felton's house. The lord pulled up his pants. Stared at his house. Then at the knight. Then at the minx. He grabbed the cord dangling over the top of her tunic and yanked it. Her cleavage relinquished the money purse with a jingling bounce. He flung the pouch at the knight.

"Well! Get started!" Felton flailed his arms . . . and his pants fell down yet again.

Peasants lined the yard and the crumbled wall of Felton's house. Felton, pants secure at last, sat in a chair in front of the crowd, flanked by his bully boys; the Minx lounged at his feet. They all watched as the dragonslayer, battle-ax aloft, spurred his horse up the hill with a shout. The dragon, perched on the mill stone, waited for him.

"When this is over," Felton whispered to the thug-at-arms behind his chair, "get my money back."

"*My* money," the minx corrected him.

Both were to be disappointed. As the knight charged, the dragon swooped out and scooped him off the saddle into his waiting jaws and scooped the horse into his outstretched claws. The crowd let out a collective sigh of dismay as the dragon flew over them, the knight's legs sticking out of its mouth, the horse squealing and kicking in its clutches.

Felton was particularly dismayed. He sprang from his chair and watched the dragon wing out across the wheatfields, disappearing into the forest.

"My money's in that dragon's mouth."

"*My* money." The minx pouted.

The water rippled in the creek as the dragon winged his way over the waterfall and fluttered slowly down to the bank, gently releasing the skittish horse. The frightened animal bolted into the water and stood there quivering. Bowen's legs still dangled from the dragon's mouth, twitching. The dragon spat and Bowen tumbled out . . . very much alive and very moist.

"Next time just carry me off in your clutches." Bowen wiped the drool from him. "Your breath is still vile."

"Sorry," the dragon apologized. "It must have been that boar I took for breakfast."

Bowen laughed and jingled Felton's money pouch. "You took a boar for breakfast and I took a boor for lunch. Both our appetites have been sated."

The knight splashed water over his face and hair to rid it of dragon spit and then doffed his surcoat and began to wash it in the creek. Following the knight's example, the dragon tended to his own toilette, shaking off the grime of battle and licking flour from his hide.

They had chosen the waterfall for their camp, liking both its seclusion and central location. There were many villages and towns within its radius, most under the control of some minion of the king. They had agreed that there was to be no killing or harming of anyone and as little destruction as possible, just enough to make the dragon's threat look effective. This first foray had been an exception, as it was in the nature of a personal vendetta between Bowen and the lord.

The dragon wondered if he had been wise in suggesting this scheme. He watched the knight lay his surcoat out to dry upon the bank. The faded emblem of the sword within the circle stood out more clearly against the wet leather, but it was very frayed and tattered. The knight started to count his money.

"And what of your other appetite, Knight?" the dragon quietly asked.

"What do you mean?"

The dragon tried to broach the subject casually, idly fluffing out his scales. "I am your livelihood, so it's in your interest to keep me alive. . . . But there is much gold in the world. When you have your fill of it and no longer need me . . ."

The dragon's tone betrayed him, and it had not come out casually at all. The knights bristled at his words. "I am a knight of the Old Code. My word is my bond," he said indignantly.

"Did you not once give your word to slay all dragons?"

"How dare you impugn my honor! If anyone has doubts, it should be me." Bowen turned from him. "I trusted a dragon once before and lived to regret it . . ."

The dragon hoped he would not live to regret his own decision to trust Bowen. He had enough to regret already. He suddenly realized that his preening and grooming of his scales had inadvertently exposed the thin red scar on his chest. He frantically readjusted his scales, just as Bowen confronted him once more.

". . . yet here I am, blithely jumping in and out of your reeking jaws like some demented jester! How much good faith do you demand, dragon?"

"Why did you put your faith in me?" The dragon was sincerely curious.

The question caught the knight off guard. He stared at the ground, as though he might find the answer there, then attempted to parry with a question of his own. "Why didn't you kill me when you had the chance?"

"We had a truce," the dragon replied simply.

"And now? This was your idea, remember? What's it to be? Partners or enemies?"

"We are not enemies," said the dragon, but he could not be sure Bowen believed it. He was not sure if he believed it himself.

"No . . . I suppose not. . . ." Bowen responded slowly, then barked a sardonic laugh. "In league with a dragon. Life is a mad caprice."

"At least it's better than death," the dragon muttered solemnly.

"Is it?"

The dragon stared at the knight, struck by the bitterness he had infused into those two words. Bowen seemed to realize it too, and self-consciously shifted tone as he waded into the water to lead his horse to the bank.

"For you, I mean—I should think you'd welcome death. The last of your race. All your friends dead. Hated and hunted wherever you go."

"Do you delight in reminding me?" the dragon snarled testily. This was not going well. He wasn't exactly sure how it should go, but not like this. "Yes, Knight, I *long* for death . . . but fear it."

"Why? Aside from your misery, what's to lose?"

The dragon's answer came without hesitation. "My soul."

Chapter Thirteen

SHEEP AND WOLVES

"Don't clutter up a clever scheme with murky morality."

Bowen moved his horse slowly through the crowd. It was market day in the village and the square was a teeming clutter of stalls and carts as peddlers hawked their wares. The knight was in no hurry. He had already sighted his prey. A blubbery nobleman made his way through the bustle comfortably ensconced in a canopied sedan chair that was hoisted by four burly lackeys. Two haughty servants preceded his lordship, clearing the path by flogging the crowd aside with horsehair flyswatters.

As his chair wended past the various booths the lord casually filched food and merchandise, much to the disgruntled but silent disapproval of the vendors. Oh, Bowen was going to enjoy puncturing this bloated pig. This one belonged to the new breed of knight that had insinuated itself into Einon's kingdom. Men filled with greed and corruption who devised bloodless ways—at least bloodless for the king—of increasing Einon's coffers and his power. They were the schemers and Einon's old guard—the retinue of brutes who had served his father—were the enforcers.

It had evolved into an efficient system. One had only to stare into the hollow-eyed faces of Einon's subjects, their expressions ashen cold, the spark of rebellion long ago extinguished. Once they had been fighters. Now they were no better than the sheep Bowen had seen grazing down by the lake when he rode into town. Docile and dim-witted and waiting to be fleeced. Einon's pilfering of their purses was nothing compared with his plundering of their spirits.

The hog-jowled lord was working his way through a gooey gooseberry pie when he casually glanced up. What he saw made his eyes go wide. Bowen did not need to turn around to know the dragon was descending.

He came in low and fast. They had agreed there'd be no fire this time. It was far too dangerous . . . and utterly unnecessary. Just one pass through the marketplace and it was pandemonium. Carts and stalls and goods went topsy-turvy. Panicked people tripped and slipped on splattered fruits and vegetables. The lord's whippers couldn't keep the frightened mob back from their master. Nor were they even trying. Their haughtiness fled and so did they, along with everybody else—including the lord's chair bearers.

The sedan chair crashed to the ground with its grand cargo. As the dragon swerved off toward the lake Lord Blubber blustered up out of the chaos of curtains and cushions and mashed merchandise, wiping away the pie that was splattered all over his face. Bowen was the first thing he saw, smiling down on him from his horse.

"Are you the lord of this village?" the knight amiably inquired.

"Not the sheep! Don't let him get the sheep!" Lord Pie-face hovered anxiously over Bowen's shoulder, watching the dragon skim over the sheep herd, sending it into a bleating stampede along the shore of the lake.

"Do you mind?" Bowen glared at the lurking lord, whose flabby lips were still crusted with the sticky, sweet stain of the pie. The fool was so close, Bowen couldn't draw back his bow without his elbow plunging into folds of the man's belly. A harsh nudge on Bowen's part quickly served to explain the problem to the lord, who obediently stepped back.

"Please . . . just don't let him get the sheep."

Bowen didn't. Sighting along his arrow shaft, he pulled the bow back taut and loosed the arrow.

It flew to its target, passing under the dragon's wing. The beast let out a screech and lurched in the sky. He clutched his chest, grasping the shaft that was protruding from it, and went into a staggering spin, then plummeted into the lake, disappearing below the surface.

The lord excitedly hugged Bowen and the crowd descended on him with jubilant shouts. Bowen looked at his bow. He loved the feel of it in his hands. He had designed it to be longer than most bows; it was almost as tall as a man. He had carved it himself from yew wood, which gave it rare resiliency and range. A special weapon for a special purpose . . . dragonslaying.

Bowen felt as though he had betrayed it.

The dragon luxuriated in the silence of the water, swimming along the bottom of the lake. It had not been pleasant to hear the cheers that had greeted his death. How far man and dragon had drifted from the Once-ways, he thought sadly.

Bowen's aim had been true. The arrow had passed easily under his wing, where he had clamped a claw on the shaft, catching it in midflight. He had yelped and twisted, making it look as though the knight had scored a direct hit. It was ridiculous, of course, to think that such a tiny little twig could actually fell a creature of his stature. Still the crowd had been convinced, the impression no doubt helped immeasurably by his spinning death dive into the lake. As spectacular as it was, it had also been humiliating; but no more so, he supposed, than Bowen's loss back at the wheatfields. The dragon knew that this awkward alliance was not going to satisfy either of them for very long. Nor had he ever intended that it should. He only hoped it would last until he could think of something better. But whatever decision he made, he knew it would lead to the same inevitable conclusion.

The water had become cold. He had swum far enough

downlake to surface safely. As he broke the water he could still hear the distant shouts of the villagers touting Bowen. Not so distant—in fact, quite close—he heard a confused, "Baaa!" A wayward sheep, having strayed from the herd, grazed along the shore.

"Hellooo . . ." The dragon's eyes gleamed as his tongue flicked hungrily across his lips. . . .

The dragon idly watched the patch of wool he had belched up bounce in the air above him as he floated along on his back, his wings unfolded just enough to catch the current of the wind. He drifted down beside Bowen who tallied the day's take as he rode through the tall grass of the plain.

"Most profitable. I should have met you long ago, dragon." Bowen clinked the money back into its purse.

"No compunctions, then?" The dragon tried to make the question sound idle. It seemed to surprise the knight in any case.

"About what?"

"Well, such deception hardly befits . . . a . . . knight of the Old Code. . . ." The dragon tried to remain blasé, playfully blowing at the puff of fleece. Rankled, Bowen angrily snatched it out of the air and wheeled on the dragon.

"That's deba . . ." he began—only the dragon was no longer there. He had floated to the other side of the knight. "That's debatable," Bowen said defensively, watching the dragon drift in circles around him. "Fleecing Einon's lordly lackeys is a service to mankind."

"Is it?" the dragon wondered placidly. "When you squeeze the nobility, it's the peasants who feel the pinch."

Two more puffs of fleece popped out of the dragon's mouth on the words *peasants* and *pinch*. Bowen swiped them from his face, even as he tried to deflect the dragon's verbal blow.

"Not my concern." Bowen sneered. "Why put my neck on the chopping block for people afraid to risk their own? Don't clutter up a clever scheme with murky morality."

Bowen's surly grumble betrayed his feigned indifference. As he spoke the dragon surreptitiously studied him. And suddenly he knew. He knew. This was the one. The one he had been waiting for. The knight had it in him. But how was he to bring it forth? The ragged emblem on his breast was like the ragged scar on the dragon's own. Old wounds that tore deep.

"So be it"—the dragon shrugged—"*Knight of the Old Code . . .*"

The subtle emphasis ignited Bowen's hot retort. "If I wanted my conscience pricked, I'd have stayed with the priest. And what does a dragon know of the Old Code, anyway?" he demanded.

"'His blade defends the helpless,'" quoted the dragon. "'His might upholds the weak; his word speaks only truth—'"

"Stop it! I remember the words. And that's all it is! A memory. Dead and gone. And nothing—*nothing*—can bring it back."

Bowen's voice was thick with emotion. He turned from the dragon.

"You sound like who one tried. . . ." spoke the dragon gently.

"And failed. . . . So I no longer try to change the world, dragon, but merely try to get by in it. Just like you."

"Yes . . ." The dragon could not keep the faint lilt of sorrow out of his own voice. "Just like me."

The dragon twisted his body and alighted on the ground next to Bowen. The grass swishing in the wind was all that broke the silence as they moved on.

Chapter Fourteen

OUT OF THE FLAMES

"I remember now. . . ."

Einon drunkenly watched the roasted pig twirl on the spit, the fire crackling its skin. Red, leaping flames prompted red, leaping thoughts. But they flickered and changed as fast as the ever-altering firelight and he soon forgot them. Just as well. He slumped in his chair and turned back to the wrestling match that was going on around him. No weighty matters tonight. He was too drunk and it was too hot. So hot that they had moved the banquet tables into the courtyard; but what with the fire and the torches, it was not much cooler there.

Sweat rolled down Brok's bare, barrel chest as he knuckle-wrestled two opponents at once. He twisted one out of his chair and the man drunkenly toppled back into the fire with a yelp. The knights and their ladies roared their approval as the servants obligingly beat the flames off the defeated wrestler.

Urged on with raucous shouts and laughter, Brok flung the other combatant out of his chair onto the table. There was a loud crack as the man's finger bone snapped, and with a howl, he went sliding past the cheering diners, sending food and crockery flying. He skidded to a stop at the end of the table. His head flopped over the edge. He groaned and then passed out, his rolled-up eyes staring vacantly at Aislinn.

Einon laughed. He was not so drunk that he couldn't

appreciate the incongruity of the moment. His mother was the only point of stillness in the rowdy revelry, primly seated at the opposite end of the table, solitarily engaged in shifting carved wooden figures in geometric positions over a board of painted tiles.

She called it chess; another strange ritual of her people. She told him it was a game of war and had tried to teach it to him once when he was a boy. But as far as Einon was concerned, it was nothing like war. This game was rigid and formal and full of silly rules. War was bloody and chaotic and had only one rule: stay alive to crush your enemies. In Aislinn's game churchmen fought and the queen had more power than any other piece, while the king cowered in the back lines of the board. A game for fools or cowards . . . or dead people like his mother's. Only Bowen had ever played the game with her, claiming that it taught strategy. But Einon had always suspected Bowen played merely out of courtesy rather than from any true interest.

Now Aislinn played by herself. Einon did not understand how a game for two could be played alone, but then his mother seemed to do everything alone. She would have eaten alone tonight, as she usually did, had he not insisted on her presence. She did too much alone. Like going among the rabble with her medicines and cures. It was unseemly and undignified. She was the king's mother and he would not have her flouting the official policies of his court. He would not have her secret and quiet and alone.

He shouted down the table at her, gesturing to the drunken wrestler who was sprawled next to her. "Can he continue, Mother?"

Aislinn lifted the unconscious man's arm off her chess-board by its sleeve and dropped it disdainfully over the edge of the table. She calmly straightened the chess pieces and resumed her contemplation of the board, never even glancing up.

"The field is the indomitable Sir Brok's, my son."

While Brok performed a victory dance to the delighted

roar of the crowd, Einon spun to Felton, who sat beside him. Nestled drunkenly in Felton's arms was a buxom blond minx, obviously a peasant, despite her gorgeous robes. Purses and stacks of coins littered the table in front of them. Einon scooped two stacks from Felton's pile and placed them on his own. "Twenty you owe me, Felton!"

Felton had started to protest feebly, when Aislinn came to his rescue.

"*Ten* . . . my son."

The correction was spoken in a flat calm voice. Einon frowned down the table at his mother, who looked up from her board. She sipped her wine, staring at her son from over the rim of her cup. Weary despair, not age, had caused her beauty to fade. But resilient strength still glittered from her straightforward gaze. It reminded Einon of another gaze, and shaking off this unpleasant memory, he turned his frown on Felton. The golden lushness of the minx's cleavage nearly popped from her gown as she squashed it on the table, leaning over to slide one of Felton's coin stacks back toward her. Felton smiled queasily at his king's displeasure and slapped the girl's hand off the coins.

"No! Rowe . . . Ros . . . my pet!" he stuttered, and scooted the coins back into Einon's pile. "The spectacle of Sir Brok's prowess is worth double the wager, sire!"

This elicited a hearty laugh from Einon, and his courtiers followed suit. Felton stroked his pouting minx's cheek and giggled giddily along. Einon reeled to his feet, snatching up a flagon to pour more wine. It was empty. He banged it on the table, grabbing the arm of a nearby serving girl.

"More wine, wench! The king's thirst must be slaked!"

The girl whirled on him, an upraised dagger in her hand. "Slake it with blood, Piglet!"

The knife plunged down. Einon jerked the flagon up. The blade rattled into its hollow, piercing the bottom of the vessel before it got stuck, stopping just inches away from Einon's eye.

Growling, Einon wrenched the flagon back, jerking the

knife from the girl's hand, and slammed her down to the ground. She fell before the fire, her red hair flying out from under her shawl. A half-dozen swords also flew out, ready to stab her to death.

"No!"

The blades halted at the king's command. Einon staggered forward, the glow of the fire and the glow of the girl's hair flickering in his sobering gaze, lighting the elusive memory in his brain. He leaned down and pulled her up by the loose leather band that was tied about her throat. "I know . . . you. . . ." Recognition emerged from the crimson fog of wine, and it too was red. "The quarry! The blind dog's whelp!" Einon laughed. "Family devotion! A fine thing!" He whirled to the queen. "Isn't it, Mother?"

Only Aislinn's resolute, unwavering gaze responded to his sneering question . . . or accusation. The queen's eyes were filled with quiet admiration for the girl. Einon turned his sneer back on his would-be assassin.

"First you beg mercy for your father's fate. Then try to avenge it." He paused. "And now you'll share it."

But the conviction in his words was fleeting, and even as Einon's sneer fled he realized it had not been a trick of distance or of the firelight that day in the quarry. The girl was, indeed, beautiful . . . even as she spat in his face.

"In your kingdom, Einon, there are worse fates than death."

In one motion, Einon wiped his face and slapped the girl across hers. His sneer was back.

"I'll think up one for you! Lock her up!"

Brok and some others grabbed the girl and dragged her off. Einon gazed at the dagger, still stuck in the flagon. He tore it free and the pitcher clanked to the courtyard stones. With the dagger, he carved a hunk of meat from the pig carcass on the spit and brought it to his mouth to tear off a bite. But suddenly he hesitated. The girl had called him Piglet. Someone else had called him that once. He flicked the meat off the blade and it went sizzling back into the fire.

Einon turned to see his mother watching him in inscrutable silence. She slid her white queen over the chessboard and took the knight guarding the black king.

"Check," she muttered, her eyes drifting back to the game.

Einon distractedly hacked at the scaffolding cross brace with the girl's dagger. Still in his night robes, he stood amid the construction rubble of his half-built tower room. The morning sun streamed through the arched portal of the single erected wall. The view was spectacular. The room would be magnificent when it was finished. Einon jabbed the knife into the brace again.

Workmen discreetly scuttled about him. Their tools banged and rasped and scraped in counterpoint to his violent whittling; the noise becoming louder in his head, swirling and jarring, overwhelming his mind and memory with other sounds . . . sounds of battle . . . clanking metal . . . ringing swords . . . crackling fire.

Einon's eyes suddenly sparked with a ferocious light. He flew down the stairs, through the castle halls, scattering servants out of his path, flinging open doors before the guards who were stationed nearby them knew he was there. He stalked across the courtyard with determined purpose, through the debris of last night's feast and the ashes of the cookfire. Then bolting through the grated doorway of another building, he charged down a passage and barged into a small, hot room, startling the red-haired girl who was chained against the wall.

The trickle of sunlight from the narrow window fell across her face as she stared into Einon's intense, unnerving gaze. He slid the dagger between the folds of his robe and idly stroked his chest with it.

"I remember now," he said, pressing close to her. "The blind man . . . your father . . . the redbeard who killed my father . . . and you gave me this. . . ."

He pushed back the robe with his blade, exposing his scar. It had thickened and hardened—a fat, ugly knot.

"I owe you," he whispered with a smile. He caressed her cheek with the dagger blade, sliding it gently down her throat, between breasts, over her jerking heart. "I remember now . . . everything. . . ."

Chapter Fifteen

LOVE AND HATE

"Those others I killed because I wanted to kill him."

The heat had finally broken. But Kara did not feel the night air's chill, even though she wore only a thin linen shift. Lying among the rumpled coverlets of the bed, she felt nothing . . . only a numb emptiness. The unspilled tears in her eyes glistened in the brazier glow.

"You weep?" Einon drunkenly asked, throwing his jerkin over his pale torso. It did not quite cover the scar on his chest. He lurched up off the bed and weaved to the night table to refill his wine cup. "You could be on the battlements as buzzard bait rather than in the royal bed. Rebels must learn to love their king."

As her first tear fell he sneered in amused contempt and downed his wine. Through the blur of the tears that followed, Kara spied Einon's discarded belt on the floor.

And her dagger tucked into it.

The dagger plunged down. But it struck no sparks against the flint. The dragon watched in amusement as Bowen scraped the knife rapidly up and down the flint. But the tinder stubbornly refused to ignite. The head of the plucked bird skewered on a spit hung limply down, its beak half-open, as though it were laughing at the knight's efforts. The dragon's sudden snort of flame sent Bowen leaping back . . . and the campfire was suddenly ablaze. So was the bird.

"Hope you like it well-done," said the dragon, wiping the black rings from his nostrils with a sniff. Bowen nodded a doubtful thanks and jerked the spit from the fire. He beat the flames off the bird and began to eat in silence. He had maintained a brooding silence ever since their conversation after the lake business. The dragon wondered if he had pricked the knight's latent conscience too soon. Perhaps he was reconsidering this alliance. The dragon cast a worried glance at the talon-adorned shield, its grim trophies glinting in the fireglow. He noticed that the knight was watching him.

"Did you hate us so much?" the dragon asked.

"I hated one of you." Bowen tapped the broken talon in the center. "This one here. These others I killed because I wanted to kill *him*. But I never found him. Never shall. If you are the last, he must be dead."

"Yes . . . What was he like? This dragon you hated."

"He had a hide that shimmered like yours. Only all over."

"It fades with time—and cares—"

"And he had only half a heart. But even one half held enough evil to pollute an innocent."

The dragon forgot himself and rose up hotly. "Einon was no innocent. He polluted the heart!"

Now Bowen rose and stared wildly at the dragon. "So you know the story, dragon?"

"All dragons know it!" retorted the dragon defensively, hoping he had not revealed too much. "What was to be their hope became their doom. A spoiled, ungrateful child was given a great gift and destroyed it."

He watched his words cut through Bowen, prodding into life a suspicion he had never wanted to confront.

"No!" Bowen vied, shivering, as though trying to shake off the doubts that had seized him. "I knew that boy. Taught him. Taught him the ways of honor and right. The Old Code."

"Then he betrayed you, even as he betrayed the dragon whose heart he broke!"

"That's a lie, dragon!" Bowen shouted, refusing to listen.

"Stop calling me dragon! I have a name!" the dragon shouted back.

"What is it, then, dragon?" Bowen shouted even louder.

This time the dragon didn't shout back. Awkward silence deflated the tension. The dragon shrugged sheepishly. "Well . . . uh . . . you couldn't possibly pronounce it in your tongue."

Bowen turned away in exasperated disgust, flinging the rest of his bird into the fire. As he did so the dragon suddenly felt the searing pain slash through his shoulder and the red glow pulsate from under the skin.

"Arr . . . er . . . awrrr . . . owshh," howled the dragon, clutching his throbbing, glowing shoulder.

"You're right. I couldn't possibly pronounce that," Bowen said. The dragon saw the knight turn around with the sudden realization that he wasn't receiving a language lesson. This language was universal—pain! The dragon fell, grimacing to the ground.

Chapter Sixteen

EINON'S HEART

"And you do not realize you are the only one."

Einon's wine cup rolled across the floor, the wine seeping over the stones like blood. It had fallen from his hand as he slumped against the wall, the dagger buried hilt-deep in his left shoulder.

"A love dart from Cupid, Einon!" Kara glared tauntingly at him from the bed, waiting for him to follow the wine cup to the floor.

But Einon didn't fall. He shook the startled glaze from his eyes and steadied himself, wrenching the blade from his jerkin sleeve. He flung the jerkin off and examined the wound. Kara gasped. A thin line of blood trickled from his shoulder, but the wound was surprisingly slight.

"No . . ." she whispered in disbelieving despair. How many chances would she get to kill this man and how many times would she fail? Even when she struck a blow, he seemed impervious to it. Her father had taught her how to handle a blade; this thrust had gone deep, she had felt it sink into his flesh, just as she had that night on the battlefield years ago. Einon laughed at her bewilderment, wiping at the blood and sucking it from his finger.

"Not as deep nor as deadly as you thought?" he mocked, lurching toward her. "Next time stab more flesh, less cloth."

"Next time I'll pierce your heart!" She raised a fist to strike him, but he grabbed her arm and threw her back on the bed, straddling her.

"You already pierced my heart, sweet"—Einon leered, hovering over her heaving body—"in more ways than one. A very special heart. Like no other."

He pressed her hand against the knotted scar on his chest.

She yanked it back with a shudder, spitting, "A black withered thing devoid of pity!"

At Kara's insult Einon brought the bloody knife to her throat. But as he gazed at the lovely face, twisted with hatred for him, he suddenly grew calm and gently wiped the knife along her cheek. Kara felt the smear of the warm, sticky blood from the blade upon her flesh. But it was not that which made her shudder. It was the pathetic, perverse look of pain in Einon's eyes.

"Then teach me pity," he almost whispered. "Pity me. Everything . . . I would give you everything. Even power. You are so . . . beautiful."

Still pressing the knife against her cheek, he kissed her reluctant lips in awkward tenderness. Kara squirmed at the taste of him and bit his lip. He yanked her back by her red hair and, laughing, kissed her again, this time with crude rough passion, then shoved her to the bed and staggered up.

"Everything . . ." He smiled, breathing heavily, eyes flashing. "Even power . . . even a throne . . ."

But Kara did not hear his wooing promises. She was staring at the wound in his shoulder. *It was almost entirely healed!* As though she had only scratched him! Einon stuck the knife into the bedpost and reeled drunkenly from the room.

Kara twisted the dagger from the post and turned the blade on herself. But unable to plunge it upward, she flung it away. It slid across the floor with a whining screech that matched her own. Fighting back fresh tears, Kara clawed at her own flesh, scraping down the curves of her body as though trying to tear Einon's foul touch from her. In thwarted fury, she ripped the covers from the bed of her despair, then collapsed upon it, the tears coming in a torrent.

"It is a poor kind of love . . . but more than he has ever shown before."

Kara jerked up at the strange, melancholy voice, searching for the intruder on her private grief. Aislinn, the queen, emerged from the shadows.

"Am I to seek solace in that?" Kara hotly asked the melancholy-eyed woman.

"No . . ." Aislinn stooped down and picked the bloody dagger off the floor, inspecting it curiously.

"How did you come here?" Kara demanded.

"I have my ways."

"Why did you come?"

"To help."

Kara laughed bitterly. "I need no help from her who bore the beast."

A slight flinch penetrated, but did not betray, the woman's eerie calm. Though worn and pale, her face was still beautiful and bespoke an even greater beauty once upon a time.

"I bore a child. . . ." Aislinn spoke softly. "An innocent child. Was it his fault that he was the bitter fruit of a seed sown without love?"

Kara was unmoved. "I would have smothered such a child in his crib!"

"You say so now," Aislinn told her. "I thought so once. But when you hold it in your arms, you do not see the monster it can become. . . . Only a small something that is a part of you, crying for your nourishment, frail and helpless. And you do not realize you are the helpless one." Sudden bitterness shattered the queen's serenity. "How could I mother him when I was less than human? Merely a bit of plunder. A creature of submission. Allowed no pleasure. No feelings. No voice. How could he hear me? What was left for him but his father's taint?"

Trembling with emotion, Aislinn tried to regain her regal composure.

"Is this the help you offer?" Kara sneered. "To foretell my

future in your past? Give me the dagger again. Let me kill myself before I am accomplice to this vile legacy."

"Why wish for death, when there is freedom?" The queen's voice was steady and calm once more.

"How?" came Kara's hushed question.

Going to the fireplace, Aislinn pressed a carved gargoyle decorating the mantel stone. The hearth slid back with a rumbling groan, revealing a secret staircase.

"I told you. I have my ways."

The staircase led down to an old Roman cistern. Aislinn ushered Kara over the stone path that ran along the circumference of the walls. Kara saw the door on the other side and started to open it, but the queen stopped her. Sliding open the small hatch in the door, she gestured for Kara to peek through. It led to the courtyard beyond, where two of Einon's guards patrolled.

Aislinn pointed to a set of stairs that led down to an iron gate, just above the water's surface. Kara nodded and headed down them. At the gate, she stopped.

"Thank you . . ." Kara turned back, but Aislinn had already disappeared into the shadows.

Chapter Seventeen

DRACO

"An old complaint that acts up now and again."

"Dogs! Fools!" Einon's insults drowned out the cry of the dying guard who clutched at his chest, reeling unevenly as he tried to kneel before the enraged king. Einon put a boot to him and kicked him down atop his comrade, who had preceded him in death and lay on the stone floor in a puddle of oozing blood.

"If you can't guard a simple girl, then go guard shades in hell!" Einon screeched, jabbing his crimson-stained sword at the guard. But the guard did not hear him. He was dead.

Aislinn watched in stony silence as Brok nervously tried to calm her son's wrath. "They were good men, milord."

Wild with fury, spittle flecking his lips, Einon spun on Brok, his blood-tipped blade at the startled knight's throat. "You dare to question your king?"

"No, sire . . ." Brok answered cautiously, and pointed to the secret stairs beneath the open hearthstone. "But how could they have known of that?"

"More importantly, how could the wench know about it?" Einon's dark gaze shifted to his mother. He slowly withdrew the blade off Brok's neck and issued a command. "Get my best men."

Brok bowed and left the room. Aislinn heard his grunt of relief as he passed her. But her eyes never left Einon. She coolly returned his suspicious stare.

"I'll send someone to clean up this mess." The queen turned and exited, sidestepping the corpses on her way out.

The dragon woke to find the pain gone and the knight dozing in the curve of his curled-up body, huddled against his scaly haunch. He must be cold, thought the dragon. Bowen had taken the horse blanket he usually wrapped himself in at night, wet it in the cool creek, and placed it on the dragon's shoulder. The wound was still glowing hot when Bowen had first put the blanket on, and steam had puffed off it with a sizzling hiss. But the cool cloth had been comforting and soothed the pain.

Later Bowen had brought him water to drink in his shield and resoaked the blanket several times when the heat of the wound had dried it out. He had stayed by the dragon, guarding him while he rested, asking what he could do to help. There was, of course, nothing else to be done. But he had asked nonetheless.

He watched the knight's head slump forward on his chest and his eyes pop open as he jerked it back upright. So tired he seemed as he rose to inspect the wound, gently pulling off the blanket and placing a hand on the shoulder, where the red glow had faded to nothingness.

"Go back to sleep. It's passed now," the dragon reassured him. Bowen turned, surprised to see him awake.

"I wasn't asleep. I was just resting my eyes for a moment." Bowen self-consciously folded up his blanket. "What happened? What was it?" he asked, and the dragon thought he detected genuine concern in his tone. Of course, there was no way to tell the knight what had happened. Not yet. Not now.

"A . . . an old complaint that acts up now and again," the dragon vaguely hedged.

"Forgive me if I upset you . . . if anything I said . . ."

"Oh, let's not stir all that up again."

"No . . . best not."

"It wasn't that. . . ." The dragon would not have the

knight think himself responsible for the attack. "It wasn't you . . . not you. . . ."

He wasn't sure Bowen believed him.

"You'll be all right?" the knight asked solicitously.

The dragon nodded. "Have you been watching over me all night?"

"I've . . . I've . . . been up thinking. . . ." Bowen stammered, too embarrassed to admit that he had, indeed, been watching over his companion.

"About what?"

"Many things . . . Mostly what to call you . . . I've found you a name."

The dragon smiled at the Bowen's sudden burst of boyish enthusiasm. "You say that as though you reached up and plucked it from the sky."

"I did. Up there. See that cluster of stars there?"

Bowen pointed to a patch of sky where a serpentine constellation shone brilliantly against the night's black curtain. The dragon stared at the pattern of stars in fervent longing.

"I know those stars very well." He sighed wistfully.

"Do you see the shape they make?"

The dragon smiled. "A dragon."

"Yes. We call it Draco," Bowen explained. "It means dragon in some scholar's tongue."

"So instead of calling me dragon in your tongue"—the dragon chuckled—"you'll call me dragon in some other tongue."

"You're right." Bowen frowned. "It's a silly idea."

"No! No . . ." the dragon protested gently as he realized the knight had thought he was mocking his offer. He had been touched. Friends called you by a name. "I would be honored to be named after those stars. Draco. Thank you, Knight."

He had embarrassed Bowen once again.

"I have a name too, you know." Bowen feigned casualness.

“Yes, I know. . . .” The dragon smiled, unfooled. “Bowen. Thank you, Bowen. Thank you for my name. . . . Draco.”

“You whisper it as though it were a prayer,” Bowen said.

“Perhaps it is the answer to one, Bowen.” The dragon gazed heavenward and breathed: “Draco.” And the whispered syllables echoed above the rush of the creek and the tumble of the falls, out into the night, across the sky, toward the glittering stars so far away.

Part IV

THE REBEL

His blade defends the helpless.
His might upholds the weak.

—***The Old Code***

Chapter Eighteen

A MAIDEN SACRIFICE

"I merely chewed in self-defense."

Bowen recognized the village immediately as he rode over the log bridge toward the rustic huts. It was here he had last seen Einon. Here they had parted ways, with the boy shouting, "The king is above the code." He could not forget this place. He could not forget that gray morning.

The goatherds had shunned him as he had ridden through the pastures on the other side of the stream. And as he rode toward the village no one came down now to greet him. But he did not expect anyone to greet him. These people had no use for men-at-arms. To them, he was just another of the king's hunting hounds. He wondered under whose domain this place had fallen. He hoped it was someone as disagreeable as that fop, Lord Felton. Whoever it was, he'd make them pay for his unpleasant memories today.

As he turned his horse down the main path, the sleepy village suddenly erupted with wild commotion. An angry mob rushed into the path, pursuing a disheveled young woman, pelting her with rotten vegetables and mud. Shouting above the crowd, the girl futilely tried to hold her ground.

"Throw off the yoke of Einon's oppression!" *Splat!* A glop of mud sprayed across her forehead.

"Madwoman!" someone shouted.

The girl was undeterred. "Raise arms, I say!" *Splotch!* A sodden cabbage plowed into her chest.

"You say too much! Leave us in peace!"

"We want no trouble with Einon."

Whack! Another cabbage smacked her face, its rotting leaves sticking to the mud already there.

Still the girl persisted as the crowd pressed her back, converging around Bowen and his horse.

"You already have trouble with Einon!" the girl snarled defiantly. Bowen admired her spirit, if not her intelligence. "Listen to me!"

"To treason!" bellowed a burly voice. A bear of a man, sporting an eye patch, brushed past Bowen's horse to confront the girl. "You father sang that sour tune once, Kara." He pointed to his covered eye. "And once was enough. We'll not dance to it again!"

"No, Hewe," the girl replied contemptuously. "Just cringe like a dog under Einon's boot."

"A cringing dog's a live one!" Hewe, the bear, reared back to toss the gooey lump of cheese in his hand, but Bowen leaned over in his saddle and scooped it from his grasp. The bear angrily wheeled about with an oath, but seeing his potential foe was an armed knight, said nothing more, eyeing the intruder warily.

Bowen smiled pleasantly and bit into the cheese. The girl laughed. Bowen looked over at her. A smile broke through her veil of vegetables and she was staring at him with a probing interest he found unnerving. He turned back to Hewe, still licking smears of cheese from his lips.

"Why waste good food on bad rhetoric?" he said, and took another bite.

"I speak the truth!" the girl snarled, her smile disappearing.

"Truth is rarely inspiring, lass," Bowen mumbled, his mouth full of cheese, "and never wins rebellions. But it can stretch rebels' necks . . . if there *is* a neck under that vegetable patch."

The crowd laughed as the girl self-consciously wiped at her face. She was actually quite pretty, thought Bowen, cleaned up a bit. Her long red hair was striking enough, even caked with mud. He grinned at her flustered attempts to reclaim her dignity and, pulling the cabbage leaf from her fiery tresses, offered her some cheese. She grabbed his hand and indignantly shoved the soft glob into his face. The crowd laughed again until . . .

. . . a woman screamed . . . and pointed skyward. The crowd gazed up. So did Bowen, wiping the cheese from his eyes.

"About time . . ." he muttered to himself as he watched Draco circle ominously overhead, then swoop down, scattering the panicked crowd.

Negotiations were going nowhere. Bowen peeked around the hut with a couple of frightened villagers. Smoke curling from his nostrils, Draco stood perched on the bridge over the stream like a hungry vulture. He had them worried but not exactly desperate. Perhaps it was time to torch a thatched roof or raid the goat herd. The bear, Hewe, peered over Bowen's shoulder.

"Maybe he'll just go away." ventured the burly fellow hopefully.

"Maybe you'll all just die of thirst," Bowen suggested, peeved. "Where is the lord responsible for this village?"

Hewe snorted. "Lord Brok lives in a fine house six miles away. He'll only blame any destruction on us and pluck our pockets to pay for it."

Bowen sucked his teeth. Brok, eh? Just as well he wasn't here. He'd just have to bluff his way through this one. "Well, I won't pluck them as deeply! It was a fair offer, take it or leave . . . him!"

He pointed to the dragon. The villagers mumbled among themselves.

"Leave *him*!" The girl, Kara, was pointing at Bowen as she shoved through the crowd, dripping mud and mushy vegetables in her wake. "It's bad enough that you grovel to

Einon. Will you be bullied by some blackmailing knight? You don't need him to get rid of a dragon!"

Bowen glared at the girl, caring neither for her insults nor her meddling. He turned to a rotund villager who stood nearby along with three rotund young girls, obviously his daughters. "That's right. Perhaps you'll part with one of your delectable daughters instead of gold. Dragons are partial to maiden sacrifices."

The rotund father fanned his arms in front of his daughters to protect them from such a horrid thought.

"Why must it be a daughter?" said Hewe, smiling at Bowen, and the knight followed the shifty gaze of the fellow's good eye as it fell on the red-haired girl.

Draco watched the group of villagers roll the rickety cart down the path to the bridge. The young girl was strapped to a pole wedged into the back of the cart. She was yelling like a madwoman.

"No! No! Please!" she pleaded.

The front wheel of the cart bumped to a stop at the opposite end of the bridge and the peasants, with elaborate bows, hastily retreated back to the village. The girl gazed up fearfully at Draco and screamed. It was a very healthy scream and it annoyed him, almost as much as this bizarre spectacle befuddled him.

"Psst! Psst!"

Draco turned his head toward the urgent hissing. It was Bowen. He had sneaked across the stream and hunkered behind a clump of bushes near the bridge.

"Don't look over here," Bowen whispered frantically, gesturing for him to turn his eyes away. Draco stared back at the girl, more befuddled than before. He whispered back to Bowen out of the corner of his mouth.

"Who's the girl?"

"A nuisance. Get rid of her."

"Why?"

"They're trying to placate you with a sacrifice."

"Whatever gave them that bright idea?"

"Never mind! They're imbeciles."

"Barbarians!"

"Just get rid of her!"

"How?"

"How should I know? Eat her."

"Oh, please! Yech!"

"My, are we squeamish? You ate Sir Eglamore."

"I merely chewed in self-defense, I never swallowed."

"Oh . . . I suppose scorching her's out of the question, then?"

"Absolutely!"

"It would impress the yokels."

"Will you listen to yourself?"

"Well, do something with her!"

Draco leaned into the girl. She screamed that annoying scream of hers again, and when Draco reached out a claw to her, she fainted. At least it stopped the screaming. Wrenching the stake from the cart, the dragon flew off with the limp girl. The crowd poured out of the village, cheering.

"Wake up. Wake up, please. Good dear. I hope I haven't frightened her to death."

The voice sounded far away and muddy as the blackness turned a hazy gray. A blurry image emerged from the fog and sharpened into . . . a dragon's peering face. Kara screamed the rest of her way to consciousness. The dragon winced and the small digit of his claw came down over her mouth. He shushed her with a maimed forefinger to his lips.

"Do you mind?" asked the dragon, and his voice was as polite as his manners. "I have very sensitive ears. Are you all right?"

Kara, not really sure, hesitantly nodded. Draco removed his claw.

"Oh, good." He smiled apologetically. "Sorry for the scare."

Really very polite . . . for a dragon, thought Kara. A bit

too polite. It made her suspicious. She edged back on the rock ledge, where she lay near a waterfall, and realized her bonds were loose. The dragon nodded amiably.

"I cut them," he explained. "You're free to go." His smile was unnerving. And his eyes too kind. It frightened her more than the smoke and the fire and the growls. She warily scooted back from this most unconventional dragon . . . and promptly fell off the rock into the creek.

She sputtered up, shivering from the shock of the cold water. And came face-to-face with the dragon's sympathetic eyes again as he craned his neck over the rock.

"Oh, dear, let me help!" Before she had time to object or run or even scream again, he slid the palm of his claw under her and scooped her out of the creek. She found herself actually grabbing hold of his talon to steady herself as he lifted her back onto the rock and gently set her down. He was smiling at her again.

"Well, you did need a bath. . . ." he suggested sweetly. "Why! You're quite pretty!"

Flustered but flattered, Kara shyly pushed her hair back from her face. She was slowly realizing there was going to be no smoke, no fire, no growls. She returned the dragon's grin with a tentative smile of her own. "A . . . th . . . thank you . . . a . . ."

"Draco!" The dragon beamed. "My name is Draco!"

Chapter Nineteen

REUNION AND RENUNCIATION

"I vomited them up"

Bowen rode through the forest, headed for the waterfall, his sour face expressing his sour mood. He had waited an hour for Draco's return to the village, all the while looking like a fatuous idiot, mocked and smirked at by the passing villagers who thought they had outfoxed him . . . particularly the one-eyed oaf, Hewe.

"Still here, Knight?" he'd taunted him. "After your generous suggestion, we've no need of you."

"One scrawny girl won't satisfy that beast," Bowen had blasély retorted. "He'll be back."

But Draco never came back. He had left him high and dry and looking like a fool. How long did it take to drop the girl someplace and return? Draco would have considerable explaining to do once Bowen got to the falls. But what if he wasn't at the falls? What if something had happened to him? Perhaps some chivalric dolt had seen him with the girl and tried to rescue her.

Just as these dire thoughts ran amok in his head, he spied something on the trail that gave his imaginings sudden substance. Hoofprints. Dismounting, he knelt for a closer look. Several riders had recently passed this way. By the depth of the tracks in the dirt, Bowen knew the horses were heavily weighted. That meant saddle trappings and weapons. A hunting party. Fearful for Draco in earnest now, Bowen quickly mounted and galloped for their camp.

Soon he could hear the splashing song of the falls from beyond the trees. But he also heard another song. It was the weird dragon song that he had heard long ago. The strange mystical trilling that had echoed in the mountains the night he had taken Einon up to the dragon cave. But the song was different now. It was not the melancholy music he remembered. This time the trill was light and happy. Joyous.

But it was not the eerie beauty of the song that thrilled him, but the knowledge that it could only come from Draco, and that meant he was safe from harm. How safe Bowen quickly realized as he broke from the trees onto the creekbed. His euphoria over the dragon's safety quickly soured to irritation as he realized it had not been disaster that had prevented Draco's return to the village, but mere dalliance.

Kara stood on the jutting rock, arms outstretched, letting the gentle, warm rush of air caress her body as it dried her clothes and tousled her wild red mane. The comforting heat steamed from Draco's nostrils as he contentedly trilled, curled up beside her.

"Such a happy song," she cried enthusiastically, and impulsively stroked his snout, its gusting warmth wafting her hair off her shoulders. Draco blushed a bright crimson.

"We dragons love to sing when we're happy," Draco purred, fluttering his eyelids coyly.

Kara laughed at his awkward shyness and continued to pet him. "You're not like a dragon at all."

Draco chuckled. "How many do you know?"

"You're the first," Kara confessed with a smile. "But what a fraud! You're supposed to eat maidens, not serenade them. I'll bet you do none of the horrible things they say you do."

"Minstrels' fancies," Draco agreed. "I never hurt a soul unless they try to hurt me first."

"Then why were you in my village?" Kara asked curiously.

"Oh . . . ?" The dragon paused, stuck for an answer, when suddenly something rattled his distracted memory. "Oh! . . . The village!"

"Yes! You remember the *village*."

Both Kara and Draco turned to the new voice. Kara frowned when she realized it belonged to that rude knight she had met earlier. He charged his steed across the stream, heading straight for Draco. But as he reached the rock Kara emitted a warlike screech and leapt onto his horse. She plopped into the saddle behind him and pummeled his back with wild, flailing blows.

"Leave him alone, you bully!" she cried, then to Draco: "Run, Draco, fly! I'll hold him." The knight tried to dislodge her from his back, but she clung to him tenaciously, snarling at him all the while. "Pick on someone your own size!"

Bowen's excited horse spun and stomped in the water and both Kara and the knight went tumbling from the saddle into the stream. The knight got to his feet before Kara, and when she saw the dragon still on the rock, she desperately floundered in the water, trying to get to Bowen before he could draw his sword. But he didn't draw his sword and Draco didn't seem at all afraid of him.

"Smite him, Draco! Torch him!" she shouted. But the dragon was too busy suppressing his laughter to torch anybody.

"You all right?" Draco asked the knight, choking back a chuckle.

"Where have you been?" the knight snapped at him, far too casually.

"I've . . . been distracted." Draco smothered another chuckle. "Bowen, meet Kara."

Bowen turned to the girl and, with an exasperated sigh, grabbed her arm to help her up. Kara slapped him away. He let go and she flopped back down into the stream.

"You should have eaten her!" the knight growled.

By this point Kara was utterly confused.

"Now, Bowen . . ." the dragon tried to placate him.

What was going on here? Draco called the knight by name. Their conversation was far too informal. Kara rose and shook the water from her. The knight continued to rant at the dragon.

"Bad enough you forgot me, but what about yourself?" the knight railed. "You were so smitten by this baggage—"

"I beg your pardon!" Kara interjected indignantly. The knight withered her with a glance and she was once more overtaken with the feeling of familiarity she had had when she first saw him in the village.

"Shut up!" the knight ordered her, and turned back to the dragon. ". . . So smitten that your alarm senses didn't even hear me ride up. If I was the hunting party whose tracks I saw back on the trail, you'd probably be extinct right now."

"Now, Bowen, don't be angry," Draco tried to mollify him.

"Why not? I was worried to death—"

"Worried? Over me?"

"Here I am, waiting around. . . . I don't know what's happened . . . where you are. . . ." Bowen sloshed through the stream, complaining and waving his arms to the uncomprehending air. "When you're coming back . . . *If* you're coming back? You just disappear. . . ." He wheeled back on Draco, only to discover he had disappeared.

Bowen glared suspiciously at Kara, as though she had hidden him. She hadn't, of course, but she'd seen Draco tense, go all aquiver as his ears perked and he listened to a sound her ears weren't capable of hearing. He had suddenly whirled and swooped behind the falls.

All this she was about to explain to the insolent knight when Draco popped his head out of the falls.

"Horses. Someone's coming." His acute senses on the alert again, he ducked back behind the falls as Bowen suddenly swerved to the sound of the horses. Kara heard them too, pounding along the ground, echoing through the trees.

"I'll handle this," Bowen instructed her. "Just act nonchalant."

Instead, Kara ran. For, as the riders emerged from the trees onto the bank, she recognized them. And they recognized her. It was Einon and his search party.

As she ran for the opposite shore Einon motioned two riders into the creek to pursue her. They were quickly upon her. Dismounting, one grabbed her and tried to hoist her to his mounted companion. As she struggled in the warrior's strong grasp she suddenly felt it slacken and he went tumbling backward. Unable to regain her balance, she went with him—he to the ground, she into Bowen's waiting arms.

In one fluid motion, the knight slung her behind him and yanked his sword from the dead warrior to meet the onslaught of the other horseman. The rider's skill was no match for Bowen's swift blade, which slashed across his throat. He pitched off his horse into the stream, and as his scream faded to a gurgling rattle, laughter boomed across the water.

"It can't be!" Einon laughed, and Brok, at his side, laughed with him. "But it is! The king's old mentor."

And it was in that moment that Kara remembered where it was that she had seen Bowen before. He was her knight. The one who had let her escape on the battlefield. The one who had defied this king once before to save her and her father. She watched his face harden as he sized Einon up, not liking what he saw. Piglet rode his horse a little ways into the creek, taking the measure of Bowen in return.

"Still giving carving lessons, I see, Bowen," Einon said amiably.

"Get off your horse and I'll give you one," the knight replied.

"I'm bigger now. Perhaps I'll give you one."

"Stick to slaughtering peasants. It's safer."

Einon laughed blackly. "Oh, we don't slaughter them anymore.They can't pay their taxes if they're dead."

"This wench must owe a lot if you'll come to fetch her personally."

"Show your future queen more respect."

Kara knew her face must have mirrored the knight's startled surprise as he turned to her. Speechless, she could only shake her head in vigorous denial. It was enough for the knight. He turned back to Einon.

"The lady seems unwilling."

"I admire her spirit." Einon shrugged.

Kara found her voice. "I'll never wed you, Piglet!" she swore vehemently.

Bowen grinned. "Do you admire her honesty as well?"

"Ask me at the wedding."

"When I go to your wedding," Bowen said, "it'll be to make your wife a widow."

Kara laughed. Einon's pale face flushed with anger for a moment, then his bland smile returned. "Your manners are as ragged as your attire, Bowen. It seems times have not been kind to you. You should never have broken with me."

"It was you who broke with me."

Einon idly stroked his chest in somber, and it seemed to Kara, perhaps even regretful remembrance. But he quickly shook off old memories with a twisted smile and unsheathed his sword. Bowen pushed the girl back and tensed with readiness as Einon started to slowly dismount.

"I'm ready for my lesson now, Knight." Einon's foot was still in the stirrup. "But first I'll teach you one!" He suddenly flung his shield at Bowen. Even as Bowen dodged it Einon was back in the saddle and bearing down on him. The knight deftly rolled from the path of the flailing hooves as Einon charged over him and swooped down on Kara. Before she could flee, he had grabbed her by the hair and jerked her head back.

"Don't go anywhere, sweet. This won't take long." He leaned down and kissed her ruthlessly on the mouth. As she squirmed from his cruel lips she saw Bowen rise from the water, Einon's shield in his hands. He slammed it against the king's back, knocking him off his horse.

"Only expose your back to a corpse. That's one lesson you never learned," Bowen jeered. Einon's men started to rush in, but the piglet came up shaking water, eyes flashing.

"Stand back," he ordered Brok and the others, and wheeled on Bowen. "You *are* a corpse! You just don't know it yet."

Kara shrank back toward the falls as the two engaged, trading fast and furious blows. It was breathtaking to watch. Bowen held fast. But Einon was younger. And more agile.

"Lie down, Knight," Einon pressed him. "Life has passed you by. You're the sorry scrap of a dead world and dead beliefs."

"They were *your* beliefs!" The fury of the knight's voice matched the fury of his attack. But Einon met every thrust.

"Never! Never mine!" It was Einon's words that struck home more than his blows. Bowen faltered in his attack.

"They were! You spoke the words! You spoke them from your heart!" Bowen shouted in mad vehemence, but he sounded as though he were trying to shout down the truth.

"I vomited them up because I couldn't stomach them. Because I knew it was what you wanted to hear!" Einon's voice had the harsh grate of the swords' screeching steel.

"Lies!" Bowen gasped, and staggered like an old man. His eyes blurred with wetness. "I taught you . . ."

". . . to fight! That's all." Einon barked. Kara watched helplessly as he drove the knight back toward her. Toward the falls. Toward an unbearable truth against which the knight was unable to defend himself. "I took what I needed from you, Knight. You taught me to fight! And you taught me well!"

It was the coup de grâce. Bowen seemed dazed, his attack was desperate. Einon's blade ripped across his shoulder and sent the shattered knight spinning back onto his knees under the splash of the falls. Kara ran to him as Einon charged in, blade upraised. But before he could deliver the deathblow, he was blinded by a swooshing spray of water.

Kara saw the glittering body of the dragon blot Einon from their view as he landed between them and the king. His wings swooped up and he roared. She heard Einon's scream and then saw him splashing through the water toward his mount. He stumbled onto his saddle and, wheeling his horse, looked back upon the dragon and shivered, quaking with fear. Draco seemed to shiver too, and dropped his wings with a gasp as Einon galloped away, his minions following.

Draco slumped down in the creek, trying to catch his breath and clutching his chest.

"Draco!" Bowen staggered up out of the water and sloshed over to him. "Did he wound you? Let me see?" Kara was surprised by the knight's concern as he tried to shove aside the scales where the dragon held his chest. But Draco rolled sharply away from him.

"He didn't touch me!" Draco snapped wearily, then softly explained. "It's just the old complaint again. Look to your own wound, Knight."

"A poke in the shoulder, that's all." The knight dismissed his bleeding arm.

Draco turned his head back over his shoulder and gazed gravely down. "That is not the wound I meant."

A troubled frown fell upon Bowen's face. Kara was also troubled by something.

"Excuse me," she said, and both knight and dragon turned to her. "Just how is it that you two know each other?"

Part V

THE CODE

Arthur unto the vale of Avalon was swept to lie among his brother knights in a grove of stone upon a tor.

—Gildas the Scribe

Chapter Twenty

SCARS

"That's the way the Wretched world turns."

A cluster of gray huts huddled on the edge of a gray marsh, all cloaked in a gray mist. A craggy tor lurked above the haze like a dawdling god in the clouds disinterestedly contemplating the dreary fate of those below. Like the distant tor, Bowen appraised the sullen village from a knolltop perch, sucking his teeth in distaste.

"You'll wring little gold from those squalid hovels." Kara voiced his silent thought. But when he had thought it, it hadn't sounded like the reproach it now seemed.

"And you'll recruit few warriors from them," Bowen snarled testily. He clawed at his wounded shoulder and looked to Draco for support. All he got was silence. Draco was staring at the glum grayness down the hill. His filmy inner lids had shuttered over his eyes, turning them dull and lifeless as they gazed beyond the village to the forbidding crag that pierced the fog. A slight trilling sighed from his closed mouth. The dragon had descended into this woebegone, distracted mood ever since the girl first discovered the true nature of the trade he and Bowen plied. Bowen had quickly curbed her scandalized tirade by suggesting that those who saved her deserved gratitude rather than vilification.

While sparing in her thanks, Kara had at least abstained from upbraiding them for the ethics of their profession. But she had hardly abstained from moralizing. Indeed, Bowen was beginning to feel like he had been kneeling in church for the last four days. The girl had tediously harangued them on the plight of the peasantry, the tyranny of Einon, and her feeble plots for rebellion. The indirect ploy to shame them was hardly subtle. But the more the girl nattered about the deplorable state of the kingdom, the more sullen and silent Draco had become. Bowen didn't need this. He would have liked to send the wench packing, but couldn't figure out where.

They couldn't abandon her to Einon's cold mercy, and her own village had used her as dragon bait. She was a nuisance, true. Still one could feel sympathy for her predicament. And even admire her unrelenting sense of purpose. There was a fine fire in her defiance and her courage . . . and in her red, red hair.

Right now it was ablaze in the sunlight, which seemed to make her angry eyes glow. Under their hot gaze, Bowen sweltered with sudden shame. He turned from her, furiously scratching at his shoulder with a frown.

"Here. Let me see." Kara came to him and slipped a cool white hand under his unlaced tunic. She tenderly eased off a poultice of matted leaves that she had soaked in herbal oils and examined the wound. "It's knitted well."

"Y-yes . . ." Bowen stammered, staring down at her head of flame. "You . . . you have the healing touch, girl. . . ."

She gazed up at him. Her bright brown eyes glittered gold. Warm like her hair. "Kara . . ." she corrected, her lips so close to his, he felt the puff of breath that carried her name to him. It smelled faintly of the wild onions from last night's stew. Bowen liked onions. He liked the smell.

"It's just a little stiff." Kara gently probed the wound with her fingers. Her touch on his skin made him jump. "Did it hurt?"

"No!" Bowen backed farther away, self-consciously working his arm back and forth. "No . . . Kara . . . thank you. I'll limber it up in the village below. In a few days it'll be just another scar."

The familiar bite returned to his voice, reminding her—and himself—of the matter at hand.

"And what's one more scar . . ." Despite her frown, Kara's voice lacked its usual condemning edge. It was softly sad. ". . . for a knight, I mean? I once knew a knight who must have had many scars. For he was a very brave knight. Once he stood all alone against an evil king and even saved a rebel leader from a blinding."

Bowen whirled around sharply, stunned by the declaration and the ghosts it evoked, ghosts that seemed suddenly to be swirling before him. Haunting specters of yokes smashed under his sword, freed men scrambling through mud and flame, the rumble of charging horses and shouting soldiers . . . and a screaming boy wearing a crown that did not fit him . . . and that he did not fit. And a girl . . . frightened, but brave, running through the confusion, toward a fleeing giant with hair like her own . . . a tousled mass of flame. And out of that scarlet memory another ghost came howling taunts at him. Another fiery jolt from the past, splashing from a bucket-headed helmet, washing over him with startled, crystallizing clarity. Red, red hair. Spilling all around the dazed face of a young girl. This girl. She was the one. The one he had spared that day. The one who had wounded Einon.

Einon.

Einon. Einon. Einon. Einon's pall had shadowed everything the last few days. Bowen could not escape him. Or his words. ". . . Never! Never mine!" Even this girl was a part of Einon, linked to him by a long bloody trail of tragedy and desire; Einon's desire to possess her and her desire to avenge the evils he had visited upon her. And they were *Einon's* evils. No more sad fantasies of double-crossing dragons. But Bowen still hated that dragon. Still hated the heart. Without it, Einon would have died. And Bowen could have gone on believing, believing he had made a difference in one life that had been snuffed out too soon. But no, Einon had to live and expose the dream as delusion.

He turned from Kara, stammering bitterly, "That . . . knight of whom you speak no longer exists. He died of his wounds long ago."

"Pity." How much regret could she breathe into one word? "His kind is missed in this world where heroes turn out to be mountebanks only looking out for themselves."

"Well, that's the way the wretched world turns!" Bowen whirled back on her. But the heat was gone from her eyes now. They were moist and brown and filled with regret. As was her voice.

"And what about those who can't look out for themselves? You could lead them, Bowen. You could give them courage and hope."

"False hope!" His retort was as harsh as hers was pleading. Why didn't she bristle? Why didn't she rail at him?

As Bowen silently asked himself these questions a wincing trill slid out of Draco. Bowen glared over at him, but he was still gazing at the tor that jutted out of the foggy swamp. Bowen spun back to Kara, tenderly assaulted once more by her plaintive stare. He grabbed her fiercely by the shoulders.

"Even if you could raise that ragtag army of yours, what chance would they have against seasoned troops? The last time they tried, it ended up a massacre. I remember! I was there!"

"You had no part in that!" The firmness was back in her voice, the determination back in her eyes. "You spared me! You spared my father."

Her fingers savagely tugged at the headband about her throat, then flexed out and clutched Bowen's tunic in agitated appeal.

"Let others stand with you and this time the end will be different!"

"So fierce in your innocence. The dazzle of your dreams blinds you to dark truth."

Bowen gentled his grip on her shoulders and gazed sadly in her flaring eyes, drinking in her angry beauty with melancholy yearning. Kara squirmed under his probing scrutiny and broke away.

"What are you staring at?"

"Myself, once upon a time . . . But you will learn, even as I did."

"God spare me such knowledge that can steal a soul."

He thought he would burn up in her glare, but she turned it from him and turned down the sloping hill, toward a mist-wreathed grove of trees.

"Where will you go, Kara?" Draco's solemn voice stopped her. The filmy hoods of his eyes retracted, giving his gaze a strange luminosity. "It might be dangerous for you alone."

One bitter bark of laughter shot from her lips and echoed off into the fog. "It *is* dangerous. And will be as long as Einon thrives. For everyone. Why do you care, Draco? Does my plea touch you?"

Bowen heard the hope that crept into her sneering tone. Perhaps she had spied a glimmer of compassion in Draco's troubled, soulful stare. Whatever it was that flitted through those large eyes, Bowen didn't like it. He knew that Draco was not the same dragon he had been before. He wondered if anything would ever be the same as it was before.

"Does it?" the knight demanded. "And does your longing for death finally outweigh your fear of it?"

Draco stared from Bowen over to Kara. Her anxious face also awaited an answer.

"No . . ." The dragon withered under the girl's searing stare. Bowen almost felt sorry for him. "I can't help you," Draco droned. "Man abandoned dragon wisdom long ago. . . ."

The girl's unforgiving glance did not waver.

"Einon will not fall in my lifetime. . . ." Draco mumbled,

and his eyes went filmy again. Kara turned and strode toward the grove.

She was already a shadow in the mist when Bowen called after her. "You silly wench! Come back here! You can't go wandering off alone. It's not safe! Einon will have you in his bed or on his gibbet within this week. You're helpless without us! What will you do?"

His echo sounded tight and shrill as it faded down into the haze of the hill. *What will you do? . . . What will you do?* Kara was already lost in the trees, but her answer drifted back through the fog.

"Try to turn the wretched world the other way."

Chapter Twenty-one

MIST, MOSQUITOES, MORALITY, AND MUD

"And what about my corpse?"

Bowen wiped sweat from his eyes, swatted at a mosquito, and watched the money sack pass from hand to hand . . . long, grubby fingers dropping trinkets of dubious value into the pouch . . . crude cutlery, glass beads, a pewter ring, some actual coins—all of base metal and low worth. A miserable ritual.

Bowen was miserable too. He smacked another mosquito off his neck and wrinkled his nose at the stink of rotting fish drying on some shabby nets near the marsh. Miserable. The village was miserable. The villagers were miserable. Towering, ragged giants, hollow-cheeked and haunted-eyed. No lord oversaw this fog-drenched, insect-swarming sweatbox. No minion of Einon's for him to gouge.

Even that fact made Bowen miserable. He silently damned Kara. Damned her red hair and her hot eyes and her hot words. Damned her for dredging up the annoying pangs of his laggard conscience. Damned her and bid her good riddance. Things would improve in a few days and he would forget the embarrassment of finding himself in this dung heap. He damned the village too, whacked another mosquito, and maneuvered upwind of the fish stench. Even the climate and livestock were miserable.

Soon the smell of smoke began to overtake the smell of

foul fish. It was coming from two skiffs, ablaze and adrift in the water. Draco's little demonstration to ante up the stakes. Not much, but then Draco balked at doing any real damage. Still it was enough. At least for this paltry job.

The chief of the village, a gaunt giant, brought Bowen his fee. Rather than plumped with the jingling music of good coin, the sagging sack rattled and clanked with its sad treasure. Bowen reached for the limp bag reluctantly, knowing it was too late to renege and that they'd have to go through with this charade.

The tall chieftain thrust the sorry wealth of his village forward in his scrawny claw, nervously staring skyward, eyeing the dragon that was now circling the swamp with lazy menace.

"Wait!"

Bowen turned to see Kara push through the towering crowd, jabbing an accusing finger at him.

"That man is a fraud!"

The chief jerked the sack back. Kara smiled in gloating triumph. Bowen viciously squashed a mosquito on his cheek and wished it had been the girl instead.

"Is this a fraud?" He yanked his dragon-talon shield off his saddle and thrust it under the chief's hawk-curved nose for closer inspection. "That girl's a wandering idiot, babbling nonsense."

"That's a lie! This knight is no dragonslayer!" Kara lashed back.

"You are mistaken, my child."

Bowen, Kara, and the chief turned to view the new speaker who had entered the debate. He pressed through the crowd, shooing a mosquito with a rolled-up scroll and leading his mule behind him.

"Gilbert!" exclaimed Bowen, delighted by the sight of his former ally. The monk threw his arms about the knight and embraced him warmly.

"Bowen, my lad! Praise the saints, you're alive! And whole! You still have your strong right arm!"

"Well, of course, where else would it be?"

"Someone's arm is buried back in that glade under a cross bearing your name. You would have been touched by the reverence of the ceremony I performed."

Bowen smiled, remembering Sir Eglamore, and tolerated Gilbert squeezing his arm just to be sure he was in fact alive. The friar turned to the village chief. "You couldn't put your trust in a better man. I have personally seen him slay almost two dragons!"

"Almost?" Kara asked skeptically. Gilbert smiled on her with the benign patience that a man of God always showed the dim-witted.

"Well, I didn't actually witness the deathblow to the second one, but since Sir Bowen is here, he must have won."

"Of course I won! I never lose." Bowen stole Kara's gloating triumph and smiled it back at her.

"And I do not lose my ballad." Gilbert gleefully clapped Bowen on the shoulders. "Now, it will have an heroic ending."

"Gratified to be a patron of the arts."

"I long to recite it for you."

"I long to hear it, brother."

"What an honor! The poet performs for his inspiration!"

"The honor is mine, Gilbert. You are too lavish in your praise."

"Nonsense! It will be my privilege to recount your courageous deeds right after you have added to them!"

At these words, Bowen paused. "Added to them?" he asked doubtfully.

"Once you have dispatched this winged marauder above!"

"Winged marau . . . oh! . . . above . . . yes!"

"Yes! Inflame my muse to even greater glories!"

"Yes! Do!" The chief, caught up in the cascade of Gilbert's adulation, eagerly thrust the sack at Bowen once more. But Kara thrust herself between the knight and his fee.

"No! You mustn't!" she cried. "He's in league with the dragon!"

The flood of enthusiasm evaporated into parched silence. Exposed by the bold-faced truth, Bowen could only strangle down a sheepish gulp, try not to look guilty, and stare at Kara, silently vowing never to rescue another damsel.

Fortunately, everyone else was staring at the girl too. Gilbert. The villagers. Their chief . . . who slowly broke into a chuckle, then a laugh; a wide, wheezing giggle displaying rotten teeth and spewing rotten breath in Bowen's face as the man once more handed him the pouch. Bowen joined the tall giant in laughter, whirling a finger beside his head as he nodded at Kara.

"Told you. An addlepated ninny!"

Everyone was laughing now. Even Gilbert, who, in pity for the poor unfortunate, at least attempted to veil his amusement with a hand over his mouth.

But Kara was used to being laughed at. "What if he loses?" she asked.

"I never lose!" Bowen brandished his shield of trophies, still laughing. But suddenly he was the only one who was so doing. The others were considering the question. Kara stole back her gloat.

"There's a first time for everything," she countered. "And if you do lose, will the dragon return your fee?"

Not much of a fee, thought Bowen. But it was all these poor brutes had. And the possibility that it might end up in some dragon's maw had to be considered. The chief was already considering it, sizing up the dragon who was swirling above. Bowen stuck his fist into the sack and rooted around. "Oh, I'm sure the dragon has great need of a . . . wooden spoon?"

Though a good—if somewhat ridiculously illustrated—argument, the chief snatched back the bag anyway and left Bowen holding the spoon he'd plucked out.

"Ninny or no, she has a point," the chief stated, and shrugged.

"Exactly!" Kara pressed her point. "Why should you be paid for work you've not done yet?"

The chief considered this also and snatched back the spoon too.

"I never lose!" Bowen's sackless, spoonless fingers flailed in frustrated appeal.

"Then you'll be sure to collect your fee"—Kara blandly smiled—"*after* you've slain the beast."

"In advance!" Bowen hissed through curled lips. She had been there when they had plotted the whole gambit. She knew it was Bowen's turn to die this time. "This monk will tell you I've been cheated before."

Surely, these gullible rustics would choose the sage advice of a priest over some strange, mad girl.

They did.

"A suggestion," Gilbert offered diplomatically. "Allow me to hold the fee as an impartial party. Would that be fair?"

The fire bolt caused Bowen's horse to rear and he nearly spilled from the saddle, juggling both his lance and the reins.

"A little close, I think!" Bowen snarled at the dragon, hovering above.

"You can't just come out and change plans at the last moment." Draco sniffed.

"You really must learn to improvise." Bowen feinted wide with his lance, but Draco's dodge made it look closer than it was. The nonchalance of their choreography was such that it didn't even interrupt the flow of conversation.

"I was all set for the horse scoop." Draco pouted.

Bowen's mount had become quite accustomed to Draco and was obligingly blasé about being scooped up . . . provided, of course, Draco didn't spook it by blowing fireballs too close to its hooves.

"Well, blame that wretched girl. It's all her fault. Been nothing but trouble since you befriended her."

"I'm glad she didn't go too far off."

"Could have gone farther for me."

"She has put us on the spot, hasn't she?" Draco smiled. "You might admire her resourcefulness."

"You admire it while you're 'dying' instead of me. You will have to, you know. Only way 'round it."

"And what about my corpse?"

"What?"

"Are you going to cart it off or am I just supposed to lie here and pretend to decompose?"

"Don't be absurd. We do the lake death again." Bowen gestured with his lance to the marsh behind them as he made a wild sally at Draco. The crowd, watching from the village, oohed and ahhed. Draco pirouetted away from the thrust and caught a glance of the mossy gray water over his shoulder.

"Dive into that muck?"

"My, aren't we delicate? It couldn't be simpler. A quick dip under and you slide out through the fog."

"If it's so simple, you do it."

"Just get on with it. God knows we've given them their meager money's worth."

"Well, if there's no profit in it, I'll just fly off and there'll be no victor."

"Except the girl. Oh, no!" Despite the logic of Draco's solution, this situation had now become a matter of pride. Bowen would not let this girl best him. Draco took another dubious glance at the marsh.

"I'll remember this when it's your turn to die."

"Can't be any worse than the inside of your mouth!"

"I resent that."

"Stop stalling! Here I come!"

Bowen jabbed the lance under Draco's upstage armpit. The dragon took the blow expertly under the wing and, with a screech, spun out over the marsh into an elaborate aerial dance of death.

A little too elaborate for Bowen's taste. Draco was a bad actor. But then Bowen had never actually seen a good one. He had attended enough palace entertainments to know that convincing realism, never foremost in the repertoire of players' posturings, was always absent in their death scenes. These were invariably interminable moments, rife with flailing limbs, rolling eyeballs, and long-winded speeches wheezed between gasps and chokes and bellowing stage whispers. Bowen suspected few of these frantic fools had ever been on a battlefield where death was either ugly and swift, or ugly and prolonged, but was, in any case, rarely accompanied by pretty prancing, heroic last words, or applause.

Even off stage, these strutting, rouge-daubed popinjays came down to earth only during the feast. They could eat with ravenous realism. Perhaps there was a correlation between appetite and the histrionic bent. Certainly, Draco not only acted like an actor, but also ate like one.

Finally Draco approached his last gasp. With a dainty death rattle, the dragon twirled and careened toward the marsh. Despite Bowen's disdain, this acrobatic scenery chewing fooled and thrilled the mob in the village, who broke out in cheers at the sight of the dragon's plummeting carcass. Bowen slapped a mosquito, waiting for Draco to disappear under the water with a plosh.

But there wasn't a plosh. Only a splat. A rather loud splat . . . and a groan . . . and waves of mud exploding into the air. Bowen's horse whinnied and reared again, and this time the unsuspecting knight tumbled from the saddle to the ground. A glop of mud came hurtling from the sky across his face.

Bowen wiped the goo from his eyes and discovered . . . Draco plopped on his back, eyes closed, sprawled in a death tableau that he did his best to make look serene.

"Well, sink," Bowen whispered frantically, while acknowledging the wild approval of the crowd. Kara was running out to them. "Sink!"

"I can't!" Draco muttered from the corner of his mouth, not breaking his pose. "This is as deep as it gets."

Before either could figure out what to do, a laughing Kara was upon them.

"Now who's the ninny?"

"Oh, aren't we the witty wench?" Bowen glared at her. "I'll get you for this, girl!"

"You'll have to get out of it first." She chuckled.

"Bowen, my lad! You've done it again!" Gilbert jostled across the field toward them on Merlin. He rattled the money sack above his head and whooped gleefully. "I shall make you greater than Beowulf!"

"Shouldn't be difficult." Draco spewed swamp water through a clench-teethed harrumph. "Beowulf, indeed! A bucolic murderous sot!"

Bowen shushed him with a hiss as Gilbert rode up and tossed the bag to Bowen. Oh, joy—a wooden spoon all his own. Provided he could get away with the goods!

"Oh, look at the brute." Gilbert admired the kill. "He's even bigger than the last one you tangled with."

"Actually, he's about the same size," Bowen corrected him with dry modesty, shoving at Merlin's front flank to shift him away from the marsh edge. But Merlin was stubborn and Gilbert wanted another look.

"No, much bigger!" Gilbert asserted positively.

"Come along, Gilbert." Bowen grabbed Merlin's reins, steering both mule and priest away from the supposed corpse.

"But his talon?" Gilbert queried. "I shall be honored to fetch your trophy for you!"

The priest rustled through a sheaf of manuscripts slung over Merlin's back and produced a dagger. Bowen grabbed for it, but Kara got there first, plucking it from Gilbert's fingers.

"Let me!" Kara beamed devilishly at Bowen, who wondered what she was up to, and knew, whatever it was, it was no good. "It's the least I can do after casting aspersions on your skill."

Before Bowen could stop her, she had waded into the marsh and was clambering up the dragon's flank. Her foot sank into his soft side with her whole weight on it. Draco, valiantly maintaining his death pose, couldn't quite muffle a groaning "Ooof!"

"What was that?" Gilbert started in his saddle.

"Ah . . . reflex action!" Bowen shouted after Kara, more for Giblert's benefit than with any hope of stopping her nonsense. "Best stay back! There might be another."

Kara stood on Draco's belly. "Not this old boy." She thumped her foot against his hide. "Dead as they come. See!"

For further emphasis, she bounced up and down on him. Draco's mouth twitched, stifling a grimace. Then his eyes popped open and crossed in pain. Bowen protectively blocked the errant eye from Gilbert's view by standing in front of it, and hoped the priest hadn't noticed. He hadn't. He was watching Kara bouncing. She appeared every bit the wandering idiot that Bowen had branded her.

"Whee!" Kara bounced over to the claw flopped across the dragon's stomach and straddled it. She rattled the knife along the talons. "Now which one? How about this?"

She gently wiggled the blade along Draco's claw. A high-pitched giggle squeaked out of the dragon's closed mouth.

"Good Lord! It's alive!" Gilbert leapt off Merlin in alarm.

"Ticklish too." Kara grinned and nuzzled the dragon's belly with the blade. Draco helplessly choked back his laughter and his "dead" carcass quivered with very lively mirth, rippling the murky water around it.

"Stand back, child!" Gilbert grabbed the hilt of Bowen's sword and slid it from its scabbard, trudging into the marsh to rescue the girl. With a sigh of exasperation, Bowen tramped in after him.

"Give me that!" Bowen wrested the weapon away from Gilbert.

"Of course, Sir Knight, I yield to your superior skill." The priest bowed and gestured Bowen forward into the fray. Only Bowen didn't go forward.

"Get down from there, Kara!" Bowen barked at her. "And Draco, shut up!"

"But, Bowen . . ." Gilbert tugged on his sleeve, confused.

"You shut up too!" Bowen waded out toward the dragon and the girl, abandoning Gilbert to his befuddlement.

Draco made a feeble effort to maintain his charade of death.

"Oh . . . Ha! . . . Please, Kara, stop!" His whispered protests were gasped out in between chuckles. "Hee . . . ho . . . oh . . . You'll give the game away."

"That's the idea!" Kara tickled him with her free hand too . . . until Bowen grabbed it by the wrist.

"Oh, no, you don't!" Bowen yanked her down into the water. Draco heaved a relieved sigh. Kara bobbed up, spitting mud and venom.

"That's the last time you'll dunk me!" She swung an indignant fist at Bowen. The blow missed, but not the spray of mud that came with it.

"You troublemaking wench!" Bowen shook himself like a wet dog and shoved her back down.

"Have a care, Bowen!" Draco admonished.

"I don't need you to take my part," Kara sputtered up. "You're just as bad as he is, bilking innocent people. . . ."

"Ah . . . er . . . a . . ." Gilbert made a vain stab for attention, but his timid intrusion was lost in the gabble of arguing voices.

"You both should be ashamed of yourselves," Kara fumed.

"What business is it of yours?" Bowen fumed back.

"Now . . . Kara . . . Bowen . . ." Draco placated—or tried to.

“Excuse me,” interjected the friar, but Bowen cut him off.

“You’d think after we saved your life, you’d at least do us the courtesy of not sticking your meddlesome nose in our affairs.”

Draco took a more diplomatic tack. “I’m sorry, Kara—”

“What do you mean you’re sorry?” Bowen shot back. “No . . . Don’t talk! You’re supposed to be dead. And close that eye!”

Even more confused by all this jabbering, Gilbert leapt into the fray once more with what seemed an intelligent question.

“Shouldn’t someone kill that dragon?”

Aghast, Draco popped his eye back open and stared at the priest, along with his two companions.

“No!”

The emphatic unison of the retort sent Gilbert sloshing back a contrite step or two as he added, almost apologetically, “I think they rather expect it!”

He pointed meekly to the villagers rushing across the field toward them. Every lean, lanky one of them was armed to the teeth with any weapon that could hack, cut, or carve meat off the bone.

“Oh, no.” Bowen had seen this before and knew it was trouble. Even if he hadn’t, he could have guessed, particularly when the scrawny chieftain led the others in a rapturously mouthwatering chant of “Meat, Meat, Meat!”

“Meat?” Draco’s head snapped up. The ravenous crowd lurched to a halt behind the fanned arms of their leader, surprised that their anticipated feast was still walking. Well, not exactly walking.

Draco was having enough trouble just trying to stand, flopping awkwardly in the mud. The chief, quick to assess an advantage—which, by the way, was probably why he was chief—bellowed encouragement to his people. “Quickly! Kill it while it’s down.”

“Get out of here, Draco!” Bowen shouted, as he splashed

from the pond and leapt onto his horse, spurring it out to waylay the onslaught.

"No! Stay back!" Bowen called to the crowd, but they ignored his threatening sword and his shout was lost amid the cries for "Meat! Meat!" As they rushed past him he wheeled the horse, seeing Gilbert drag an excited Merlin from the crushing path.

Draco floundered in the mud, fluttering his wings like a duck skimming the water in prelude to flight, but the viscous mire made both skimming and flight slow going. Realizing her joke had gone dangerously awry, Kara tried to propel him forward by shoving her whole body against his rump and pushing. At last mud gave way to momentum, and as the swamp dwellers slogged into the marsh to descend on him, Draco swooshed upward in a backwash of mud and water.

No longer braced by Draco's back end, Kara plopped into the mud at the feet of the chief, who had been drenched in the spray of the dragon's ascent. He dripped water and suspicion down on her.

"Don't blame me," she growled at him. "I said it was a fraud."

But the chief's raised cleaver suggested that if he now agreed with her assessment, he also thought she was a part of the fraud. Luckily before the cleaver could come down, the chief did. Splat into the swamp. Felled by the village money sack flung by Bowen. Bowen splashed his horse through the confused crowd.

"No dragon, no charge." Bowen smiled down at the dazed chief, then turned to Kara. "Those wooden spoons have some heft." He hauled her onto the saddle and wheeled his horse to circle out. But instead, the circle was closing in . . . on him! No longer confused but angry, the villagers were forming an ominous ring about him. Every gap toward which he whirled his horse became filled with scowling swampers brandishing crude cutlery. Apparently the return of their meager purse was not as crucial to them as the thwarting of their massive appetites. They pressed in, leaving no way to turn.

Save one—up. Draco swooped in, scattering the swampers like a pack of squealing pigs. His wings enveloped the horse and riders, and when he swept skyward again, both horse and riders were gone. The splashing villagers were the only ones left in the swamp. A mocking neigh directed their frightened glances upward.

"Had to use the horse scoop after all!" Draco shouted delightedly above the rush of the wind and the surly curses of the cheated villagers.

"Worked like a charm." Bowen laughed and looked at Kara, who was cringing in the saddle, clinging to him. "If you had kept your mouth shut, we could have done it straight off and all've been a little drier."

But Kara was too frightened to spar with him. She wrapped her arms more tightly about his waist, trying not to look down. A windblown tress of her flame hair brushed across his lips, but all he could taste was the mud streaked in it. He spit it out and laughed at the discontented brutes below, shaking their fists and axes at them. The horse joined Bowen's laughter with a raucous whinny. It was answered by a lamenting bray.

"Draco . . ." Bowen's eyes followed the movement of the swampers as their gaze shifted abruptly downward and across to the edge of the swamp.

"Yes?"

"Care to try a double scoop?"

He pointed to the new object of the swamp folk's ire—Gilbert. The poor baffled priest still gazed upward, unaware that an entire village was now staring at him with vengeful malevolence.

"Bowen?" he plaintively cried out his bewilderment. But Bowen was too busy digging in his saddlebag to answer. For he had already seen what Gilbert saw when he turned his gaze earthward again—the savage sneer of the swamp chief!

"You vouched for him," the skeletal giant snarled, and again hoisted back his cleaver to strike. And again, he hit the ground before the cleaver hit Gilbert.

This time a half-eaten venison joint was the agent that delivered the blow. It fell at Gilbert's feet along with the chief and the cleaver. Bowen had pulled the makeshift bludgeon from his saddlebag and dropped it from above. Gilbert picked it up and examined it briefly. Very briefly. For the outraged peasants were upon him by this time, having stopped their advance only long enough to peek skyward to locate the dragon and ascertain whether or not any more dangerous food was being dropped. None was. But Draco was closer than any of them cared to have him.

He sliced down between Gilbert and his pursuers, a taloned claw extended to snare the priest. Gilbert screamed, ducked, and flung the meat into the air.

The claw missed the priest by inches.

"Damn!" Bowen muttered, for the intent had been to nab Gilbert out of his predicament, not frighten him out of his wits. "Run, you fool!" Bowen shouted back at him, and pointed to the villagers, now reassembling for attack. Fortunately, they were momentarily waylaid by a fight that broke out in the front ranks, where, it seemed, the lust for revenge had been sabotaged by the lust for the savory manna from heaven which had laid their chief low and which Gilbert had inadvertently tossed in their path.

As several tussled over the joint Gilbert took Bowen's advice and ran . . . after Merlin, who was already running ahead of him, spooked by swooping dragons and an insane, shouting mob hungrily waving about cutting tools. The mule was wiser than the master, Bowen observed. After all, if dragon meat wasn't available, mule might do. That venison joint wasn't going to feed the whole village. And even a mule would be an improvement on the reeking bounty they culled from the marsh.

Gilbert managed to grab his saddle horn and jam the wrong foot in the right stirrup. Half in, half out, he hopped alongside the excited mule as a rawboned woman charged up and took a wicked slice at him with a filleting knife. Prodded by this encouragement, Gilbert yelped, dived, and slopped sideways over the saddle, his face smothered in the satchel of manuscripts.

This spared him the sight of the dragon plucking him and Merlin into the air.

"A double horse scoop!" Draco's voice boomed in Gilbert's ear. Startled, the priest shoved aside the scrolls and saw the villagers behind him . . . and below him. Gilbert spun frantically, coming face-to-face with three other faces. Kara's was yellow and queasy. Bowen's smiled in amusement. The horse's whinnied in bland contentment. Merlin hee-hawed back nervously. And Gilbert screamed.

As Gilbert took stock of his new predicament Draco banked and headed toward the swamp. Bowen saw the village chief slowly lumber up to dazed consciousness only to go down again, ducking the low-flying dragon and the eight kicking hooves dangling from his clawed clutches. The poor fellow had hardly gained his feet when he was nearly run down by this own shouting people, still giving hopeless chase.

The dense fog that enshrouded the heart of the marsh drifted around them as Draco gained altitude, adjusting to the extra weight of the priest and mule. The chief avoided being trampled by his people and called them back as they sloshed out into the swamp or boarded skiffs in desperate pursuit of their vanishing prey.

"No!" ordered the chief. "They have wrapped themselves in the shroud of Anwnn. They belong to the dead now!"

Bowen heard the ominous words over the rustle of Draco's wings, the terrified bleats of Merlin, and the whimpered ones of Gilbert. And as the chieftain pointed with his cleaver Bowen's eyes followed its direction . . . toward the craggy tor jutting out of the mist.

Chapter Twenty-two

OLD HAUNTS AND OLD SINS

"There must be an answer!"

Einon sheathed his sword. No dangers seemed to be lurking. The cavern had long been abandoned. With day-light drifting in from its mouth, the place had shed the eerie mystic aura he remembered. Now it was only a cave. An empty cave.

He had not visited the spot in the last four years, not once since that first night. Strange how vividly he remembered the place, how vividly he remembered everything. It had been dark and he had been dying, and, at the time every-thing seemed a blurred delirium. But there were scholars and priests who claimed that in the final throes of death came great clarity. Perhaps when he lay dying, he had stored in his mind a vision that he could not perceive at the time. Sometimes he had dreams of astounding clarity that, in the instant of waking, became muddled and lost. Perhaps his memory of this place was like that . . . only here the reality was clear and that dying dream of long past was muddled.

Perhaps that was why he could remember the ledge where the dragon perched and held the sword before his eyes. And there was the stone on which he had lain, where he had sworn an oath in exchange for a heart. Gained life for the price of a few paltry words. Cheated death with a lie!

Even as he remembered it he felt no guilt. It had gotten him what he wanted. Just as he had lied to get what he had wanted from Bowen. Bowen and the dragon. He had never thought to see either again.

Bowen had been a surprise. The dragon had been a shock. Any dragon would have been, leaping from the falls like that. But it was when the beast had spread his wings and the scales fell back from his chest, exposing the jagged red scar, that Einon knew he was beholding *his* dragon—and his death—and he had screamed.

But death had not come. And he realized it was not only the scar that had made him scream. It was not only the scar that had made him know. An undeniable intuition had throbbed in his terrified heart as the dragon towered above him. It was the heart the dragon had given him . . . pounding, aching with secret sharing.

Had the dragon felt it too? Had that wrenching moment of recognition stopped the creature from crushing him? Why had he let him escape? Whether the dragon had known him or not, why let him escape? Einon distractedly ran his fingers along his chest as this and other confusing thoughts besieged his mind.

He had gone in search of the girl and had found Bowen. And then the dragon had appeared. All three had played a part in the miracle of his transformation from dying prince to living king. All three he had lost the first day of his reign. All three he had found again . . . together in one place. A disturbing sequence of coincidences . . . as though all his darkest betrayals had conspired to converge upon him. But it could be no conspiracy . . . unless it were fate's. Just coincidence. Bowen and the girl had wandered into the dragon lair just as he had. He wondered if they had survived the dragon's fury. Bowen was of no consequence, but he would lament the loss of the girl.

He had seen no sign of them at the falls when he rode back with Brok and a large troop. Only the two men Bowen had killed, bloating on the bank in the sun. Einon was not sure why he had returned. Perhaps in search of answers to the questions that now tormented him. Perhaps to slay the dragon, to purge himself of his old sins in an orgy of blood and violence, the way he solved all his problems and answered all his questions. Perhaps to see if the dragon had slain Bowen and the redhair. Whatever the reason, he had come back with his questions still unanswered and his sins still to be answered for.

"It's peaceful here, isn't it, my son?"

The cave was not quite empty after all. Einon saw Aislinn emerge from the shadows on the ledge and step into a pool of sunlight that sprayed through a crevice in the cavern roof. She looked down on him with her strong, sad eyes.

"I come here to be alone sometimes." Alone? She was always alone. Even at court, when the castle was crawling with people. "You did not find the dragon at the falls?"

"No," Einon muttered tersely. He did not like his mother finding him like this. He felt weak before her . . . as if she knew his secret fears.

"Bowen? Kara?"

"No. Only the bodies of my men. The dragon must have eaten Bowen and the girl."

"And not your men? Picky eater." She was laughing at him. He knew. She wasn't even smiling. She never smiled. But she was laughing at him nonetheless.

"Why didn't he eat me, Mother? Why didn't he kill me? I broke my vow to him."

"Yes, you did."

There was still no smile. But he knew she had stopped laughing at him. "Then why?"

Her face was impassive . . . and beautiful. "I can't answer that."

"Can't or won't? Yours was the dragon clan. It was you who brought me here!" His voice echoed through the cave. "There must be an answer!"

"Perhaps it is in your heart, my son." As she spoke these words a cloud passed over the sun and smothered Aislinn in shadow once more.

Chapter Twenty-three

THE TOR

"A land of mist and water."

Mist swirled everywhere. Gilbert could not see a thing. He wasn't sure whether he himself was shaking or it was the quivering mule beneath him that made him shake. He looked down at the crippled claw that clutched them. He looked above them at the scaly neck extending into the powerful jaw. The rustling wings made the air howl around them and sent his scrolls to shivering.

"Saints preserve us!" he prayed hoarsely as he had prayed a dozen times already, and crossed himself, grateful that so far the saints had preserved them.

"All's well, Gilbert," Bowen assured him, even though Gilbert could not see him through the fog.

"Well?" The priest was incredulous. "I nearly have my bald pate trimmed at my neck. I find you in league with a pair of rogues—"

"I am not a rogue!" Kara's voice cut through the haze.

Gilbert ignored her. "One, a dragon who kidnaps me—"

"He saved you!" Kara protested again.

Again, the priest disregarded her. "—only to get us lost in this dreadful fog."

"Not lost." Draco's firm voice shushed Gilbert's whining, as did the sight that suddenly loomed out of the thinning mist.

A circle of eerie stone columns rose upon the crest of the tor—an ancient ring that grew larger and larger as the dragon swiftly descended and gently deposited his cargo on the ground.

Hee-hawing, the skittish Merlin bucked Gilbert into the mossy grass and bolted off among the stones. The priest sat up to find Bowen at his side, ready to give him a lift up. But Gilbert had had enough of being toted about and, disdaining the helping hand, got to his feet himself. Straightening his rumpled cassock with obvious annoyance, he stared fearfully through the gloomy mist, and shuddered.

"What deadly, unholy place is this?"

"Most *holy*, priest."

Gilbert turned to the dragon's voice along with Bowen and the girl. He was solemnly perched on the most massive of the monoliths in the stone ring. He gazed out on the darkening sky, watching night come creeping through the haze and spoke quietly. "More than death dwells here."

"W-what more?" Gilbert asked, not sure he really wanted to hear the answer.

"A spirit. Beyond death. Alive and eternal. That remembers the Once-ways and the glory of one who shared our name."

"What one?" Again, the priest could not refrain from asking.

"Pendragon," came the answer.

"Pen—*Arthur* Pendragon?" And suddenly the stunned priest knew where he was. "A land of mist and water . . ." And he knew what the stones were. He crossed himself and moved among them in reverent awe, quoting the bits of lore and legend he had memorized in his head, and in his heart. "'Arthur unto the vale of Avalon was swept . . . to lie among his brother knights . . .'"

"'. . . in a grove of stone upon a tor,'" Bowen finished for him, remembering the words too. Gilbert smiled over at the ashen-faced, unsettled knight.

"Not a grove . . . the Round Table of Camelot!" The friar quivered with emotion, tears rolling down his rosy cheeks. He stood in the center of the ring, pointing out the stones. "This is where Sir Gawain sat. And here Sir Percival. There Galahad. And Sir Kay. And there Lancelot . . . at the right hand of—King Arthur!"

His trembling finger pointed to Arthur's stone. The tallest one in the circle. The one atop which Draco sat perched.

"I have found you as foretold, brave Arthur. Let the end of my quest be the beginning of a new Camelot."

Bowen slumped sullenly against Lancelot's stone, listening to Gilbert's prayer as the priest and Kara knelt before Arthur's stone. Draco, still perched atop it, gazed out at the star-filled sky.

"Let us who remember the glories of your golden kingdom feel your noble spirit, O Sainted King," Gilbert intoned. His voice had none of its usual rhetorical pomposity, just a quiet, fervent clarity. "And let the song of Excalibur echo in our enemy's ear. Amen . . . Ready, child?" He rose and helped Kara to her feet.

Both turned to Bowen. "And you, Bowen?" Gilbert asked, vague hope in his voice.

Bowen glanced upon the stones. He was impressed. He had been moved, like the others. But he could not be moved to madness. He shook his head at the priest.

"My son, this is Avalon!" Gilbert's voice was still laced with earnest, kind dignity. "The shadow realm of the Round Table. It is a divine omen!"

"Omens and shadows won't win battles." Bowen rose. "Nor will you. You'll find out when you try to raise your . . . army." He sneered the word at Kara. "You already know the courage of *your* village. They're very brave at pelting girls with vegetables."

Kara calmly stared his sneer down. "It must start somewhere." She turned to Draco. "Will you wish us luck, Draco?"

The dragon ignored her, still staring at the stars peeking through the misty veil of night. "Look at your cluster of stars, Bowen." Good old Draco. Only he would think of reducing Gilbert and Kara's futile rebellion to hopeless stargazing. Bowen wondered what the dragon had up his sleeve and played along.

"The ones I named you after," Bowen said, looking up at the dragon constellation. It sparkled through the haze, brilliant in the black sky.

"More than mere stars," Draco replied, and Bowen instinctively shivered at the solemnity in his voice. "Long ago, when man was young and the dragon already old, the wisest of our race took pity on man and shared with him our secrets. And when this Wise One was dying, he gathered together all the dragons, making them vow to watch over man always. Even as he would watch, once he was gone. And at the moment of his death the night became alive with those stars."

Bowen heard the dragon's words in a daze. As though they crept toward him through the mist of the tor like slow-moving shadows . . . strange and foreboding shapes that so fascinated him he was helpless to stop the doom he knew they brought. He could only listen in fearful silence as the dragon continued.

"Through the years, the Wise One's shimmering soul was joined by others as the dragons kept their pledge to serve man . . . until the heavens were aglow with stars. But then man grew arrogant with the gift of our power and shunned our guidance. And fewer stars ascended the sky to hold back black night."

Bowen followed the dragon's forlorn gaze to the constellation once more. It seemed to pulsate with a glittering glow. Draco sighed. And that sigh seemed to encompass all the sadness of the world.

"All my life I've longed to perform one deed worthy of those forever shining above. Finally my chance came. A great sacrifice that would reunite man and dragon as of old and ensure my place among my ancient brothers of the sky. . . . But my sacrifice became my sin."

And Bowen knew. He turned to the dragon. "It was you. Your half-heart beats in Einon's breast."

Draco bared the scales on his breast, revealing the jagged crimson scar over his heart. "Yes. My *half*-heart, that cost *all* my soul. Even then I knew his bloodthirsty nature, but I thought the heart could change him. I was . . . naive."

Bowen barked a short, savage laugh; then he felt surging melancholy overwhelm the bitterness within him.

"Naive? No more than I . . ." The knight's voice sounded different somehow, quiet and hollow and small. "Always I dreamed of serving noble kings and nobler ideals. The Old Code was already a creaking relic when I became a squire. But dreams die hard. And you hold them in your hands long after they've crumbled to dust. And in your heart long after they've soured to bitter poison . . . I will not be that naive again."

Draco descended into the circle of stone and Bowen turned from the pity he saw in his large eyes. Pity, but not solace.

"Too long I've been afraid," Draco explained. "Afraid to die. Afraid to confront the evil I have wrought."

Bowen could not face him. He stared into the night. Up at Draco's stars . . . now obscured behind dark scudding clouds. Somewhere in the distance thunder rumbled. He heard the dragon turn to the others. "I will go with you."

Bowen walked from the circle. He sought the shadows of the stones. He was alone now. Draco's voice called after him above the roll of thunder. "So be it, Bowen. Farewell."

Farewell. So be it. He was alone now. Alone.

Chapter Twenty-four

PENDRAGON AND EPIPHANY

"A knight is sworn to valor."

The rain came in a big, bellicose torrent. Kara, Gilbert, and Merlin took shelter under a rock overhang while Draco, oblivious to the downpour, waited it out on top. Kara had drifted off to sleep after a while, leaving Gilbert fussing over maps and charts and histories of old Roman campaigns that he constantly seemed to conjure up out of his scroll bag.

A crack of thunder woke her. She stirred and found Gilbert swaddled in parchment, poring over a diagram of tactics by the light of the small fire that hissed and sizzled as the angled rain spit at the edges of it.

She snuggled into the blanket the friar had given her and smiled. She was thinking what Hewe the Bear's reaction would be when she showed up in the village not only alive and whole, but with Draco at her side. His one good eye would pop out of his head.

Hewe was not a coward, she knew that. He had planned the rebellion with her father and had fought hard beside him. The others of her village were not cowards either. But the wounds Einon had inflicted upon them the last time were still too fresh, and had weakened them, whereas he had grown stronger. Fear did not hold them back, only a sense of futility. They would fight again if they had any hope of victory. Now she was bringing them hope. Draco would be their hope.

The priest had been right. Avalon was an omen. Everything had been. Her finding Draco and Bowen. Why couldn't the knight have seen what was so obvious? Only he marred her happiness. He, who had stood against Einon when there was no hope, would now deny himself his heart's desire. Oh, to be so strong and splendid . . . but so stubborn. What would it take to reach out and release the glory and greatness that lay hidden within him?

She closed her eyes, and the memory of his haunted face wavered in the darkness as sleep came to reclaim her once more. But the lashing storm called her back with a bellow of thunder. Or perhaps it was the rustling swoosh from above that made her stir. In either case, she leaned up from where she lay, suddenly alert. She looked out into the rain, then suddenly rose and ran out into the torrent.

"Kara?" she heard Gilbert call behind her and the shuffle of his scrolls as he abruptly stood. She turned to him, soaked, and pointed at the sky. Lightning flashed and in its momentary clearness Draco's silhouette was caught, winging through the gloomy rain toward the distant tor. The firelight flickered over Gilbert's perplexed, worried face. The rain was cold. As cold as the hope in her heart.

The wind howled. The rain lanced through the ever-present mist. Bowen huddled under Arthur's monolith. Huge as it was, it could not keep out the cold bite of the rain. He pulled his cloak around him.

"Valor . . . valor . . ."

It came on a hoarse whisper. Bowen at first thought it some aberration caused by the rain spilling over the stones. But it came again. An echoing whisper. Bowen sprang up, peering into the rain and mist and windswept night.

A knight stood in front of the stone opposite him. No, not stood—*floated* in front of the stone. Pale and as wispy as the swirling mist. Slashed by the rain. Wavering in the wind. Bowen instinctively went for his sword. But the ghostly image did not move from the stone. Whose place at the

Round Table did Gilbert say that was . . . ? Gawain, was it?

"A knight is sworn to valor . . ." The words issued from the apparition of Gawain. He was answered by another voice.

"His heart knows only virtue. . . ." Bowen whirled to the new voice. A shadowy wraith arose from Sir Percival's stone. Beside him, from Kay's stone, a third specter appeared.

"His blade defends the helpless. . . ." whispered Sir Kay.

"His might upholds the weak. . . ." Galahad's ghost fluttered from another stone. Then Bedivere: *"His word speaks only truth. . . ."*

Their hollow voices echoed and overlapped in the wind. Bowen fell back and another voice hissed over his shoulder. He whirled round as Lancelot loomed before him. *"His wrath undoes the wicked!"* The words sliced through the wind and the rain like damning accusations. Bowen staggered back into the center of the circle as Lancelot raised a ghostly hand and pointed to Arthur's stone.

Eerie and majestic, Arthur's spirit rose from his stone, holding aloft the heavy sword in his hand. Bowen collapsed to his knees, his heart crashing against his chest. Golden light seemed to spray from the blade, sparkling through Arthur's misty, mighty form. The king spoke in a rumbling rasp that seemed to cow the chaos of the storm.

"Inside the table's circle,
Under the sacred sword,
A knight must vow to follow
The code that is unending,
Unending as the table—
A ring by honor bound."

Again, the unearthly voices took up the invocation of a knight's duties. Other spirits of the Round Table joined their ghostly brotherhood, converging on Bowen, chanting the words of the Old Code in a crescendoing cacophony, accompanied by the roaring thunder and the driving rain, whirling about Bowen in a mad dance with the whipping wind.

Bowen thought his heart would break. He was drenched in rain and tears. He covered his head from the jumble of sight and sound, reciting the code himself in a breathless rushed litany, trying to shout down the mad singsong racket of the spirits, trying to hold on to the sense of the words and retain their meaning.

"A knight is sworn to valor . . . his heart know only virtue . . . blade defends the helpless . . . upholds the weak . . . speaks only truth . . . !"

He stopped, realizing his was the only voice he now heard. Only the rain echoed in the circle. The spirits were gone. All but one . . . Arthur still drifted before his stone, slowly lowering his sword.

"His wrath undoes the wicked. . . ." The golden light had dimmed. Arthur's image was fading into the mist and rain . . . fading into the stone. But still his voice whispered across the circle to Bowen.

"The right can never die,
If one man still recalls."

Bowen rose and staggered to the rock, speaking the words with the faint voice.

"The words are not forgot,
If one voice speaks them clear."

The voice was still now. Arthur's wraith had disappeared into the stone. Bowen stumbled to it, embracing it. Its wet hardness was somehow reassuring, comforting.

"The code forever shines,
If one heart holds it bright."

Thunder roared. Lightning crackled. In its jagged light, another shape seemed to loom out of the rock like a new vision. . . .

Draco! It was Draco! Sitting atop the stone. Bowen flung up his arms, reaching longingly out to him. The rain streamed down Draco's face, into his kind eyes. He stretched down his wings and enfolded the knight in them.

There they stayed, wrapped together around the rocky symbol of their once-lost dreams and their newfound hope . . . two reclaimed souls cleansed and purified in the heavenly rain and reunited in a common purpose.

Chapter Twenty-five

A KNIGHT OF THE OLD CODE

"Save your strength for the fight against Einon."

Gilbert felt the shattering sting in his hands as the one-eyed giant's quarterstaff smashed down upon his own. Cheered on by the milling villagers with shouts of "Hewe, Hewe," the burly cyclops beat Gilbert back with rough, wild blows. Gilbert was mystified by the brute's success. True, he outweighed the priest and his reach was longer. But Gilbert had strategy, which was superior to strength. After all, he had practiced these moves for years. Of course, it was only against imaginary partners . . . with tree limbs or shepherd's crooks, in glades or on hillsides or merely miming empty-handedly on the back of Merlin while he traveled. But he had followed the diagram meticulously, even as he did now, although he had to confess his performance was somewhat awkward. But at least he was defending himself. And oh, how his hands ached! And it was hard to swing into the next position when the blows came so fast. Where had a cheese maker learned to fight like this?

A vigorous stroke by Hewe tumbled Gilbert to the ground at the feet of Merlin, who brayed and shied back. The priest thought the villagers' laughter showed an unsportsmanlike regard for his valiant albeit brief effort. One must always be gracious in victory. He would need all the Lord's patience to whip this rabble into shape.

"We should have waited for Draco." Kara knelt beside

him to help him to his feet. "He'll be back. He must." But she didn't sound convinced.

Nor was Gilbert. He didn't know the dragon as well as Kara, of course, but in all his vast years as a historian and a scholar, he had never encountered such a fantastical legend as the one the dragon told. Both the literary and biblical traditions belied the dragon's claims. Was he to totally discount Perseus and Siegfried, and what about St. George? That brave knight would have to be uncanonized, if one believed the dragon. Gilbert just didn't know. That dragon made a muddle of many cherished things. But then he had believed in the Pendragon and he had brought Gilbert to Avalon.

Gilbert scanned the sky along with Kara, but the air was filled only with the mocking jeers of the peasants. He gave Kara's hand a comforting pat as he rose and took the scroll she held for him. The quarterstaff fighters in the diagram were rather crudely rendered, but the positions and instructions beneath them were clear enough.

"Aha!" Gilbert threw his hands up in miffed exasperation and turned to Hewe. "I thought so! It's parry, parry, thrust. Not parry, thrust, thrust. You're not following the rules of combat!"

Hewe crumpled the scroll with a downward blow of his staff and snarled at the priest. "The rule is to win! Which is more than we'd do if we followed you and this daft girl, priest." He spat derisively. "You'll lead us against Einon. To hell, more likely."

Gilbert tried to smooth out his crushed scroll. It seemed simpler than smoothing out his crushed pride.

"When the dragon gets here, you'll show us some respect, Hewe," Kara snapped at him. All this brought was more laughing jeers from the crowd. For an oppressed people, they were entirely too cheery, thought Gilbert, and traded doubtful glances with Kara, still unsure whether Draco would show and make good her threat. The village had been quite surprised to see her, considering the fact that the last look they'd had of her was flying away in the clutches of a dragon. But while they couldn't disregard her obvious escape, they weren't giving any credence to the rest of her tale, even if she had a priest to back her up. Gilbert certainly saw no gullibility in the one-eyed, scowling face of Hewe.

"*If* the dragon gets here, he'll find you've been sent packing," Hewe bellowed. "We've had enough of your moon-eyed mischief, Kara!"

He raised his staff to menace them off, but an arrow suddenly embedded itself in it.

All eyes turned to a rider in the pasture beyond the stream. Slinging his bow, he galloped over the bridge into the village and brought his horse to a rearing halt between Gilbert and Kara and Hewe.

Gilbert didn't recognize him for a moment . . . all scrubbed and shaved. His clothes and mail, though still frayed and worn, were clean and mended as best could be. Even the ragged emblem of the sword within the circle seemed brighter. But it was not as bright as the fierce fine visionary fire in the rider's eyes. Bowen! No, thought Gilbert, a knight of the Old Code.

"Save your strength for the fight against Einon," Bowen said to Hewe as he leaned forward in his saddle and plucked his arrow from the staff.

Hewe pulled it back with a contemptuous jerk. "There isn't any fight against Einon," he stated.

Bowen smiled at him. "I'm going to start one."

Gilbert turned to Kara, but she only had eyes for the knight. Hewe spat at Bowen's news. He was very good at spitting.

"You and what army, Knight?"

"He'll enlist!" Bowen gestured across the stream to the ridge beyond.

There, the massive form of Draco was rising up from behind the horizon, his hide magnificently aglow. Like fire. Ablaze against the morning sun.

Part VI

THE REBELLION

The sky's untouched without the reach,
The dream's no good without the dare,
And one must fight for what one wants,
'Tis purpose God attends, not prayer.

—Gilbert of Glockenspur,
"The Psalm of Survival"

Chapter Twenty-six

A BOW, A BIRD, AND FELTON'S FURTHER MISFORTUNE

"Is that dog wearing a sword?"

"Hungry, pet . . . ?" Brok removed the hood from the falcon that perched on his gauntleted wrist. He stroked the feathered tuft on the bird's head and cooed at it. Felton found it a revolting exhibition and thought how nice the tuft would look in one of his hats.

The whole afternoon had been revolting. He had ridden over to discuss the business of the realm, not to join in the lout's hunt. But Brok had been insistent and an insistent Brok was a Brok not be to denied. It wasn't that Felton's company was valued; he was there only to provide at least one easy target for the brutes Brok had gathered together. In fact, game had been sparse, but the jests had been plentiful . . . and Felton had been the butt of most of them. And he had yet to introduce the matter he had come to discuss. He had just begun to launch into the details when Brok interrupted him to fuss over his feathered fiend.

"Peasants disappearing every day, Sir Brok . . ." Felton sighed, picking up where he had left off. "More than a hundred from my village alone. The king wants you to look into it."

"Why should I have to look after your flock, Felton?" Brok laconically muttered, and blew kisses at his falcon once more. The bird pecked back at his beard.

"It's not just my village," grumbled Felton. Didn't the dullard pay attention? "But every village."

"Not mine, I'll wager. The scum wouldn't dare."

"Nevertheless, Einon instructed me to inform you—"

"You have! Now shut up!" Brok cut him short and stroked his bird. "Don't worry, Felton, we'll find your filthy little runaways for you. Just like she finds her prey. Eat, my pretty."

He released the bird and watched with bloodthirsty amusement as it soared skyward toward a screeching crow. But the huntress never reached her prey. An arrow ripped through the falcon's breast, sending it plummeting earthward.

"I say! What a splendid shot!" Felton exclaimed, forgetting himself.

Brok turned and scowled at him. "Idiot!" he growled, and with a wail of anger, whipped his horse off through the forest in the direction of his fallen bird. The others rode after him.

Felton figured he'd better follow suit.

The stone hit the straw man's shoulder and the crow perched there cawed an angry shriek and winged off it. Hewe threw another rock at it for good measure, but it was already out of range, berating its tormentor below with its persistent croaking.

"You're up, priest," Hewe snorted with disdain. Gilbert could hear the tittering murmur of the other archers behind him. He squinted at the straw man on the other side of the glade. It seemed very far away. He nervously took his position and, notching an arrow, tried to remember everything Hewe had dismissively barked at him a moment ago.

Gilbert knew he should be happier than he felt. The rebellion was going well; word had filtered through the towns and villages about the secret weapon that would ensure victory against the tyrant. Men had come with their crude weapons and brought their families with them. Their tents and shelters spread out from the borders of the village along the stream and across the pastures. Under Bowen's command, inept bungling progressed to discipline and skill. Each man was assigned to a unit and had duties beyond his training periods—whether it was to provide food for the camp or to build weapons. Even the women and children helped, making arrows and collecting metal farm implements that could be melted down and remolded into swords and spears.

Gilbert's own duties included the roles of historian, scribe, and spiritual leader. He helped Bowen draw maps and plot strategies and kept the recruitment records. He bolstered skeptical spirits with rousing eloquence and spine-stiffening sermons. And in the waning hours of the night, when his duty to the day's cause was done and campfires dotted the fields, he would find a few quiet moments of inspiration and scribble his fancies across parchment, celebrating the glorious adventure in which God had granted him a role.

And though Gilbert was grateful to God and thanked Him every night in lofty and lavish prayer, he longed for a bigger role. Bowen would have exempted him from arms training altogether, out of regard for his priestly vows, but Gilbert would not be dissuaded and would quote himself by way of explanation:

"The sky's untouched without the reach,
The dream's no good without the dare,
And one must fight for what one wants,
'Tis purpose God attends, not prayer."

But while he tackled his training with enthusiasm, he performed less than proficiently. And that was the source of his discontent. He had already abandoned the quarterstaff as his weapon of choice; though he understood it intellectually, his manual dexterity was no match for his mental agility. He was clumsy and inept. This also proved the case with the pike, the mace, and the ball and chain. And he had shown, at best, only a middling competence with a sword. He was beginning to fear that he would strike no blows for God and Arthur on the battlefield and that his only part in the fight would be to bless the troops and bury the dead.

Archery was more or less his last hope. There were aspects about it that made Gilbert hopeful. For one, you could take your time. You could stand behind a tree or a rock and assess the situation before acting. No one was battering at you with another weapon, giving you no time to think, moving too fast for you to effect the intricate strategies of your defense, let alone your attack.

Today he had come with Hewe and his mates into the forest for instruction. It was cool and green and quiet, and nice to be away from the crush and hum of the village, with its blasting forge fires and clanging weapons and chattering crowds.

"Higher with that bow hand, priest, unless you're shooting gophers!" Hewe's condescending instruction was accompanied by the crow cawing above. Both disrupted the idyllic calm and interfered with Gilbert's concentration as he tentatively pulled back the bowstring. He heard Hewe's peasant pals snickering behind him. Ignoring them as best he could, Gilbert took a breath and composed himself, sighting the target once more.

"You're aiming with the wrong eye!" Hewe growled. Gilbert could tell the man was performing for his friends.

"Yes, well, it's easier for you, of course," Gilbert drolly remarked, and silently asked God to forgive him for mocking another's afflictions.

Hewe the Bear glared at the priest with his good eye and bit his words off with deliberate slowness as though he were speaking to a dimwit. "Sight along the arrow. . . . And get your fingers off the feathers!" He groaned as though his pupil were hopeless and threw up his hands. "Anytime you're ready."

Gilbert heaved a sigh of his own and sighted down the

arrow as instructed. The straw man seemed to loom large and enticingly at the end of his shaft; not quite so far away as he first thought. He let loose the arrow.

Thwack! The arrow buried itself right in the middle of the straw man's heart. Gilbert let out a yelp of delighted surprise. He couldn't believe it and turned to the dumbfounded peasants—their mouths agape; they couldn't believe it either. Trev, a tinker, a short fellow no bigger than his bow, let out a long soft whistle, impressed. Hewe cut short the whistle with a stern glance.

"Beginner's luck!" Hewe frowned down Gilbert's proud smile. "Try again!"

Gilbert eagerly notched another arrow, consummately performing every direction Hewe had given him, and let fly.

It hit the dummy right between the eyes.

Trev twittered his eyebrows at a stunned Hewe. "'E's a natural, 'e is!"

"Shaddup!" Hewe grumbled, and shoved the short fellow aside. Yanking the bow out of Gilbert's hand, he suspiciously examined it as though Gilbert's skill were the result of some trick.

"I like this!" Gilbert exclaimed. "I thought you said it was hard."

Hewe shoved the bow back at him. "Again," was all he said.

Gilbert was only too happy to oblige. "Bow hand up. Sight along the arrow. . . ." His bow snapped with a hearty twang. And the arrow scored another direct hit, right in the dummy's crotch.

There was a collective wince from the group—all except Trev, who whistled again and exclaimed, "A natural!"

"Anything else I can try?" Gilbert asked of a dour Hewe. The bear squinted his eye up at the abrasively cawing crow circling above. It was as though he shared Gilbert's mocking amusement and his cries were directed at Hewe personally.

"Now for a moving target," Hewe said slyly, and pointed skyward. "That pesky crow . . ."

The peasants oohed at the challenge. But Gilbert was feeling cocky and he accepted it without hesitation. Notching another arrow, he drew his bead and fired. As the arrow sliced through the air another bird suddenly appeared in the sky. Both bird and arrow converged upon the crow. There was a shriek and a flutter of feathers and one winged creature plummeted downward, an arrow in its chest. It was not the crow, whose cawing turned triumphant. Gilbert had already dashed across the glade to claim his kill.

"Look! Look! A falcon!" The priest came running back, gleefully waving his arrow with the dead falcon still impaled upon it.

Hewe was unimpressed. "You were aiming for the crow."

"Would've 'ad it too," Trev offered, "if that falcon 'adn't got in front of his shot."

"Who asked you?" Hewe towered over the short fellow, but the debate was abruptly ended by the thunder of hoofbeats as a hunting party of knights and nobles burst into the glade. Realizing that one of them must be missing his falcon, Gilbert quickly hid the arrow and the bird behind his back.

"Which one of you scum shot that bi—" The brutish knight stopped in midtirade as he pointed at Hewe, who was clutching the sword at his side in readiness. "Is that dog wearing a sword?"

"They are all, Sir Brok!" a fop answered the brute. Gilbert recognized the man. It was Lord Felton. He rode up to the wary Hewe and gazed down on him with contemptuous indignation. "A sword is a noble's weapon. Where did *you* get it?"

"I made it," came Hewe's surly retort, umembroidered with a "sir" or a "milord." But Felton didn't notice the breach of etiquette; he was too busy laughing. His fellows joined him—save for the brute called Brok. Felton leaned forward in his saddle.

"I would have a closer look at the blade's workmanship."

Felton imperiously gestured for Hewe's sword. "Let me have it."

Hewe smiled, suddenly all deference, as he bowed. "With pleasure, lord." As he came out of his bow his blade came out of his scabbard, and with a lunge, he sliced off Felton's hand. "Close enough for you?"

Felton stuttered a scream, staring at his blood-spurting stump, and slid from his saddle. Brok and the others stared in stunned disbelief. Gilbert was stunned too, but through his daze he heard Hewe the Bear's growling threat.

"That's the last time you'll reach for anything of ours!" A dozen drawn swords answered the bear's taunt and Gilbert hoped that Hewe's reckless bravery was matched by an ability to calculate odds. It was. The bear whirled to his men and shouted, "Run!"

Gilbert did.

Chapter Twenty-seven

BROK'S DISCOVERY

"That's it . . . one fluid stroke."

Kara swung the heavy battle-ax through a series of exercises. Like Gilbert, she was in search of the weapon that best suited her needs. She had not had much luck with stabbing blades; she'd try the hacking ones. If she ripped into Einon with this, there'd be no missing her mark. Imagining him before her, she whirled the ax above her head with a savage heave. The momentum threw her off balance and sent her staggering.

"Easy . . ."

Sturdy arms caught her and stopped her fall. It was Bowen.

"Oh . . . Thank you . . . " she said shyly. She could feel the metal studs on his surcoat pressing into her back. But she made no attempt to move. Nor did he seem in any hurry to release her.

He just stared at her . . . somewhat stupidly, she thought, but sweetly. And she wondered if she was staring back as stupidly. Self-conscious, she turned away, but he did not let her escape his strong arms. She shivered as he gently slid his knee against her inner thigh and nudged her legs apart.

"Here . . . widen your stance," he suggested, and gripping her wrists, guided her arms up, swinging the ax aloft. "Up . . . then down."

Their arms swung down together. Their bodies swayed

forward. Again, she felt the studs pierce into her back, his loins tightly clinging to her from behind.

"That's it . . . one fluid stroke."

The downward arc of the ax almost threw her off balance again. But Bowen's enfolding arms steadied her. She was glad for the support. She was beginning to feel light-headed. Too much time in the sun, she thought. The knight's face was crushed into her hair, and as she turned to free him of its tangles, her lips almost touched his cheek.

"That could cleave a man's skull," Kara said of the maneuver. Her voice sounded husky and strange to her own ears.

"Like a pudding," Bowen agreed.

He still had not let go of her. She wondered if he was going to show her another move. Well, no hurry. She could wait until he made up his mind.

But as it turned out, Gilbert made up Bowen's mind for him.

"B-bow . . . K-K-Kara!" the friar breathlessly stuttered as he came running up, gesturing excitedly with an arrow, a dead falcon impaled on it. Frantic spittle and feathers were flying everywhere. Ei . . . Ei . . . Ei . . ."

"You . . . you . . . you . . . what?" Bowen batted the bird away and grabbed Gilbert by the shoulders. It seemed to compose the priest.

"Einon's men!" Gilbert blurted out, and pointed with his arrow toward the woods beyond the pasture.

Bowen snatched the ax from Kara's grip, and shouting "Find Draco," dashed off.

Gilbert caught his breath, then smiled at Kara and held up his arrow, the bird flopping limply on it. "Look, a falcon!"

Kara sighed and marched off in search of the dragon.

Brok bore down on the short peasant, amazed at how fast the man could run on such stubby little legs. These mad dogs were going to pay deeply for their effrontery. This sort of thing didn't happen in his shire. Not that he gave a damn for Felton. The fool could bleed to death, for all he cared. But that falcon had been the best he'd ever had. And with their arrows, they had brought down three more of his men while on the run. Well, run they may, but they wouldn't escape. Did they think they could retreat to their village and hide among the folk there? Brok remembered what enough of them looked like and he might just be willing to stretch a few innocent necks in order to flush out the others or even just as payment for his bird.

The short peasant was breaking from the forest. Fool. He wouldn't stand a chance across open ground. Brok raised his blade and spurred his horse. But as he tore out of the forest and down the ridge, he suddenly reined the steed up quick.

So this is what Felton had been jabbering about!

Brok had found the runaway peasants. They littered the landscape. Hundreds of them! And they were well armed. A troop of them rushed toward the one-eyed rebel as he and his band came tearing down the ridge. They were led by a knight on a charger. Brok recognized him. Bowen!

Suddenly a roar echoed out over the valley, an alarm that alerted the whole camp to readiness. Bowen turned in his saddle and signaled to . . . a dragon!

The creature was perched on a rocky cliff behind the village, roaring out the alarm. At Bowen's signal, he swooped off the crag, winging toward the ridge.

Brok did not wait for the dragon to reach his destination. He waved what was left of his party back and, whipping his horse around, sought the cover of the woods again. He had not come a-hunting for this!

"Oh, no! His scum wouldn't dare run away!"

Half-concealed behind an arras, Aislinn watched from the balcony as Felton screeched his sarcasm at Brok and the king.

"No, they'd only host the whole bloody rebellion right under his hairy nose!" Felton flipped his stump at Brok. The wrapping was spotted with blood. "I may not have known where my peasants were padding off to, but at least I knew something was going on! You oaf! You cretin! You beefy, bullock-brained dolt! You're responsible for this! Look at my hand, my liege!"

"Shut up, you screeching popinjay, or your neck will match!" Brok roared back.

"Shut up, the both of you." The stark quietness of Einon's tone cut short their bellowed bickering more effectively than a shout. The king stared at Brok. His eyes, dazed and distant, seemed to be seeking something, a memory. "Bowen . . . and the dragon . . ." His fingers ran along his chest and Aislinn thought she saw him shiver.

Bowen and the dragon, the queen thought. Fate, cruel for so long, had now chosen to be kind. Now all was inevitable. The time had come. Aislinn went to her chamber, and there, under the shadows of the cross and the watchful dragon icons, she proceeded to write four letters, which she sent off by courier that night. She hoped they would arrive in time. Four letters to five men. She knew they would answer her summons. She knew they would come. The dragon would lure them. She knelt in her chapel and prayed for forgiveness. The jeweled eyes of the dragon statues glittered in the candleglow.

Part VII

THE VOW

His word speaks only truth.

—The Old Code

Chapter Twenty-eight

THE SWORD WITHIN THE CIRCLE

"You are my confidence."

Bowen dreamed of dragons, the dragons he had slain. In his dream, he slew them again. Like somber statues of the dead, they perched on the gray, crumbling stone pedestals that littered the Roman ruins. He stood among them, listening to their trilling song of sorrow. And the sorrow swept over him and brought him to his knees. He begged for forgiveness and longed for the song to cease.

But it did not cease. And the large grieving eyes of the dragons held no forgiveness in them, only a baleful wretched contempt. The stones seemed to crowd in upon him, the dragons loomed over him. Then their wings spread out in unison with a gusty flap that sounded like a death rattle. And they descended upon him, swooping and diving, a swirling, spinning blur of glittery motion and crescendoing sound.

The flutter of their wings, the rustle of their wind surged and tore at him, howling discordant accompaniment to the trilling dirge. The song spoke mournfully of pain and loss and guilt, thrumming and echoing in his ears, deepening inside his head, overwhelming him with its agonizing beauty. Like Odysseus in the thrall of the Sirens, Bowen thought he would go mad. He screamed to blot out the woeful wailing, but his cry was drowned in its welling pool of pathos. He drew his sword and tried to strike down the exquisite horror, slashing out at the sparkled flesh as it came flying by. Ripping into it. Tearing. Rending. Brilliant scarlet light shimmered in the swath he hewed with his blade.

Soon all was a blood-colored dazzle of blinding brightness. There were no more dragons to hack. Only a glowing red haze, which made the sweat glisten on Bowen's skin as he wildly pivoted to the reverberating lament, vainly trying to carve sound out of color.

Suddenly a sliver of silver sliced through the crimson curtain and clanked against his blade, driving him to his knees. At the hilt of the intruding sword stood Einon, pale and white against the red. He smiled and slashed. Bowen sprang to his feet and fought. Driving. Driving. He had one purpose. To kill Einon. And to atone for his sins. To silence the dreadful dragon song. He was lightning. A shooting star. The winter wind. Flash and speed and cold steel. Einon could not stand before his onslaught, could not hold back the whirlwind of his blade . . . could not stop smiling! Bowen's sword slid into his chest. Einon lurched forward . . . and still smiled! His fingers clutched out and grasped the blade. Bowen yanked it back and Einon's pale hand turned to a scaly claw, its talon scraping along the steel like screeching death, digging a jagged groove into the blade. Bowen looked up to see Draco plunge backward off his sword, spiraling back into the crimson glow that suddenly became a garish blur, rippling and swirling and being sucked into the dragon's wound.

Bowen was pulled into the vortex as the red was overcome by black. The glare and the dragon were gone. Only the blackness now, a dizzying dark void into which Bowen floated and fell and spun, shouting for Draco. Shouting silently. He felt the words forming in his mouth, felt them throbbing in the muscles of his neck, felt them straining in his throat and bellowing from his chest. But he heard nothing . . . only the singing despair of the dragon trill seeping through the darkness, pervading his soul; becoming louder and stranger, distorting to a jarring thunderous peal. . . .

He woke with a startled jerk, sweat drenching his face and bare torso. The deafening blast that had pierced his slumber sounded again and his groggy gaze squinted into the bright light invading his tent.

Kara stood in the open flap, a twisted ram's horn in her hand.

"Battle trumpet!" She held it up for his approval. "Good tone, don't you think?"

No, Bowen didn't think. He had slept miserably, when he had slept at all; he was still tired. He reeled wearily in his cot and started to sink back sleepily. Kara threw his pants in his face.

"Sun's up, Knight," she announced cheerily—far too cheerily. "So's the army. Why aren't you?"

As he struggled to put his pants on under the blanket, he thought of suggesting that Kara turn her back for discretion's sake, but he could only muster a grumpy mumble. Ignoring his demure gyrations, she stuffed a hunk of bread in his mouth.

"Breakfast!" she said.

Bowen just groaned.

"Too dry?" She yanked the bread out of his slack-jawed mouth. He puffed his lips and sleepily tried to blow the sprinkled crumbs off them. Kara dipped the bread in a goblet of wine.

"Here, sop it in some wine." She crammed the soaked bread back in his mouth. It was last night's wine and stale, like the bread. Both dribbled down his chin.

"Come on! Time's a-wasting." Kara hustled behind him. "Wash up." Bowen felt something cold and wet slap his back and yelped his first word of the morning.

"Jesu!" Bowen jumped up, his pants fortunately and finally done up.

"Well, good morning to you too. A little cold?" Kara held a bowl of water and a wet cloth.

"A little fast!" Bowen snatched the cloth from her and wiped the sleep from his eyes. "What's the hurry?"

"There's much to be done!" Kara pushed him back on the cot and flung his tunic at him. "Troops to train, strategy to plan, crises to resolve!"

Bowen pulled on his jerkin. "What crises?"

"Well, that beard for one." Kara grabbed his jaw in her hand and, squeezing his cheeks, jerked his head one way then the other. "It could use a trim." She slipped behind him and, tilting his head back, grabbed a battle-ax. Bowen slid his chin out from under her hand and leapt away.

"Oh, don't worry." Kara sliced the ax smoothly through the air. "You taught me well."

"To cut throats, not to shave them!"

Kara shrugged and set the ax down. "Well, if you don't want to look like a victorious general . . ."

"I'm not yet," Bowen reminded her. "Don't get overconfident."

"You are my confidence," said Kara. "I've never been more sure of anything in my life."

Her smile was as bright and bold as the sun that shone into the tent and haloed her red hair. She held out her hand to him. "Come."

Bowen took her hand and she led him from the tent.

Outside waiting for them was a delegation of peasant warriors led by Gilbert and Hewe. Kara still held his hand. Her brown-gold eyes stared at him, warm with pride. "Tomorrow we will look to you . . . glowing at our head like a shining beacon."

She gestured to a cross pole draped in a heavy cloth and Hewe whipped off the covering . . . revealing a set of glistening armor—a coat of mail, a leather surcoat, a helmet, and a shield. Both the shield and the surcoat were emblazoned with the symbol of the sword within the circle. But it was slightly altered. Dotted through the circle was a pattern of stars, golden and bright . . . the constellation Draco.

"They made it for you"—Kara gestured to the assemblage—"all of them, all contributing what they could.

Gilbert designed it. Hewe hammered and polished it. And over your heart . . . the Pendragon and Draco entwined as emblem of your courage."

"It was all Kara's idea." Gilbert handed Bowen the shield. Bowen took it in stunned silence, gazing at Kara. Her eyes were still warm, but shining with something more than pride.

"A knight's armor should shine as bright as his honor," she said softly.

Unable to stand the beauty of her eyes any longer, Bowen cast his down, admiring the shield. His fingers lightly caressed the line of stars threaded through the sword within the circle. He felt honored and unworthy. Arthur and Draco. He scanned the cliffs above the village, seeking out the dragon, longing to look upon him, remembering his dream. But his gaze was not rewarded.

Something brushed against his face, and startled, he turned. An old woman pressed her hand to his cheek in silent reverence. Then others reached out to him. Warriors, women, children. All pressed close to touch him or give a word of thanks. It was too much. Overcome, Bowen bolted into his tent.

Outside, they shouted his name. He stared at the shield in his trembling hands. And he thought his heart would break.

Such faith . . . such faith they had in him.

"They want to see you in it."

Bowen straightened himself, wiped the moisture from his eyes, and turned to Kara, standing in the entrance with his mail and surcoat.

"Shall I help you put it on?" she asked.

"Please . . ." Bowen said, hearing the tremor in his voice. Kara held the coat of mail out for him and helped to pull it over his head.

"How rapidly your heart beats," she noted, her palms resting on his chest as she smoothed out the mail.

"They expect much."

"They will give much."

"And if I don't lead them to victory?"

"Then you will have led them farther than they ever dared go before. . . ." Kara helped him into the leather surcoat, her strong fingers swiftly fastening the straps. He watched her work. So close. So beautiful. As she bent over to cinch the final buckle, her hair billowed in a fiery wave beneath him, beckoning. He lifted a hand and reached out to stroke it. But just then she finished her task and leaned back to inspect him, and losing his courage, he dropped his hand to his side.

She tossed her red hair from her face and admired him. "There. All done."

"Not quite," Bowen said; her hair still beckoned. "It is custom to bestow a favor on a knight."

"A favor?"

"A veil or a scarf that he wears into battle as a token from his lady fair," Bowen explained, moving close, unable to resist the luring blaze of her hair.

"Do you have a lady fair?" Kara asked hesitantly, aware of his proximity, but not edging away.

"I should be honored to wear your favor." Bowen moved closer still and his fingers laced through her tousled locks. He had frightened her. He had thrilled her. Both his request and his touch. Flustered, she turned.

"I . . . I have no such finery. I am a peasant," she stammered nervously.

"You are the woman I love," came his blunt confession. He saw her back stiffen, and as he gently turned her to him she trembled uncertainly, her brown-gold eyes full of disbelief . . . and another, deeper feeling, a feeling of anguish. . . .

"How can you . . . ?" she whispered.

"How can I not?" Bowen asked, not understanding her dismay. But even as he pulled her close she broke from him.

"I can give no favor." Kara spat out the words, tears welling in her eyes. "I can give nothing. The one thing that was mine to give Einon stole forever."

Bowen seized her shoulders. "It doesn't matter."

"It does to me!" Again, Kara pulled away. "It was all I had. My only dowry. My only treasure . . . love's first blush . . . now scarlet with shame!"

"Not your shame!" Bowen insisted. But Kara was not to be soothed.

"It is easy for you." Kara spoke with numb sorrow, her cheeks stained with tears, her brown-gold eyes drowning in them. "Lost honor can be recovered. Not so lost youth. What washes away the stain of soiled innocence?"

Bowen knelt before her.

"Einon's blood. I swear."

It was a holy vow. Made at the altar of his goddess. And the goddess was touched. She held out her hand to her acolyte, who reverently took it in his own, pressing his lips to it in one chaste kiss.

Chapter Twenty-nine

A DRAGON'S BEQUEST AND A MOTHER'S GIFT

"Fear not the dragon, my son."

Bowen rode up the narrow trail to the crest of the cliff. The valley below was alive with cookfires, gleaming in the darkening twilight. Music and shouts and sounds of merriment trickled up from the camp, joyous and carefree, as though none of the revelers were facing death the following day.

Draco had claimed this lonesome bluff, where he spent long hours, sleeping little. But he knew he had chosen the best watchtower and that he was the best watcher. Who could see or hear as far as he? There was little chance for a surprise attack with Draco at his post.

But even though the enemy had discovered their camp, and sent out a few scouting parties, they made no move against them. Bowen had drilled enough tactics into Einon to know the boy wouldn't dare risk an attack. He was at a disadvantage in terms of open ground and numbers, as Einon's spies surely had told him. He would wait for Bowen to bring the battle to him. Well, thought Bowen, he would not have to wait long.

Bowen heard the soothing beauty of Draco's contented trilling before he saw him, curled at the cliff edge, dreamily gazing down on the camp.

"Hello, Bowen," Draco greeted him without turning around. "I heard another hundred and fifty families found their way into camp today. The eve of battle and still they come."

"So many, so fast . . ." Bowen said. "There's not been enough time, they've not been properly trained."

"What they lack in training, they make up in passion." The assurance in Draco's voice was like the assurance in his dragon song . . . comforting and peaceful. Both allayed Bowen's concern. The dragon turned and smiled at him. "You've done well."

"Because you have made me better than I was." Bowen longed to take pride in the dragon's praise, but he could not. Not yet. His dream of this morning still haunted him. He leaned back in his saddle and unhooked something from it. It clanged as he slung upon the rocks in front of Draco. It was his talon-trophy shield. "I have not always done well."

"Oh, Bowen," the dragon said sadly, "the Once-ways were long forgot on both sides. And wrongs by both committed in ignorance and misunderstanding. You, like these you slew, were merely a creature of sorry circumstance. Surely God forgave you any sin in this."

Bowen dismounted and knelt before Draco. "I do not seek God's forgiveness. Only yours."

The forgiveness was in the dragon's eyes. "I can find no fault in you, Knight of the Old Code."

"A knight of the Old Code needs no such adornment." Bowen picked up the shield of his shame and offered it to Draco. "Perhaps you know what should be done with it."

"I know. . . ." Draco smiled again and leaned his shoulder down. "Climb up and bring your shield."

Bowen obeyed, mounting Draco and clinging to his neck. Draco's elegant wings unfolded and Bowen felt the kiss of the wind upon his face as they hurtled heavenward.

They soared higher than Bowen ever remembered soaring. The last gray streaks of dusk gave way to the oncoming night, its advent lit by an escort of stars. Draco's constellation dangled across the sky like glittering diamonds spilled on black velvet. How clean and white they were. And

Bowen spoke his silent thought: "Like a promise of hope."

"Hope is not so far away, Bowen," the dragon replied, gazing longingly at the stars. He swerved and swooped away. "Look down!"

Bowen did so . . . and gasped at the panorama that filled his eyes. The landscape was dotted with the campfires of his people, as though some stars had fallen to earth and now glowed both above and below him.

"There lies your hope, Bowen," Draco said. "The one I've waited for. Man must now make of the world what he can. . . . The day of dragons is done. . . ."

"Not done for you!" Bowen protested. "If we are victorious tomorrow, we'll need you."

"You'll have victory," Draco assured him. "But no need of me. Listen to them, Knight of the Old Code. The Once-ways are in their songs and their laughter and the cries of their children. Listen. And look."

Perhaps it was only the hollow howl of the wind that made Draco's words sound cryptic and wistful. But they sent a suspicious shiver down Bowen's spine nonetheless. He looked, watching the patches of light flicker against the dark. "What do you see?" he asked the dragon curiously.

"Everything," Draco replied. "It's yours now. . . ."

The night was dirty and loud. Aislinn watched from her chamber window as Einon and his knights surged through the crowded courtyard, bustling with war preparations. Men drilled. Armorers and blacksmiths sweated over forge fires. Weapons were cached. Wagons rolled into the castle gates with food and provisions for storing.

As Brok and the others tried to keep up with his fierce pace, Einon strode across the stones inspecting everything. He was dressed only in his night robe and carried a torch. As the entourage moved to a cart stationed below her window, Aislinn was able to catch bits and pieces of the conversation.

". . . entire towns and shires deserted, milord," Brok was dourly reporting, ". . . peasants all gone . . ."

"And gone with them the best of my crops and livestock!" Einon snapped out the words. He had leapt into the cart and his torch exposed a meager load of apples. Picking up one, he bit into it, made a sour face, and spit the morsel out. He flung the apple against the castle wall in disgust. It hit with a pop and clung there—an oozing glob.

The torchlight danced grimly across his face. It seemed whiter than normal, almost ghostlike. The rage in his pale eyes dwindled to a fixed reflective daze as he stared up. Aislinn pulled back from the window so that she would not be seen. But he wasn't looking at her. His intense gaze sought the night sky, as though trying to bore a hole into the darkness, in search of some light to chase the shadows from his disturbed soul. He shuddered and his fingers crawled inside the folds of his robe, stroking his chest in agitated distraction.

The unctuous tones of Felton trickled over the din as the lord slithered forward to try to appease his troubled king. He gestured grandly with his stumped wrist, now covered in a leather cuff studded with jewels that caught the torchlight and sparkled. Aislinn had observed that he had several different cuffs, dyed in different colors to match the variety of his wardrobe. This one was brown, matching the soft deerskin tunic and pants he currently wore. "Do not worry, sire, a few dirty peasants are no match for us."

"A few, fop?" Brok growled. "Hundreds, all armed and spoiling for a fight."

"You should know, Brok." Felton sneered, amiably. "It's your land they're on. But any noble is worth a hundred peasants."

Brok tapped Felton's leather cuff. "Guess you're only worth fifty."

Felton snatched his arm from Brok's touch and held it up proudly. "At least I have proven my valor to my king. Do you preach caution because you're afraid, Brok?"

Brok certainly wasn't afraid of Felton, and snarling at the man's insult, he charged the noble. But Einon leapt from the cart to stand between them, and waved Brok back with his torch, putting a protective arm about Felton. The torch flickered over the king's calm smile.

"My brave Felton." Einon patted the noble's cheek. "A regiment unto himself."

Einon chuckled. Felton giggled. The others joined the merriment. Then Einon savagely clawed the cheek he was patting and whirled Felton around by it, slamming him against the wheel of the cart.

"Idiot!" Einon's fingers slid from Felton's cheek and his palm thrust under the noble's quivering chin, stretching his neck back over the rim of the wheel. Felton's startled eyes stared straight up—where they met those of Aislinn, gazing down. In the torch glare, she could see the red welts where Einon had torn at his cheek.

"I know this man who leads them!" Einon barked, and released the fop. Gasping, Felton slumped against the wheel as Einon whirled on his other knights, shouting, "You're all idiots! I am served by dolts and fools! The only clever man in this kingdom is my enemy! And I will destroy him! But I will not underestimate him! Him or the dragon! Now begone! All of you!"

The knights quickly dispersed into the commotion of the courtyard. Einon, torch in hand, stormed into the castle. Aislinn knew where he was going and waited and watched. A few moments later her suspicion was confirmed when she saw flickering light ascend past the arched windows of the tower stairwell.

The queen turned to the five burly men who waited behind her. "Come," she said, and led them from the chamber.

Einon stood in his partially constructed tower room, holding back the surrounding dark with his torch. Its blaze danced wildly to the rough whistle of the wind; the gusting song muffled the racket drifting up from the courtyard far below. The wooden window shutter in the one erected wall swayed on its hinges, groaning against the portal with an abrupt hollow bang. *Groan. Bang. Groan. Bang.* It reminded him of the wretched scum condemned to the hell of his quarry. Groan, as they swung their hammers back. Bang, as the hammer struck stone. *Groan. Bang. Groan. Bang.* A rhythmic dirge of doom.

Memories of the quarry inevitably brought thoughts of Kara in their wake. Einon had done his share of wenching, but he understood little of women's ways. The only woman with whom he had had any lengthy relationship was his mother and he understood her not at all. He had always been awed by her beauty and intimidated by her sad, knowing eyes. It was as though she had the power to look into your soul and steal your secrets. Kara was like that too, he thought. Knowing eyes and frightening beauty. But it was beauty that could only belong to a king! He knew that such beauty was the reason his father had taken his mother as his queen. Einon also knew why his father had taken Aislinn as he had. To show her who was the strongest. To claim possession and, at the same time, to purge his fear of her. But despite being taken and possessed so ruthlessly, the look was still in his mother's eyes. And it was still in Kara's as well. And it chilled him, and made him more afraid than before.

As Einon considered these thoughts, the torchlight fluttered in the wind. It reminded him of Kara's untamed fiery hair blowing free. She belonged to him. But she was with Bowen, his betrayal of each of them binding them together. Bowen must see her every day. Did they talk often of him? he wondered. Hate him together? Plot his downfall? Share their secrets of him behind his back?

An ache tore suddenly through his heart, and with a whimpered cry, he thrust the torch into a pile of sandy mortar, extinguishing it. He sighed as the gloom embraced him and he slipped his hand into his robe, pressing it against his throbbing chest. He didn't want Bowen talking to Kara. Didn't want him seeing her. Looking into her dangerous eyes. He didn't want Bowen to know what he had done and said to her the night they had been alone. She belonged to him!

When this was done, he would stick Bowen's head on a pike up here in the tower room and possess the girl in front of it. Let her writhe and struggle under him while Bowen, gory-necked and slack-jawed, watched with sightless eyes. That would blot out the searing defiant light in her own eyes. That would strip away her power and Einon would never be afraid of her again.

His fingers ran across his naked breast, gingerly tracing the knotted scar there. His heart careened against his chest, and on curious impulse, he looked up into the sky. The blackness seemed to ripple with strange movement.

"Fear not the dragon, my son."

Startled, Einon spun sharply to find his mother, holding a torch, emerging from the stairwell.

"I fear nothing! Nothing! Do you understand?" he insisted, and wondered how she alway knew what he was thinking. The witch. He shot an uneasy glance skyward. "It's just that . . . sometimes I seem to sense him. Feel him. As though he were close." His heart had beat like this before. At the waterfall. How big and ragged the scar on his chest felt. He turned back to his mother as she stepped from the stairwell. "But I do not fear him!"

"Nor need to . . ." Aislinn assured him, and gestured with her torch as five barbaric brutes rose out of the stairwell behind her and stood in an eerie tableau. All were armed to the teeth. Einon stared at his mother curiously.

"A mother's gift to her son," Aislinn explained. "Sir Uhlric, Sir Ivor, Sir Cavan, and the brothers Tavis and Trahern. The finest to be had . . ."

All five bowed to Einon. He looked from them to his mother again. "Finest what . . . ?"

"Dragonslayers."

Taken aback by this uncharacteristic kindness, Einon's look of disbelief slowly shifted to sly amusement. His mother. Always silent. Always alone. Always thinking. And he had never known what. But he knew now. Blood above all. Just as she had saved him years ago, she would not fail him now. He impulsively grabbed his mother's hand and kissed it. As he glanced back up into her unfathomable face, he saw the sky waver behind her like a black tapestry rustling in the wind.

Bowen watched the blackness seep into Draco's scales, overwhelming their natural color and making him indistinguishable from the night. Even sitting atop the dragon and clinging to his neck, he could barely make out where dragon ended and the night began. It was like riding a piece of sky.

The camouflage allowed Draco to circle low over Einon's castle. Austere and forbidding, its gray shadow sprawled across the mountain ridge. The light of the torches and forges in the courtyard washed over the wide, massive battlements. One could march a regiment across them ten abreast. It was impregnable, but not pretty. In some places Einon had incorporated the old Roman ruins. But most of its sleek lines and ancient elegance had been sacrificed to create a lumbering edifice that defied the landscape and tortured good taste . . . a hulking monument to one man's arrogance and ambition.

"It's a strong fortress." Bowen surveyed it glumly, mourning the crumbling stones and the tall grass where he had taught a boy how to defend himself . . . and had failed to teach him how to defend an ideal. He mourned his own failure too.

"Yes, it *is* strong," Draco agreed. "But your plan is stronger. Never fear Einon will fight *your* battle. . . . Tomorrow, find me in the thick of the fray!" He might have meant the last as an eager war cry, but Bowen had caught the doleful lilt in his voice.

"What do you mean?" the knight asked.

Draco did not immediately answer. "Your shield, Knight!" he said at last. "Fling it to the four winds."

Bowen unstrapped the shield from his arm and, with both hands, spun the shield out into the night. As it spiraled through the blackness Draco smote it with a streak of flames from his nostrils. It exploded in a blaze of red light, the talons that hung upon it burning furiously, glowing with a supernatural brilliance.

All the clamor of the courtyard below ceased as Einon and the dragonslayers stared at the strange, sparking fire in the sky.

"A comet," one of the brutes whispered fearfully. And Einon also feared. A comet foretold cataclysm, disaster, the death of kings.

"Not a comet," Aislinn's calm voice reassured them. "See! It hovers. It does not fall like a comet."

"What, then?" Einon turned to his mother. He could not control the quaver in his voice.

"I have heard the elders of my clan speak of it when I was a girl." Her eyes watched the light in curious fascination. Her voice was soothing. "In the Lands Beyond the North Seas, once home to my people, this sky fire blazed often in the night. It was said to be the torches of the dead come from paradise to bless the living left behind. I believe it is your father, Einon."

"Father?" Intrigued, Einon cocked his head and stared at the mystical fire. His mother placed a hand upon his shoulder.

"Yes; Freyne." She spoke softly, serenely. He felt the heat of her torch against his face. "Come to tell you he is proud and to destroy his enemies once and for all. To claim the mantle of his clan and do what he could not. Slay the dragon!"

"The dragon . . ." Einon repeated as though in a trance.

"My people say that if you whisper, the wind will carry a message back to the spirit." Aislinn herself was whispering, her lips were almost against his ear. "Speak to your father, Einon. Pledge to him the death of the dragon. Give him the prize that was denied him."

And Einon whispered as she desired. "I swear, Father! The dragon will die!" And as the wind swirled his vow away the flame in the sky was snuffed out and the only light in the dark was the stars. Excited voices echoed up from the courtyard. Einon spun questioningly to his mother, her beauty ablaze in the torchlight. She smiled, strangely, a smile that was like nothing Einon had ever seen her make before. Her eyes were tender and tragic and moist as they looked on him. For the first time he no longer feared them.

Her hand smoothed the tenseness in his cheek. "He heard, my son. He heard."

Had the wind carried the whisper so far so fast? Einon stared out into the night again. The sky was alive with black motion.

Part VIII

THE BATTLE

His wrath undoes the wicked!

—The Old Code

Chapter Thirty

FIRST BLOOD

"Four years hasn't improved them any."

The volley of fire arrows bounced harmlessly off the castle wall and sputtered out. Einon laughed and watched Bowen ride down the line of his pitiful rebel force, shouting orders. They had crept up the mountain road near the gates just after noon. Einon watched the amusing spectacle from the battlements with his knights and generals.

"Seems Sir Brok overestimated their numbers." Felton chuckled, gesturing with his jewel-cuffed stump. Today it was a black cuff, to match his black armor.

"There were more," growled Brok.

Another pathetic volley of flaming arrows plunked against the parapet wall. One of the barbs actually managed to eke its way over the wall. Einon calmly reached out and caught it in midair in his guantleted hand.

"More or less, four years hasn't improved them any," Einon said, blasély inspecting the still-burning arrow.

Felton chuckled and smirked at Brok. "No. Hardly worth the effort. They'll get bored and go home before dark."

"Why wait?" Einon smiled. "We'll send you out to chase them off. After all, 'One noble is worth a hundred peasants,'" he quoted. "The numbers are about right. Just save a few for the rest of us."

Felton gulped uneasily as Einon wagged the fire arrow in his face. But a worried Brok was unamused.

"There were more," he insisted. "And where's the—" He

choked on the question and the blood drained from his face as he stared skyward in stunned surprise. A sudden shadow blotted out the sun, and as Einon turned to ascertain the cause of Brok's astonishment, an explosion of fire sprayed the battlements, sending soldiers screaming and leaping for safety. Einon dashed for cover with the others. Above the flames he saw the dragon hovering in the sky, framed by the sun's golden orb.

The cheers of the rebels echoed up from below as the beast rained more flames down upon the battlements. Einon whirled to his dragonslayers. Cavan, dressed in mail made of dragon scales and wearing a helmet rimmed in dragon fangs, cocked a large catapult while Uhlric loaded it with a jagged-edged pike. The brothers Tavis and Trahern maneuvered the catapult, Ivor directing them by waving his giant battle-ax this way and that as he scanned the skies for the dragon's position.

When he emerged, it was not where they were expecting him, but bursting out of a cloud of smoke. As the dragon loosed a firebomb at them, burning scaffolding and falling rock came shattering down on the dragonslayers. Uhlric, struck by a flaming beam, careened against the catapult, pivoting it and unintentionally triggering the firing mechanism. Immediately the pike shot out—and impaled Ivor, who was driven back, stunned, and skewered against the wall as the lance embedded itself into the stone. He hung there, dangling, his now useless ax still clenched in his fist.

The dragonslayers frantically regrouped, commanding a small force of soldiers to a specially constructed platform upon which were mounted four catapults armed with grappling hooks.

Cavan gave the order to fire as the dragon swept into view. But as the hooks raced skyward the dragon rolled, dodging two of the hooks and grasping the other pair in his claws. Rocketing upward, he yanked the chains that were attached to the hooks with him. Men scattered as the platform trembled and cracked beneath them. Some were not so lucky, being crushed as the platform was ripped from its foundations and slammed into the wall.

Dust belched past a livid Einon, who drew his sword and shouted to his knights, "Well, do we stay in here like sitting ducks or crush those rebellious dogs?"

Brok led a chorus of war cries and barked orders. Battle horns sounded and men scurried into position. Einon briskly descended the stairs into the courtyard, where his horse awaited. As he mounted he again gazed up at the battlements.

Sir Cavan ran along the wall, screaming at the dragon and whirling a grappling chain with a hook at either end. As the dragon dived in he loosened the chain and snared the beast's back foot.

Cavan now scurried to secure the other hook, but before he could do so, he was carried away by the dragon. Hanging on to the chain, Cavan spun in the air as the dragon slammed him into a tower, driving the fangs that adorned the dragonslayer's helmet deep into his thick skull.

The slain hunter slid down the tower wall, plummeting to land at the hooves of Einon's horse. The horse reared and Einon frowned down on the dead dragonslayer. "Oh, lovely . . ." he murmured.

He gazed up at the dragon. The grappling chain had hooked itself to the ledge of the tower, and the dragon was whirling madly in the air, caught. He rained fire down on the three remaining dragonslayers, who rushed in, lobbing spears at the creature. Einon hoped the louts got lucky before the dragon razed the entire castle. But meanwhile there were other problems to attend to.

"Open the gates," Einon commanded.

They were opened. Down the road he saw Bowen and his puny force, and scowled in savage rage. He knew more of the dogs were hiding in the woods. He knew that Bowen wanted to lure him there, hoping that a battle waged in the forest would give them an advantage over skilled fighting men. For no matter how long and how hard Bowen had drilled this rabble, they were and always would be peasant scum, not warriors. And he, Einon, would crush them.

As Einon considered his enemy's strategy Bowen stared across the short distance directly at him. In his eyes was a challenge. He wore the fighting grin that Einon remembered so well from his youth. Cocky and condescending. Einon thought he had wiped it off his face that day at the waterfall. Now he'd *carve* it off.

"Madman. Does he think he can defy me with only trained apes and arrogance?" Einon muttered to himself. "Well, today his code dies. Once and for all." Motioning his men forward with his sword, he bellowed, "Pave my road with peasant corpses! But leave the knight for me!"

They thundered out of the castle, foot soldiers following the mounted knights, and the peasant force broke and ran for the forest at the foot of the mountain without a blow being struck.

Einon laughed deliriously at such a spectacle. "Shear them like the sheep they are!"

From her tower window, Aislinn watched Einon rout the rebels into the forest . . . but she knew their defeat would not be achieved that simply. The sight of dragon only confirmed her suspicion. He hovered at the end of his chain, oblivious to the spears of the dragonslayers, watching the retreating rebels . . . almost smiling, she thought.

Chapter Thirty-one

MORE BLOOD SPILLS

"Scatter or die!"

Bowen reined his horse and waited at the far end of the forest glade. Treetops echoed with the rumble of hoofbeats, the rattle of metal, and the shouts of men.

This morning, as they had marched out in the predawn light, Bowen had felt confident and strong. Kara and Gilbert had ridden at his side. Banners that bore his coat of arms crackled in the breeze. His motley but determined warriors had fallen in sharply behind Hewe and the other commanders, and once Bowen reached the crest of the ridge, he had looked back to see the proud line that extended, seemingly without end, through the pasture and over the bridge behind the village huts. The women and children and those soldiers left to guard them flanked the long procession on either side. Then Draco had swooped down from his cliff perch, skimming along the line, dipping a wing in salute. A thousand raised weapons answered the salute and the dawn had erupted in one great shout of exaltation.

But now, as he waited, nervousness overcame confidence and he hoped that Einon's own confidence would prove to be his undoing. He had taught the boy strategy. He knew Einon expected to collide with the rest of Bowen's force here in the forest. That the boy had taken the bait told Bowen that Einon underestimated the peasant army. But Bowen asked himself, had he indeed overestimated them? Would their courage hold?

As Einon broke into the glade with his men, Bowen raised his new shield. As it sparked in the sun it roused a spontaneous cheer from his own small band of men. Their battle cry went up with a rattle of staffs, swords, and spears.

The cry was answered by the rattle of more weapons. From behind every tree and shrub the shout rolled out in a deafening roar. At the rear of Einon's cavalry, Hewe swung out of a tree on a rope, a blazing brand in his hands. He dipped the torch in a trench filled with pitch that was hidden under a dead shrub. Fire immediately burst out, and ran across the glade and around the horsemen, cutting them off on three sides. The horses panicked as the walls of flame rose. The only way out was through . . .

. . . Bowen! . . . and the hundreds of peasants that emerged from the shelter of the forest, swelling the ranks of the knight's small band. At the sound of screams and cries rising from another part of the woods, Bowen knew his troops had engaged the cutoff foot soldiers. He motioned his men forward with his sword and they charged en masse. Pikemen picked knights off horses as they tried to jump their steeds through the flames. Others descended on them with swords and axes.

"Scatter or die!" Einon shouted, and leapt his mount over the fire. Others followed his example. But even as his force split up, overwhelming numbers of rebels appeared to finish them off in hand-to-hand combat.

The peasant assault was swift and surprising and deadly. Bowen's heart swelled with pride. Their courage had held.

Felton gripped his sword and slunk through commotion from tree to tree. He had lost his helmet and his horse and he was still not certain how he had gotten through the ring of flames and all those weapon-wielding madmen. He had already played dead three times to avoid fights and now desperately sought escape or at least a place to hide. After all, having only one hand put him at a terrible disadvantage;

it was unfair of Einon to send a wounded man into battle. He had risked limb in the service of his king; he was not inclined to risk life with similar disastrous results.

He crept around the bole of a tree and nearly collided with a pitchfork that was suddenly thrust in his face. He jerked back, falling into a shrub, and the tines of the fork embedded themselves in the tree trunk.

"Have mercy! Have mercy!" Felton struggled out of the bush and fell to his knees before his adversary, holding up his stump. "Please, please! I'm a poor cripple forced to—*You!*"

His conqueror was none other than his erstwhile minx! Felton forgot his embarrassment in a flash of stunned rage.

"You traitorous wench!" he screeched, clambering to his feet. "After all I've spent on—done for you!"

She sneered and tried to yank her pitchfork from the tree. But Felton snapped the shaft in two with his sword blade. The minx staggered back, holding the broken end.

Felton advanced on her. Bad enough she was a rebel, but she was also a badly dressed one. Her superb voluptuousness was hidden under the most unseemly bulk of men's clothes. In fact, he realized with horror, they were *his* clothes! He recognized the brocaded trim . . . and his calfskin boots! Oh, did her betrayal know no depths?

The minx faced his naked blade with only her broken shaft. Felton hesitated in his thrust. She was a clever thing. It would be a pity to pierce her lush tanned flesh, to say nothing of his garments.

Nonetheless, his garments were pierced . . . but it was the very ones he was wearing. He heard the thunk and felt the pain in his backside almost simultaneously. Sharp, searing pain. He yelped and grabbed at the wound, feeling a feathered shaft protruding from his left buttock as he staggered back.

"Turn the other cheek, sinner!" The words came from a priest, who was sitting up a tree in an archer blind, crossing himself. Felton recognized him—that friar from his wheatfield. And next to him was that one-eyed brute that had dared to sever his hand.

"'Allelujah!" proclaimed a short rogue who sat on the other side of the priest and was also crossing himself. Even he looked familiar. But Felton couldn't remember where he'd seen him. And at the moment he couldn't really care. He felt the blood dribbling down the arrow shaft onto his fingers. God knows, it wasn't as bad as his hand. Still and all . . . life and limb! Life and limb! Oh, the things he endured for his king.

At the maiming of his hand he had been in shock. He preferred that state to the taste of vomit that he now swallowed back down. He felt like he was going to swoon. The minx helped him on his way. She turned his other cheek by whacking him on the jaw with her broken pitchfork shaft. He crumpled to the ground, his back flopping against the tree. He heard the arrow crack underneath him and felt its point tear deeper into his flesh. Life and . . . the minx's face became a hazy blob as she leaned into him. Everything started to jumble and go gray, then a jingling brought him back to consciousness just in time to see the minx filch his purse.

"Finally some money you can't take back!" She rattled the purse in front of Felton's blinking eyes. Actually, she looked quite fetching in his clothes, he decided. Or maybe it was just the hazy mist clouding his eyes. What had she said? Money. Mon . . . his money! Felton lifted his stump to protest. He felt the girl grab it and saw her lovely eyes grow wide as she inspected the jeweled cuff. Promptly she snatched it off his wrist. The mist grew heavier as her laughter grew fainter. He heard a groan. He thought it came from him. He wasn't sure why he was groaning. The pain had stopped and everything was getting dizzy and dark . . . and peaceful.

Hewe sputtered in exasperation. Felton had been his target, but Gilbert struck before he could get off his shot. The noble had not even hit the ground when Gilbert had already notched another arrow and whirled to the other side of the tree they perched in. Hewe could not believe the speed with which the priest fired. Nor his unerring accuracy. But never with deadly accuracy; Gilbert shot only to incapacitate and to help out his fellow rebels. It seemed to Hewe a waste of arrows not to use them to maximum effect, especially when one's eye was that good. And though Hewe hated to admit it, the priest's eye was that good.

Gilbert drew a bead on a grinning knight who swept in on a horse, shouting with savage glee as he swiped at a peasant armed with only a club. The priest's arrow neatly sliced the stirrup strap and the knight jerked from the saddle and tumbled to the ground with a crunch. The peasant rushed in with his club and there ensued a few more crunches.

"Pride goeth before a fall, brother." Gilbert crossed himself and sadly shook his head.

"Amen!" shouted Trev, also making the sign of the cross. Hewe frowned and rolled his one good eye. The little git thought the priest walked on water and had all but become his apostle. Next he'd be passing the plate around after every shot.

Piqued, Hewe turned and found a new target—Brok—who came crashing through a phalanx of peasants, scattering them with a mace and chain. Hewe aimed and drew his bowstring back and . . . another arrow struck the mace and tore it from Brok's hand. It was Gilbert's arrow.

"The meek shall inherit the earth!" Gilbert exclaimed, as the peasants rushed Brok.

"'Osanna in the 'ighest!" echoed his disciple, Trev.

Brok wheeled his horse out of the onslaught. Gilbert was already aiming another arrow at the fleeing knight, but Hewe shoved his bow aside to take a shot and snarl a biblical quote of his own. "Vengeance is mine . . ." Hewe released his arrow, but it went wide, and Brok disappeared into the woods.

". . . saith the Lord . . ." Gilbert finished the quote for the mortified archer, and wearily shook his head.

"And it's a sorry sight in the 'ands of an incompetent," added Trev, who also shook his head.

Hewe said nothing . . . limiting himself to breaking his bow over his knee and flinging his quiver at Gilbert. Drawing his sword, he uttered a bloodthirsty yell, leapt from the tree, and stalked off to pursue prey in less competitive circumstances.

A whoosh of wind rippled past Draco's outspread wings as he felt the tug on his leg and was jerked downward. A dozen men on the battlements slowly reeled in the chain snared about his foot and anchored securely on the tower ledge. He spewed a bolt of flame at them, but one of the dragonslayers deflected it off his shield. He was yanked another foot closer to the two brawny louts who cast spears at him. He spun and dived, easily dodging them, and he wondered why.

Wasn't it time?

The blaze of Bowen's trench fire could be seen through the treetops. He had heard the screams and shouts. The rebel strategy had been successful. Isolated patches of the king's force already staggered from the forest, wounded and weaponless. Somewhere in the melee below rode Einon, his violent presence the only obstacle to the utter rout of his army. An obstacle that Draco could crush with one decisive blow.

Draco resisted the pull of the chain. Victory was just a short distance away. Just a spear cast. Another few heaves of the chain. So close. But he would never see the triumph on Bowen and Kara's faces; he would not share their joy, hear the jubilation of their rebel band. Would they remember him? Would they know that for him there was no victory? Only a dark windless void where sensation ceased and the stars never shone.

Draco strained against the chain, lurching upward, out of range of the dragonslayers' spears. The soldiers were dragged or thrown from the chain as it pulled taut and tore loose from the ledge, taking a section of tower with it. The battlements were sprayed with tumbling stone and fire from Draco as he broke free and soared into the glare of the sun.

Just a little longer, a little longer. Just some scrap of victory before the end. Let it be the climax, not the end. Let it be the reward, not merely the anticipation of reward. And let it come in a blaze of glory; his way, his choosing, not at the sordid hands of these murderers. He would not fail them. Bowen or Kara or his rebels. He would not fail. He would do what must be done. But now he needed wind and light and speed and the warm sun caressing his body. He spiraled up into its glow, blinded by the golden dazzle, and wished he could fly into its fire and feed its light forever.

Chapter Thirty-two

GILBERT HITS HIS MARK

"Devil's work."

Smoke and confusion. And noise. Violent noise. Horses screaming. Men screaming. The screams of metal against metal and the high piercing screams of arrows. The cries of the living indistinguishable from those of the dying. A chaotic crush of weapons and bodies and blood.

Einon sliced his way through a mob of rebels and freed himself from the press of their sweating bodies. He reined his horse and wiped the sweat from his eyes. His army was in tatters. Outnumbered. Outmatched. Outthought. Twice he had seen Bowen, but each time he had been unable to penetrate the whirlwind of slaughter to challenge him. And so he ended up challenging no one. His entire fight had been defensive. Not once had he been in control. The field and the day belonged to Bowen.

The axes sparked and locked at the hafts. Kara saw the two soldiers rushing up to aid her foe. She wrenched loose and whirled, striking away the blade of one of the approaching swordsmen and ducking the ax wielded by her adversary. The blade skimmed her flowing hair as she tumbled backward on the ground. But as the two swordsmen dived in for the kill, a rider galloped his horse between them and, extending his legs, kicked both of them into the dirt as he rode by. It was Bowen!

But Kara had no time to rejoice—the ax man was

hacking down at her where she lay. She rolled and sprang to her feet, and before her foe could spin to meet her, her own ax swiftly rose and fell. The soldier fell too, Kara plucking the ax from his limp grip as he careened past her to the ground. She smiled at Bowen as he leapt off his charging horse and ran to her.

"Like a pudding!" Kara whirled both axes with proud skill.

"More pudding behind you!" Bowen jabbed his sword under her arm and stabbed one of the swordsmen who had regained his feet and was lunging behind her. He fell with a groan. "Only expose your back to a corpse!" Bowen admonished her as the other swordsman was joined by four of his fellows emerging from the forest. As the five circled the pair Kara clenched her axes and, out of the corner of her eye, caught a glimpse of Bowen at her shoulder. He was grimly grinning as the five men charged.

Three went for Bowen, who quickly made it two with one swipe of his blade. The other two came at her, one snarling, "Is your blood the color of your hair, wench?"

"Yours is!" Kara's ax sliced a red ribbon across his neck that soon turned to a gush of blood. The man staggered back and crumpled in the grass next to Bowen's victim.

"That evens the odds," Bowen shouted to Kara, admiring her handiwork as he drove his adversaries back.

"Hardly!" Kara laughed, tossing her red hair. "They were always in our favor." The last of her attackers gave ground before her flashing axe blade.

Suddenly a rider burst from the forest and, galloping between Kara and Bowen, whipped his horse up the hill heading for the castle road. Kara gasped as she recognized the rider, and nearly was decapitated in the moment.

"Einon!" she cried, and dodged the blade, her ax cutting into her foe's shoulder as she knocked him aside and ran after the horse. She flung one of her axes at the fleeing rider. But it went far wide.

A savage war cry turned Kara around and she saw Bowen execute a dazzling maneuver that took both his men out with one stroke of the blade. Then another blade flashed before her eyes. Her wounded opponent was upon her again. She jerked back and caught the sword inches from her face. But even cut, the man was strong, and he trapped her ax with his blade as he drew a knife with his other hand. It flashed up . . . and dropped from his fingers as they convulsively jerked open. His eyes rolled up and his body went limp. Bowen stood behind him, glaring fury. But not at her. He looked beyond her, at Einon, as he galloped off to his castle.

"Gilbert!"

The priest emerged from the forest, routing several of Einon's men on the road home with well-placed arrows. He'd been having a good day. He turned at the sound of his name and saw Bowen and Kara down the hill amidst a pile of bodies. They apparently had been having a good day too. The two were running toward him, waving frantically. He waved cheerily back.

"Einon! Einon!" Bowen screamed, and pointed. A rider almost parallel to Gilbert was dashing up the road to the castle. The priest recognized the king. The arrow was out of his quiver and notched instantly. Einon turned about to cover the retreat of his men and, in so doing, gave the priest a clear target of his breast. Gilbert hesitated, grimly aware for the first time of the full power of his remarkable talent.

"Shoot! Shoot!" Bowen and Kara were almost upon him. Gilbert noticed how white his fingers were as they tautly, tensely, pulled back the bowstring.

"Thou . . . shalt . . . not . . . kill . . ." Gilbert spoke the thought of his wavering conscience. But his bow arm did not waver.

The arrow sped straight and true. Einon jerked in the saddle as it pierced his mail and embedded itself deep in his heart.

But the howling screech of agony was not Einon's.

It was Draco's!

Gilbert jolted up at the sound along with his companions and they all three watched the dragon recoil in midair and claw at his chest, which was glowing a throbbing red! Then he spiraled and fluttered down inside the castle walls.

"Draco!" Bowen wailed, and Kara restrained him as he instinctively started forward. She pointed across the way. Gilbert looked too. Einon still sat his saddle. He had not fallen. He did not even seem to be in pain. He too had watched Draco fall into the castle. He looked down at the arrow in his breast and, his pale cold eyes glinting with understanding, calmly pulled it from his chest.

"Einon!" Bowen screamed, and breaking loose of Kara, charged for him, sword aloft. Einon, alerted by the cry, smiled when he saw the knight and spurred his horse toward him.

But a wailing trill from behind the castle walls stopped both men. Sudden panic swept over Einon's gloating face and a savage, startled cry tore from his lips. "Nooo!"

He wheeled his horse and rode madly back to the castle, leaving Bowen choking in his dust. Bowen screeched after him in hysterical fury. "Come back and fight, coward!"

But Gilbert thought Bowen was well out of this fight. He looked to Kara. Her eyes mirrored his own dark thoughts. She had seen what he had seen. She knew what he knew. "It was a true shot, Gilbert, straight to the heart."

Gilbert nodded and crossed himself. "Devil's work."

Draco had fallen into the rubble of his earlier devastation. Through the mist of smoke and dust and his own dazed pain, he saw the three remaining dragonslayers swarming in to finish him off. So, the end would come in a pile of broken scaffolding and smoldering stone, lying limp and helpless, awaiting the deathblow . . . and the eternal nothingness that would follow. A stout spear plunged out of the smoke above his head. Then a sword flashed in the sun-streaked haze and knocked the spear back. Draco heard hooves clatter on the courtyard stones and a voice shouting.

"No! I want it alive!"

A wild Einon beat the confused dragonslayers back. "Alive! I want it chained and bound!"

"Why?" a dragonslayer gruffly demanded as Einon dismounted.

"To keep it safe . . ." Einon replied, kneeling by Draco's head. Through half-closed lids, Draco saw the young king's demon leer. He knew. He knew the secret of the heart.

"No . . ." Draco gasped.

"Yes . . . Safe for all eternity." Einon gently stroked the dragon's neck.

Draco shuddered at his touch.

Part IX

THE HEART

The right can never die,
If one man still recalls.
The words are not forgot,
If one voice speaks them clear.
The Code forever shines,
If one heart holds it bright.

—The Old Code

Chapter Thirty-three

THE RESCUE

"I go to save the dragon."

Draco's melancholy trill echoed from the castle, through the night, and deep into the forest where the rebels camped. Bowen could not bear to hear it.

"Why does he keep him alive?" he railed helplessly at Kara and Gilbert. "He must be torturing him!"

"No," Kara said flatly. "Einon will not torture him. He will not harm him in any way."

Bowen turned to her, not understanding, and caught her furtive glance at Gilbert. The priest nodded solemnly to her. Gently, she took Bowen's hand and suddenly he felt like a small child about to receive bad news from his mother.

"'Einon will not fall in my lifetime,'" Kara quoted.

The words were familiar. Bowen had heard them . . . somewhere.

"Do you remember?" Kara asked of him. "Draco's words to me once. . . ."

Yes—Bowen did remember. Outside the swamp village, when Kara had first tried to incite their dormant anger. Draco had mumbled it as an apologetic excuse. "I saw Draco go down. No one, nothing touched him. It was when Gilbert shot Einon."

"What are you saying?" Bowen's question came slowly, his voice harsh and tight.

Gilbert patiently tried to penetrate the knight's incomprehension. "When my arrow pierced Einon's heart, that was when Draco screamed and fell."

But Bowen could only stare at them in dim disbelief. He refused to consider what they were suggesting.

"Don't you see?" Kara implored, tears in her eyes. "It's the heart! The dragon's heart. For Einon to die, Draco must die!"

"No, no . . ." Bowen fiercely denied them. "Gilbert must have missed. It doesn't matter. Nothing matters except that Draco is still alive!"

Turning toward his men, the knight leapt upon a stump and shouted, "I go to save the dragon. Who goes with me?"

There was no rush to volunteer—just muttered oaths and sullen faces.

"You were winning this battle!" Bowen reminded them angrily. A few short hours ago these same men had stood in the forest surveying the carnage they had wrought with grim satisfaction. Savoring the first taste of victory in their lives. Now none dared look him in the eye.

"The battle's over, Knight," the diminutive Trev said bleakly, and pointed toward the castle. "Does that sound like victory?"

Hewe stood up. "We cannot defeat the invincible, Bowen." He was blood-spattered and wounded. He must have fought hard and well. "What do you expect of us?"

"Not to desert a friend . . ." Bowen answered him. "Or yourselves."

He turned from them in disgust to find Kara holding out his sword. "You do not go alone," she said.

"No . . . not alone . . ." Gilbert picked up his bow. "This ballad is yet unfinished, and be it heroic or tragic, at least let it end in honor."

Chapter Thirty-four

AN ASSASSIN DIES

"A sorry end . . ."

His whole body throbbed from the impact of his plummeting fall. From the barbed nets and piercing spear points of the dragonslayers. From the tight manacles and biting chains used to stake him out in the courtyard.

The dragonslayers had been efficient but hardly delicate in performing that task. Draco sighed and winced. Splintered wood from a broken piece of scaffolding was still lodged under his right flank, intermittently piercing his thigh.

Yes, they had been good, these Celtic brutes. Artists in their own bloodthirsty way. Oh, they were initially stymied by Einon's order to keep him alive. But once they realized that subtle torture could be as entertaining as outright slaughter, they took to their work with real relish. With a savage enthusiasm and equally savage taunts, they used their lances to prod and shift him this way or the other. Ragged metal raked across his sore flesh. They had had their sport with him while obeying the king's command.

And what mattered it to Einon? These superficial tears and bruises to the flesh he felt not. Though he held half the heart, only the great pains linked them . . . only the deep wounds . . . the ones that were felt all the way to the heart. But the heart bore other burdens that only its original possessor could feel. Draco felt the weight of one of those burdens now. Pain that taunted him more vilely than the dragonslayers' insults. Each aching pulse beat was like the jabs of their lances, mocking him with the memory of his mistake. And with that memory, all the other throbs of his battered body merged into a single racking throb of his battered heart.

The broken scaffolding poked his thigh every time he shifted. Which, mercifully, was not often. The shackles they had used to bind him allowed almost no movement. All four feet as well as his tail were fixed tightly to the ground, and a thick-linked chain around his neck and head prevented him from blowing fire on his restraints.

His chin upon the rough stone, he could only stare at the wall straight ahead of him . . . or out of the corner of his eye, where he saw Uhlric, on guard, leaning on his spear shaft, glaring at him in surly appraisal.

"Finally, a dragon worth slaying," the dragonslayer muttered through rotten teeth, "and this madman wants to keep it alive."

He shook his matted mane and spat in distaste. So, pig, thought Draco, now that the torture's done, you want to finish doing what you do best. Yes, must have been a long drought for you and your fellow thugs these last few years . . . Oh! . . . Oh, what a marvelous idea! Why not? Yes, this fool would be easy to provoke. A few well-laced epithets about his obviously dubious heritage . . . or better, a slur on his skill. Yes, that's it. A gibe and a dare and this muck-brained mountain will lick his filmy tongue over those ugly teeth and come running with an upraised spear and a laugh on his pustuled lips. Then he and Einon would no longer trade heart pains back and forth, but share one final agony. Draco was ready for it. He had to be. The time had come.

A footstep interrupted Draco's musings. Uhlric heard it too. Challenging with his spear, the dragonslayer edged forward toward a shadowy archway just behind the dragon. Draco caught Uhlric's lopsided grin of recognition as he passed out of view. And though he could not see the intruder lurking in the arch, Draco knew who it was.

Uhlric's gruff voice growled out a greeting. "Oh, it's you. Come for a peek at the royal pet?"

A surprised, strangled gasp made Draco think that Uhlric got a peek at something he had not expected. More than a peek. Draco heard the staggering scuffle of feet. Then the dragonslayer weaved into view, holding his throat. Blood spilled through his fingers. Blood spilled through his clenched ugly teeth. He collapsed to the ground, his armor clattering against the stone. His heavy spear dropped from his lifeless fingers, rolling almost to Draco's snout.

Out of the corner of his eye, Draco saw a dim figure creep slowly along the wall, shrouded against the dark stone. He heard the short, uneven breaths.

"Come from the shadows, Aislinn," Draco bade. "Stand where I can see you."

Aislinn came forth. Sheathing her bloodstained dagger, she gazed down on the man she had killed . . . then up at Draco.

"You know why I've come?" Her voice was calm. Even. Almost wistful.

"I know."

"A sorry end . . ."

"The only end," Draco assured her with flat resignation. "In the giving of my heart, I have taken on every pain and poison stirring in his black breast. Even the pain of his death must be mine. Too long I've waited."

"No one would blame you. . . ." She sat beside him, gentle fingers lightly stroking the line of a cut along his snout. "Death without immortality—"

"That was not the only reason. . . . To rid the world of Einon would not rid it of evil. I *had* to wait. Wait for a time when mankind would not repeat my sin and let tyranny thrive. When there would be those who remembered the Once-ways. Remembered that even in the darkness there is still light and those who watch over them. . . ."

Draco's gaze wandered up, but his shackled head would not allow it to travel beyond the towering stone of the castle.

His voice came in a hollow, desperate whisper. "I cannot see. Are the stars shining tonight?"

"Brightly, my lord, brightly." Moonlight spilled on Aislinn's pale upturned face, mingling with her spilling tears, glistening in its glow.

"Then there is light enough. My soul need not flicker above."

"It is *my* sin, Dragon Lord." Aislinn wept as she spoke. "For me, for a mother's misguided heart, you gambled eternity and lost. . . ."

"It was my choice. Quickly now."

Aislinn obeyed. As her people had always obeyed the dragon. She rose, picking up Uhlric's spear. It was heavy, but she managed.

She turned to Draco. "Forgive me."

"Strike deep . . . clear to the heart."

Draco shifted, exposing as much of his chest as his chains would allow. But even as Aislinn raised the spear to strike, Draco saw the hand reach from the shadows and wrench it from her grasp.

Einon emerged from the shadows like a demon emerging from hell. His hands clutched the spear shaft like a pair of claws. His eyes glowed with cold heat. Aislinn met the gaze unflinchingly.

"I know why you brought me the dragonslayers, Mother." He spoke with none of his usual smirking veneer of pleasantness. Just harsh chilling hate. "You wanted them to kill him. You wanted me dead."

He spat out the last word with all the hurt disappointment of a spoiled child, as though stunned by such an inconceivable thought.

Aislinn stared wearily into the contorted face. "I wanted to correct a mistake made years ago when I saved a creature not worth saving."

"How unmotherly of you."

His voice was ice. Aislinn backed away, more out of instinct than fear. Her son stalked her steps, sending her back farther, an eerie dance of death taking them into darkness, behind the dragon, beyond his sight.

But their silhouettes wavered on the wall before him. His shackled head held him a captive spectator to the horrifying shadow play, as one black shape raised a shadow spear to strike.

Draco closed his eyes against the hideous image. But he could not shut out the sounds of Aislinn's gasping sigh of death. Nor the throbbing. The throbbing agony of another's treachery that ripped through his heart. Agony that could not even be unleashed in his howl of despair.

Chapter Thirty-five

A LADY'S FAVOR

"This was my father's."

The dark water shivered in the torchlight as Draco's shattering lament chased itself around the walls of the Roman cistern in a whirling, hollow echo.

"Draco!" Bowen's own echo repeated his tortured cry as he pushed through the iron gate and up the stone steps to a wooden door.

"No! Not there!" Kara's whispered shout halted him and she ran up the stairs, Gilbert following her. Kara slid the hatch in the door. Bowen peeked through it to see an inner courtyard. He could not make out the form of Draco, but he heard him moaning.

"Too dangerous that way," explained Kara.

"Then that's our way."

The three turned to see the iron gate creak and Hewe step into the cistern. Trev was behind him and a half-dozen others.

"We're got to open the gates for the rest of us waiting outside," Hewe continued as he mounted the steps.

"If we don't all die first," Trev added dourly.

"At least we'll die like men," growled the bear, and cracking the door, took a cautious peek outside, then motioned his men through. He had just started to slip out after them when Bowen stopped him. Hewe turned questioningly. Bowen just silently stared. He wanted to thank the man, to offer the encouragement such valor deserved and that a good commander should offer good men. But emotion made him mute. Yet Hewe understood—and it was enough encouragement for him. The bear smiled gruffly and slammed a paw on Bowen's shoulder.

"Go save your dragon, Sir Knight," he said, and closed the door behind him.

Bowen sighed and turned, examining the cistern. There were two passageways leading off the far-side wall.

"Which one?" he asked Kara.

She pointed to the left one. "It leads to Einon's room. From there you can see the whole courtyard."

They crossed the ledge along the wall that led to the other side. Through the passage portal, Bowen saw the stairway dimly lit by torches and started for it, but Kara held him back. Untying the leather headband around her throat, she gazed at it lovingly as she smoothed it between her palms.

"This . . . was my father's," she explained haltingly. "It's no fancy bit of silk"—her brown eyes locked on his—"but if you would still carry my favor into battle . . ."

"I should be honored," Bowen said, and offered his arm. She tied the bit of leather to it. Once more their eyes met.

"Carry this too," said Kara, and she leaned up and kissed him. Bowen enfolded her in his arms.

Gilbert discreetly cleared his throat. "I can wait, but I'm not sure Draco can."

Reminded of their purpose, the lovers broke their embrace and Bowen led them up the passage.

Brok found Einon with the dragon. He scratched his beard and waited for the king to finish giving orders to the brothers Tavis and Trahern.

"Protect every scale on his hide or yours will be flayed from your bones."

The dragonslayers listened to the command with stoic calm, but Brok knew they were not pleased. Finished with them, Einon turned and sidled up to Brok before the knight could even bow.

“Yes?” the king softly inquired in his ear.

“Just as you said. The cistern passage.”

“Alone?”

“The girl is with him.” Einon perked up at the news. Brok scratched his beard and continued. “And one other. I couldn’t make out who. I came as soon as I saw him enter the entrance outside the wall. Shall I tend to it?”

“And deny me the pleasure?” Einon asked, looking at him askance. “Most certainly not . . .” He moved to the dragon and knelt beside him. “Fear not, dragon, your rescuer comes. I knew he would. You are a comrade-in-arms. And Bowen is a knight of the Old Code.”

The dragon struggled futilely in his chains. The dragon-slayers laughed. Einon withdrew into the shadows. Brok scratched his beard.

Chapter Thirty-six

THE FINAL LESSON

"You lost before you began."

Bowen looked up at the stone slab as it slid into the ceiling and red light began to seep down the stairs from the room revealed above. As he ascended the remaining stairs he realized that the source of the light was the fireplace. The sliding stone had been the hearth. Kara slowly crept up behind him. Bowen suddenly spied the glint from the bed and immediately sprang into the room. The laughter that met his action also came from the bed, on which Einon was sprawled comfortably. The lambent flames caught the flash of his smile and the sheen of the blade he held in his hand.

"Well, well, what a pleasant surprise!" The king chuckled. "I expected you, Knight. But my bride-to-be as well . . . ?" Just then Gilbert popped his head up out of the secret opening and Einon laughed again. "And a priest to wed us."

"To bury you, Einon!" Bowen charged, stabbing only bedclothes, as Einon spun off the bed, arrogantly grinning.

"Well, to bury one of us." His blade met Bowen's in midstroke. The knight felt the stinging power of the blow all the way down his forearm. But his only response was to offer his fighting smile, and to lunge again. Again, blade met blade and the two men whirled across the floor, dancing to the swift song of death sung by the steel.

The clanging swords brought two guards from outside the chamber. From the corner of his eye, Bowen saw Kara and

Gilbert intercept their charge. Einon drove him back toward the fireplace. He had to leap over the corner of the opening in order not to fall into the empty hearth. Einon was good. Very good. Bowen had taught him well. Every thrust, every feint, Einon matched him.

"We know each other's every move." Einon laughed, as though he had been reading Bowen's mind. "But I am younger and faster."

As if to demonstrate, he executed a flashy spin and dipped his sword into the fireplace, flicking a burning branch at Bowen. The knight reeled back, dodging the flaming wood. He feared that Einon's taunt was true, and was already sore and weary from the battle. He didn't want a prolonged fight.

"After I've slowed you down, you won't get any older." Bowen ducked a wicked slash of Einon's blade and, bracing himself against the mantel, shot a foot out and caught Einon with a boot that sent him careening down the stairwell of the secret passage.

Bowen checked on his companions just in time to see Kara's ax rip into a guard's belly.

"A pudding!" he cried, and leapt down after Einon.

Einon was slumped lifelessly on the stones steps. Bowen rushed down to the limp form, and nearly got decapitated for his trouble as Einon's eyes flicked open, glowing pale death, and he flipped backward to his feet and lunged, all in one motion.

Angered, Bowen attacked with a wild sally. Einon coolly deflected the blade and forced Bowen back into the cistern. As the pair fought along the perimeter of the cistern pool, Bowen realized he was fighting recklessly and unintelligently, but the boy was tiring him, and besides, he seemed to emanate an eerie confidence, as though he truly thought himself invincible.

"Practice what you preach, mentor," Einon asserted as he drove Bowen back. "Purpose not passion, remember?"

The gibe only intensified the knight's wild attack. This

was, in part, because he knew the king spoke true. Pupil had become teacher and now he felt like the stumbling boy in the old Roman ruins.

"Nerve cold blue . . ." Einon continued to taunt him. Bowen thrust viciously at his head. Einon nimbly ducked and his blade slashed across Bowen's calf. "Blade blood-red."

Bowen buckled and teetered on the cistern ledge. Einon savagely swiped at him and Bowen leapt . . . over the water onto the opposite ledge. He felt a twinge in his leg, but still managed to land standing, bracing himself in the portal of the other cistern tunnel. Even Einon was impressed.

"Still have lessons to teach me, eh, mentor?" Einon barked a laugh.

Bowen smiled back. The wound had renewed his cool vigor. "Just one more."

"And what, pray, is that?"

"The last one your father learned."

Einon's lip curled, and with a yell, he rounded the pool and set upon Bowen. Blue sparks flashed across their blades as they moved into the dark tunnel.

As the guard sagged to the chamber floor and Bowen leapt down the cistern stairs, Kara rushed to follow him. Then she heard Gilbert.

"Parry, parry, thrust . . ." The thrust was followed by a groan. It sounded like Gilbert's, and Kara spun around. The priest's opponent had backed him to the wall, and Gilbert, flushed and sweaty, held him at bay, awkwardly counting out his beats. It wasn't so much Gilbert's skill, which was minimal, that kept him alive, but his persistent precision that utterly disoriented the guard.

"Parry, parry, thrust . . . Parry, parry . . ."

Frustration finally got the better of bewildered fear, and with a growl, the guard slashed out and slapped the sword from Gilbert's fist.

"Thrust!" Kara lunged between them with her ax and the guard hit the floor only moments after Gilbert's clattering sword.

"God forgive me. . . ." Gilbert crossed himself.

"Don't you mean me?" Kara grinned. Gilbert only groaned again and slid down the wall, leaving a bloody streak against it in his wake.

"Gilbert!" Kara knelt beside him, noticing for the first time that the right side of his cassock was ripped and soaked with blood. "He's cut you!"

Gilbert shrugged and winced. "The sword is not my weapon. Leave it! Leave it!" He slapped her fussing fingers away and was immediately contrite. "Forgive me. It's more messy that lethal. I'll be all right."

"Are you sure?" she asked, and knew he had caught her anxious glance toward the cistern passage. He grimaced a smile.

"Go to Bowen, my child, I just need to rest for a moment," he gasped. "Go! Go! Bowen needs you more than I. And Draco. I'll be along."

Kara raced to the hidden stairway then hesitated, looking back at the priest. He unslung his bow from his back and held it up, wincing again. "Don't worry. Anyone comes in, they won't get very far. *This* I know how to use. I'll be along. Get you gone!"

Kara tore down the steps. Gilbert was right. The wound was messy. But it didn't look too deep. And Bowen did need her help more than the priest. He was fighting a man he could not defeat.

The stairway was frighteningly quiet. All she heard was the scuffling of her boots upon the stone. Nothing from below. If the duel was over, there could be only one outcome. She flew down the stairs, lurching wildly into the cistern. It was empty!

Felton could not sleep. If he lay on his back, his arse hurt. If he lay on his stomach, his jaw hurt. They both hurt when he lay on his side. They both hurt anyway. He limped along the battlements and rubbed his swollen face. Of course, he really wasn't all that tired. He had gotten plenty of sleep on the battlefield, thanks to his minx. He supposed he should be grateful to her. After all, it was she who had gotten him out of the fight.

Hello? What was this?

He saw the red-haired wench run across the courtyard below, recognized her, and wondered how she had managed to get in. She was coming up the stairs. He ducked behind the wall, drew his sword, and waited. *Clack, clack, clack.* Her boots scuffed along the stairs. *Clack, clack, clack.* Frantic and fast. He wished they were faster. It hurt his arse, squatting like this.

Kara ascended the steps and stopped, gripping her ax, debating which way to go. Suddenly a sword was at her throat, then the man was sweeping out of the shadows behind her like an oily spider. An oily, mangled spider. One whole side of his face was a swollen purple welt. She recognized him anyway. It was the fop, Felton.

"This will put me in good with His Majesty," he announced, leering triumphantly over his shoulder, then his puffy-lipped face shuddered. His snakelike eyes popped wide in stark surprise and the sword slid harmlessly from her throat. Kara spun, ax to the ready, but Felton was already reeling and slurring through his bruised lips, "Then again, maybe not . . ."

The lamps went out in his eyes and he collapsed on the stones with a loud crack. If he survived, his whole face was going to be purple. But Kara had her doubts about his chance for survival. Hewe the Bear stood behind the fallen man, his sword dripping blood. He motioned his men from the shadows and down the stairs.

"I'm in your debt," Kara said.

Hewe shook his head. "I'm in yours. Your father would

be proud." He saluted her with his blade and dashed after his men.

Gruff old bear. Her father would be proud of him too. Twirling her ax up, she stepped over Felton and took off along the battlements.

The guards on the gate had gone to hell as quietly as the sentries along the battlements, never knowing what hit them. Trev and the others dragged the bodies from the path. The army outside the walls had seen the signal to move up the road and would be waiting for the gates to open. Hewe was drawing up the crossbar and flinging the doors wide . . . when he was shocked to find an outer gate beyond it! It too was guarded. The alarm was sounded before Hewe and his men could cut them down.

Kara heard the blaring of the ram's horn as she scrambled through the wreckage of the dragonslayers' catapults. The sound surely meant Hewe and his men had been discovered. She had to find Bowen! She turned to get her bearings when there, on the wall in front of her, suddenly loomed a huge shadow hoisting a huge mace!

Kara wheeled to confront the shadow's flesh-and-blood counterpart. She thrust out her ax, but it was no match for Brok's whirling ball and chain. The impact of the brute's weapon tore the ax from her hand and sent her colliding against the brawny chest of another warrior. She screamed and lurched back, and Brok's ball and chain smashed into his comrade. There was a crack of ribs, but the man didn't budge. He couldn't.

He was already dead, impaled to the wall on a giant lance. A wild Celt. One of the dragonslayers. Kara saw now that the man's feet did not touch the ground, making him appear taller than he was. She also saw the giant broad-bladed ax in his hand. Her mind had barely taken this in when Brok's mace spun down at her again and she rolled to the far side of the dragonslayer's body, to retrieve the corpse's ax. The mace smashed into the corpse's thigh. The body bounced at the blow and the ax jerked forward in the flopping arm.

Kara sprang out and grabbed the ax pole, trying to wrench it from the dead man's grip, but he wouldn't relinquish it. Just then Brok's mace came slamming down again. With both hands Kara hoisted up the heavy shaft, still attached to the dragonslayer's hand, to ward off the blow. The spiked ball cracked right through the shaft, breaking it in two. Kara was jerked to safety, swinging back with the dead arm and the ax, which finally gave in the corpse's hand. It clanked to the stone and Kara leapt to retrieve it as Brok's mace whizzed by her. He wheeled and she came up with the ax. The spiked sphere lashed out and Kara caught it on the broken ax shaft. She snapped it forward and the entangled ball whipped forward too, bashing in Brok's face. His scream mingled with the crunch of bone and a squish of blood as he sank to the stones, dead. Not as neat as a pudding, thought Kara, but effective nonetheless.

Hearing the clash of arms and voices sounding from somewhere in the castle, she assumed that Hewe and his rebels were at the gates. But above this chaotic clamor came another sound. Rattling chains. Close by. Kara sought the sound out . . . and found Draco. He lay in the shadow of the great tower on the opposite side of the cistern from which she had just come. Heavy iron spikes driven into the courtyard stone secured the weighty webbing of chains and manacles that imprisoned him. His body heaved and rocked as well as it could under the confining restraints, making the chains quiver with a forlorn ring.

Two wild-maned, spear-wielding barbarians flanked him—Celts, like the other dragonslayer. Like the dragon, the two brutes shifted uneasily, hearing the noise of battle. But something else distracted them as well and Kara heard the sound even as she followed the dragonslayers' gaze upward. It was the rhythmic, swift rasp of scraping blades. Kara's heart listened and leapt with hope. For though that sound foretold inevitable death, it also meant that Bowen was yet alive. She saw him, even as the dragonslayers below did, in the tower—one of two shadowy figures dueling as they ascended the torchlit stairs.

Bowen and Einon rose up the stairs, their blades flashing furiously in the torchlight. They had heard the gate sentry's alarum. They heard the fighting in the distance.

"My rebels are storming your castle." Bowen grinned, driving Einon up the stairs.

"Pity you won't live to see them fail." Einon laughed and lunged, but Bowen parried and his sword plunged into Einon's arm with a splash of blood. Einon staggered back into the open portal of the window and Bowen was immediately upon him. The blades crossed and Bowen pushed Einon back, leaning him over the sill. Over the boy's shoulder, he could see Draco below, struggling in his chains.

"Listen to him squirm, Knight." Einon sneered between the wedged blades. "It's him you wound, not me!"

"Liar!" Bowen bent Einon farther back over the sill.

"Is this a lie?" The king held up his slashed arm. The blood had dried. The cut had closed over. Bowen staggered back and Einon charged, putting the knight on the defensive once more and driving him up the stairs.

The dragon writhed in his chains, muttering.

"Fool! Poor fool! It will do no good."

"Quiet, dragon!" Tavis gripped his spear and looked to his brother. Trahern shrugged uneasily, obviously as mystified as he was. What was going on? A moment ago the dragon had shuddered and gasped and one of his legs had flared a fiery red as though it had been wounded. But neither of them had touched the beast. They had obeyed the king's order, as demented as it was. All this mystery was very fraying on the nerves. The battle racket from the gates, the duel in the tower above, and now the antics of a dragon they were not allowed to kill. No amount of gold was worth this indignity. He and Trahern had decided. Come morning, they would take what gold was due them and leave. They would nursemaid no dragon.

Suddenly an armed body of the king's men rushed across the courtyard, heading for the gates. Tavis looked to Trahern again. His brother shook his head, shrugged again, and spat. Tavis spat too. Come morning, they were gone.

These gate guards were a stubborn lot. They just would not die. Two of Hewe's men were wounded and the odds were now four to three. Then he heard the clatter behind him. More soldiers coming. Oh, no! Don't let it end here. Not like this. Boxed in and slaughtered, only three measly men away from flinging the gates open and the whole rebel army rushing in.

"Kill them!" the bear exhorted his men, and bashed at one with his sword. And the man went down. But not under his blade . . . with an arrow in his side. Another arrow slithered into another guard's leg and he crumpled with a yelp. Before he hit the ground, an arrow had struck the upraised sword arm of the third guard, who went reeling back against the gate. This latter intervention spared Trev, at whom the guard had been aiming his sword, from being beheaded. The little man knew who his savior was before he even looked around. "A natural!"

Hewe looked too. Gilbert stood weaving in the courtyard, notching another arrow. "Well, you great lummox, don't stand there gawking with that cyclops eye. Open the gates!" Gilbert groaned and sagged to his knees, but even kneeling, he continued to fire off arrows at the approaching soldiers, holding them at bay.

"Gilbert . . . Open the gates!" Hewe shouted to his men, running to the priest. The gates opened and the rebel force surged through them.

Tavis and Trahern spun from the clamoring at the gates to see the dragon, who was wildly straining in his chains, lamenting to himself.

"Stop, heart! Stop beating!"

"I'll stop it, if you don't!" Trahern snarled testily.

"Then do it! Do it!"

This was too much. A dragon begging to be killed. Trahern edged back, glaring at the dragon in confused suspicion. Then at his brother, who seemed equally baffled. They both stared at the dragon again.

Though he could not move his head, the dragon's eyes gazed up desperately at the tower. The brothers looked up too. The two duelists were now atop the tower, their clanging blades sparking against the night.

Bowen fiercely fought Einon, dodging building materials and scaffolding all the while. He also fought his doubts, trying to blot them out. He did not want to know how Einon's wound had healed. He did not want to think of why Draco thrashed below. He did not want to remember Kara's words, "It's the heart, the heart." It couldn't be. It mustn't be. There were logical answers for all these things. Answers that would come with Einon's death.

There was no time for such speculation as Einon slashed wide at him and his blade cracked against the one wall of the room and broke in two. Bowen did not hesitate to seize the opportunity, feeling no remorse or mercy. Even though his doubts assailed him in the instant of his lunge, he knew the answer to them all. Einon's death.

"Once you held this blade in sacred oath," Bowen hissed in cold hate as he drove the blade home. "Which you broke. Now embrace it again."

Deep into Einon's heart the blade penetrated. The king buckled and gasped. But he did not fall! And then . . . he smiled . . . Smiled like he had in Bowen's haunted dream . . . and as he did so Draco began to howl!

Stunned, Bowen staggered back, pulling his hand off the sword hilt as though it were cursed. Draco's scream chilled his blood. So did the sight of Einon, still smiling, calmly pulling the sword from his chest. Bowen reeled back, dazed.

Einon pointed the bloodstained sword at him. "Fool! You lost before you began. I am immortal!"

He laughed with malicious glee, eyes glinting like a madman, and charged. Bowen stumbled back through the debris as Einon cut and chopped at him in bloodthirsty abandon. The blade rippled his tunic as he swung himself onto some scaffolding. Einon's frantic hacking sprayed wood chips everywhere as Bowen leapt away.

"Bowen!"

Kara was at the head of the stairs. She threw him the ax as he was still in midleap. Catching it, he landed and banged it against Einon's slicing blade. The impact spun the king back through the clutter toward the edge of the tower. Bowen sent the ax flying. It shrieked through the air, just missing Einon's head and burying itself in a heavy wooden window shutter, which whined on its hinges. Still off balance, Einon lashed clumsily at Bowen. Leaping beyond the thrust, the knight jumped on the low sill to yank the ax free. It wouldn't budge.

Einon snarled a laugh and lunged. Bowen pushed off from the sill and, clinging to the broken ax pole, rode the shutter as it swung out over nothingness. Unable to stop his momentum, Einon spilled through the open window, hurtling into nothingness as well.

Clinging to the ax handle, Bowen watched the body spiral down, crashing through scaffolding, sending building materials careening, and plunging through the wooden roof of the cistern in an explosion of clutter and dust. Einon disappeared beneath the wreckage into the watery depths.

Kara ran to the window. Bowen smiled grimly at her. "So much for his immortality."

But as the din of Einon's descent dissipated, the agonized groans of Draco echoed clearly up above the noise of the rebel invasion. The knight looked down. The dragon's body was glowing red torment!

"Draco!" Bowen screamed. But he wondered if the dragon could hear him over his own wails. His weight against the shutter would not allow it to swing back. He held his hand out to Kara for her to pull him back to safety. She reached out and almost had him when the ax embedded in the shutter suddenly gave.

"Bowen!" she cried as he slipped away from her. He dangled one-handed by the broken shaft. Then the blade unwedged itself completely from the wood and Bowen plummeted into the dark night.

Trahern feinted at the thrashing, moaning dragon with his spear, watching the red glow ripple wildly under his hide. "Enough, lizard! Or by God, king or no king, we'll have your head!"

The dragon snorted a harmless bolt of flame the only place he could . . . directly in front of him. "The king's in the drink, you dolt! Who do you think fell? He can't stop you now!"

Trahern looked to his brother and both stared at the wreckage of the cistern in dumbfounded suspicion. "The king?"

Draco rattled his chains and, grimacing in pain, taunted them. "You want my head, lummox, then take it, don't talk about it."

Trahern didn't care whether the king was at the bottom of the cistern or not. He had had enough. Standing here being insulted by a mad dragon while brawls were going on all around him. Even now he heard the violent ruckus elsewhere in the castle. He was tired of being left out. He'd give this dragon something to glow about. Incensed, he jerked back his spear to strike. But Tavis was still suspicious and cautious.

"Steady, brother, steady!" He stepped forward to restrain Trahern.

"I'll not be taunted by some slime-headed reptile!"

"Cowards!" mocked the dragon. "What sort of dragonslayers are you?" Both men whirled on him.

"I can best you even in chains." The beast hissed a flash

of flame. Tavis, almost in the line of fire, got his beard singed. And his cool head boiled. He wheeled on the dragon with a growl. The dragon smiled.

"That's it, dolt, strike!"

Tavis's spear drew back. . . .

Chapter Thirty-seven

THE PRICE OF VICTORY

"You are the last."

Bowen did not fall far. A pulley rope was dangling from the tower and he managed to make a one-handed grab. The flesh tore from his hand and he felt like his arm would be yanked from his socket, but he held on. He also held on to the ax as he tangled his arms and legs about the line.

The line was weighted on the other end, but Bowen was heavier, and the rope rattled through the pulley, Bowen riding it down . . . down to Draco!

He could still see glowing patches of Draco's wounded hide flare up and saw the dragon spray fire at the two giants, menacing him with spears. As the line sped down he heard their yells and Draco's bellow. Another line of fire spewed out, nearly hitting one of the dragonslayers, who wheeled on the dragon. They were getting closer. Bowen was practically above them. They loomed closer and closer. There was more shouting, then one of the giants hoisted back his spear. Bowen swung the line into the wall, bracing his feet against it and pushing back out. The dragonslayer's spear never came forward. Bowen swooped down upon him, the great ax slicing the dragonslayer's throat.

Bowen hit the courtyard stones before the body fell in a swishing spray of blood. Wailing grief and rage, the other brute charged.

A mistake. Draco unleashed a huge fireball as the Celt stepped in front of him. Flame whooshed up the dragonslayer's burly body, burning it to a crisp. His charred corpse collapsed on the stones in front of Bowen.

"Almost too late!" Bowen smiled at Draco as he ran up to him and smashed the ax down on his neck shackles. Once. Twice. Three times. The locks shattered!

"Too soon," said Draco, stretching his free neck.

"What?" Bowen asked, and stood up. He heard someone behind him and whirled. It was Kara, breathless, in the stairwell door of the tower. She glanced curiously at Draco. She had heard him too.

"You should have let them do it," Draco explained to the knight. "Now *you* must."

"What?" Bowen repeated dully. His mind was in a fog. He didn't understand. He didn't want to understand. Again, he looked to Kara . . . silent and solemn as she moved toward them.

"Even as the heart binds Einon to me in life, it binds us in death."

"That is not true." It was a flat rejection.

"You've seen that it is! Through the heart we share each other's pains and power. But in my half beats the life source. For Einon to die, I must."

Bowen remembered that Kara had said this to him as well. "For Einon to die, Draco must." He had refused to believe it then. He refused to believe it now. He wouldn't believe it.

"No! Einon *is* dead!"

"He lives!"

Kara gasped. Bowen turned to her. Why? Why, did she gasp? She saw. She knew.

"He's dead! As soon as I free you, I'll fish his broken battered body from the wreckage and show you!" He wheeled on Kara again, imploring her. "Tell him, Kara!"

"I . . . don't . . . know. . . ." Kara stammered uncertainly.

"You saw it!"

"I don't know!"

"You saw it!"

"I know what I saw!" said the girl, confused tears in her eyes. "But I also know Draco. . . . Perhaps Einon is not dead!"

"He lives!" came the dragon's insistent hiss.

"Then I'll kill him again!" Bowen swore hotly.

"No . . . You'll kill me."

Bowen felt desperate, afraid.

"Even if what you say is true, what does it matter? Don't you hear it?" He gestured toward the battle noise. "Our rebels . . . our silly, sorry little band of rebels have stormed the castle. All on their own. For you! Alive or dead, Einon's beaten. We've won."

"You will never win until Einon's evil is destroyed. If you cannot do it, then free me so I can."

"I will not!"

"Unchain my claw!" Draco demanded. "Let me tear the hated thing from my breast!"

"There must be another way!"

"None!" Draco nodded toward the mountain crest beyond the castle. "Once, upon that mountaintop, you swore your sword and service were mine. To call when I had need of you. To ask what I would of you. I ask now! I need now! I hold you to your vow, Knight!" The dragon suddenly winced in pain. His eyes darted wildly. "He's coming! Coming to stop you!"

Bowen turned to the cistern. Kara was already cautiously checking it. She shook her head at Bowen. Nothing . . .

"Strike before it is too late!" Draco begged.

Bowen turned back to him, torn by his plea. "You are the last. . . ."

"My time is over. Strike!"

"You are my friend."

"Then as my friend, strike! . . . Please!"

"I cannot!" Bowen's voice shook. A blinding rush of tears stung his eyes. "I cannot send you soulless into hell!"

"Then I will make you!" snarled Draco. With a roar, he

lunged at Bowen with snapping fangs. Bowen spun back, evading the blow. Again, the dragon lashed out, trying to provoke him, but the knight merely leapt out of his shackled range. Draco rattled his chains wildly, growling.

"Fight back, dragonslayer!" Draco tried insulting him. "Kill me or I'll kill you!" He shot a bolt of flame at Bowen. It struck at his feet. Kara screamed, but Bowen held his ground.

"Defend yourself!" the dragon bellowed, but there was more desperation than anger in the cry.

Bowen flung the ax behind him. It skittered across the courtyard stones. Draco loosed another streak of fire. Closer this time. Bowen recoiled back.

"Pick up the ax!" Another flash of flame skimmed past Bowen, exploding on the wall behind him. Suddenly Draco jolted in pain and moaned in despair.

"No!" exclaimed Kara, in tears. "I will do it, Draco!"

She ran for the ax. Bowen spun and ran to stop her.

But someone else stopped her first.

Einon shot up out of the cistern in a spray of water and wreckage. Bloody and battered but very much alive! Cold depravity gleamed out of his pale eyes. Draco wailed in misery.

Leaping from the debris, the king descended on the petrified Kara, grabbing her arm and whirling her to him. Bowen's sword blade was in the king's hand and at her throat. Bowen snatched up the ax.

"Yes!" Draco urged him.

"No!" Einon commanded. "Or she dies."

Stalemate.

Hewe came barging into the courtyard with an advance party of rebels. He and Trev supported a wounded Gilbert between them. When they saw Kara and Einon, they froze. Einon laughed.

And Draco viciously sank his fangs into his own crippled claw.

Einon's laughter shrieked to a scream and he dropped the sword, his right hand clutching convulsively in pain.

In that instant Bowen accepted the truth he already knew. And he accepted his fate as well. Lunging forward, he yanked Kara from Einon's grasp and, shoving her to safety, spun around, his back to the king, and raised the ax—aiming for Draco!

Draco lifted his breast as much as he could to receive the blow; his scales fell back, revealing his red scar.

"Only expose your back to a corpse!" Einon hissed behind Bowen, and the knight heard a knife slither from a scabbard.

The ax left his hand and, twirling in the air, buried itself in Draco's chest, which flashed a brilliant crimson.

Kara stifled a scream as Draco reeled to the ground, his grateful eyes gazing on Bowen as his lids fluttered down. Bowen's own eyes flooded with tears as he felt Einon's dagger slide harmlessly down his back. He turned.

The blade had fallen from Einon's hand. The king clutched at his chest. His eyes filled with stunned disbelief, his mouth agape in a silent scream. He reached out to Bowen, grasping his shoulder. The knight brushed the hand aside, sneering at him through his tear-dimmed eyes. "You *are* a corpse."

And he was, collapsing to the ground. Dead. Bowen felt dead himself.

As he shambled toward the still form of the dragon, he heard his rebels pour into the courtyard. He heard Hewe shout to them, "The tyrant's dead. We're free." He heard the shout echo and more rebels crowd in and the triumphant rejoicing. It all sounded distant and unreal.

He knelt by the dragon's body and gently stroked his head.

"Your victory, Draco," said the knight softly. "Only you cannot hear it. And they already begin to forget its bitter cost. Soon it will fade, like your lost soul, to nothingness. . . . And only I will remember."

But others remembered. Kara and Gilbert joined Bowen in his vigil, oblivious to the celebration about them. Bracing himself on his bow, the wounded priest quietly intoned some Latin and crossed himself. Kara knelt beside Bowen as he buried his face against Draco's cold cheek.

"What now, dragon?" he cried bitterly. "You abandon us alone in our freedom! Without you, what do we do? Where do we turn?"

"To the stars, Bowen. To the stars . . ."

The voice was a whisper, warm and reassuring. It was Draco's voice. Bowen lifted his head. Kara and Gilbert had not heard it. He could tell by the bewildered way they regarded him. Did he look that strange? Had he heard it or just sensed it? Or merely gone mad?

No . . . The sudden light on his face was no delusion. It came out of Draco's wound . . . an eerie, ethereal glow of translucent red iridescence, oozing out like a mist, covering the body and spreading out over the ground.

Bowen and Kara rose and stood back. Draco's body dissolved in the mist, became one with it, as the strange glow began to float upward. Past Bowen and Kara and Gilbert. Past the rebels, who became hushed, their faces awash in the glittering scarlet radiance as it rose above the castle walls and ascended into the sky. The light swiftly swirled behind the mountains and suddenly the night became alive with celestial color, flashing across the black horizon.

Then sound filled the air. This time Bowen knew he heard it. Kara and Gilbert heard it too. So did the rebels. *Trilling. Draco's dragon song!* But not his melancholy lament. This was his happy song; the one he had sung for Kara that day at the waterfall. It echoed clear and sweet. It was a joyful noise.

Bowen gazed heavenward. Expectant. Waiting.

The light behind the mountains spun and congealed into a shimmering streak. The stars suddenly dimmed, fading from the sky as the light, like a ruby comet, shot through the darkness toward the constellation Draco. There, the flashing glow erupted into a blazing star, whirling with dazzling splendor into the formation, becoming the eye of the constellation.

Bowen thought the whole cluster was shining brighter than he had ever seen it shine before. But just for an instant. Then it faded along with Draco's song as the other stars returned to the heavens.

Kara wept and hugged him. Gilbert crossed himself and the rebels cheered once more. Bowen could only gaze at the stars. The new star still shone brightly . . . more vivid, more lustrous than the others, its gleaming rays beaming down upon them. He could feel its light upon his face. Kara and Gilbert's upturned faces were bathed in its glow. Its brilliance seemed to shut out the noise. It was as though they were in a pool of shining peace. A trio of stillness amidst the raucous celebration of their fellows.

How small they must look, seen from above, he thought. As all things must look from heaven. All that kept them from blending into the surging mass was the beam of Draco's starshine as it fell upon them. Smiled upon them. It felt warm and safe and seemed to gleam ever brighter. And brighter. Until the dark was swept away and all was . . .

. . . *exquisite light!*

This is the tale of a Knight who slew a Dragon and vanquished evil.

The Chronicles of Glockenspur, Detailing the Historie of King Einon and the Rebellion Under His Reign as Set Down by One Gilbert, a Friar.

Acknowledgments

Dragonheart, both as a film and a novel, has been a dream project for me. And there are a lot of people to thank: Patrick Read Johnson, without whom there would be no *Dragonheart;* to Raffaella De Laurentiis, who, for four years, stood shoulder to shoulder with me in the trenches, believing in my script and my talent; to Hal Lieberman, who stood up for me when it counted; to Steve Rabineau, who indulges my economically imprudent whimsy (and calls me the Howard Roark of screenwriters, an accolade I don't really deserve but which flatters me nonetheless); to Nancy Cushing-Jones, who thought my writing the novel was a good idea and had the patience of Job to wait for it while I cleared my desk of other obligations; to Paul Weston, John Lees, Gerry Crampton, Giorgio Desideri, Alberto Tosto, Michael Menzies, Pete Postlethwaite, Wolf Christian, Lee Oakes, Jason Isaacs, Dan "The Shadow" Hadl, and Hester Hargett, who all kept me sane in Slovakia during filming; and to Adeena Karsseboom and Steve O'Corr, who held down the fort at home. And a special thanks and all my love to my wife, Julieanne, who put up with five long years of angst and read and edited more drafts of script and book than anyone should have to, but still always cried in all the right parts.

—Charles Edward Pogue